The School for Scoundrels

The Lost Map of the Prows

Sandra Dennis

First published in Great Britain 2017
Copyright © Sandra Dennis, 2017

www.sandradenniswrites.wix.com/sandra-dennis

Twitter: @sdenniswrites

ISBN No. 978-1-7872-3130-6

This book is a work of fiction. Names, characters, places and incidents are either a product of the author's imagination or are used fictitiously. Any resemblance to actual people, living or dead, events or locales, is entirely coincidental.

Cover design: Luke Stevens
Copyright © Luke Stevens, 2017

For Isolda

Also, for those of us, both young
and old,
who love adventure

Chapter 1
Message in a Bottle

Thomas Prow was sulking.

Grandpa would tell him that sulking would *not* help, but he threw the stones deliberately hard into the water nonetheless. There were only two days of the summer holidays left and he wanted to make sure he planned them well, before he had to return to school. There he would be stuck in a classroom full of musty old books and stressy teachers, unable to get outdoors where he really wanted to be; outside and kite-boarding across the wide open sea. A place he could never seem to get enough of.

Earlier that day, he had felt a rush of excitement as he sped through the waves with a swiftness the birds would envy; taking off and spinning through the air like a rapid, flying beast. His mate Sam falling behind as the wind caught Thom's kite and lifted him further out upon the waves. The taste of salt on his tongue, the tingly feel of the sun on his face and the shouts of glee from the kite-boarders – freedom!

At the beginning of the summer holidays, the weeks seemed to stretch out endlessly before him: promising adventures with his friends around the bays and rocks of their small village; voyages on his grandfather's fishing boat out into the vast waters which surrounded their small, fishing community and time alone to explore the hidden caves on the nearby Isle of Bos.

Thom perched on a grassy bank, his legs dangling over the edge, watching the river rushing past his feet into the sea inside the harbour where the two waters met. Terraced, fishermen's cottages stood either side of the river, descending the hill to the harbour.

Carefully scanning the skyline, he awaited the return of Grandpa's fishing boat that he could see approaching from a distance. Grandpa had been delayed that morning, due to mechanical problems with his boat. Some vessels, including Skipper's – Grandpa's best friend - had returned ages ago with their catch and were bobbing up and down on the surface, either anchored or tied to the harbour wall. The afternoon's sun's rays were glinting off the water making Thom squint. The gulls screamed overhead, searching for anything the fishermen had left behind on which they could gorge themselves.

Thom observed a Common Tern dive at something dark moving up and down on the water just below his feet: a dark-red bottle. The current grasped the bottle in its clutches and carried it to the jetty where the water was shallow.

Curious, Thom dragged himself up and walked to where the bottle was being washed in and out on the waves. Although fairly small, it was unusual in that it was blood-red, had a large bulb-shaped bottom, a short neck and a cork inserted into the top. On closer inspection he could see there was something inside ... a message in a bottle? He laughed to himself as he picked up the bottle, uncorked the stopper and pulled on a deteriorating strip of leather that was attached to the note. Surprised, Thom could see that it was addressed to 'William Prow', his grandfather. Frowning, he turned the piece of paper over:

> *William.*
> *The boy must sail the high seas ... it's time.*
> *23.58, Isle of Bos, high tide, two days from now, August 29th*

Thom read the note again. It made no sense. The pealing of a bell interrupted his confused thoughts. Looking up, he could see that Grandpa was almost at his mooring point. Thom rolled the note and stuffed it into the small bottle then placed it in his jacket pocket and waved to his grandfather. He would help Grandpa tie up the boat and unload the catch then he could question his grandfather about the message. First, there was work to be done.

"Hello, boy," called William Prow, smiling at his grandson. He tossed the rope onto the quay for Thom to fasten to the huge iron ring that lay on the harbour wall.

"How was the catch, Grandpa?" he shouted above the engine, taking in the smell of oil and fish and the continuous screams of the gluttonous gulls circling above their heads. It was the same every day, but Thom treasured it. He watched his grandfather's burly figure moving the baskets about on board; his thick, blue-wool jumper with its sleeves pushed up to his elbows and his bushy, greying-beard.

"Good, better than yesterday. What adventures have you had today, then?"

"I rowed out to Bos with Sam. We explored the caves and did some kite-boarding, it was awesome. The wind to the south of the island was perfect today."

They continued to chatter as they unloaded the crates of fish onto the quayside. Once the work was complete, the two of them ambled up the hill towards their cottage at the top of the village.

Thom was aware of the solid lump inside his coat pocket, but for some reason it didn't feel like the right time to discuss it. The mystery of it sent his imagination running wild as he remembered a tale his grandfather had often told him about an ancestor of his.

"Grandpa, tell me again about great-great-grandpa, Seamus Prow, and how he was caught smuggling one dark and moonless night."

Grandpa laughed. "Ah, yes, not told this one in a while. Well, Seamus Prow, a bit of a wild one according to legend, was one of the ringleaders of the smugglers that hid stolen goods in the caves on Bos – some say that there might even still be gold in them caves."

Thom imagined a figure, not unlike Grandpa, struggling down the hill with stolen goods, under the cover of darkness; transferring their booty to the Isle of Bos, where the caves were deep and great at keeping secrets.

"He came to a bad end though ..." continued Grandpa, with a warning tone.

"What happened?" Thom knew exactly what had happened, but loved the way that Grandpa theatrically bent his neck to one side, whilst holding an invisible rope and sticking his tongue out to the side of his mouth; making a choking sound in his throat.

Thom chuckled.

"Well, boy, this is where he and many of our ancestors have lived as far back as we know, not all in this cottage, but around these shores," stated Grandpa as he opened the front door to the cottage in which they lived. "Better get inside before Gran burns the supper."

An aroma of home-cooking greeted them, along with the sound of Gran humming in the kitchen. Having removed his boots, Thom walked through to speak to her. "We're back."

"Oh, there you are," she said, holding her hand to her chest, warm, brown eyes welcoming.

"What's for supper? I'm starving."

"Shepherd's pie. Go and fetch some beans from the garden, will you?"

Thom nodded and slipped on his grandfather's boots that sat by the back door in the utility room. He sniggered as his feet slid up and down in them as he stumbled down the garden to the vegetable patch at the bottom.

Having picked the beans he returned and, overhearing his grandparent's conversation as he took off the boots, he stood for a moment and listened.

"How are we supposed to pay for a new fishing boat?" asked Gran.

"I don't know, Ellie, I was hoping 'Bessie' would keep going until I retire in a few years, but Bob says if it goes wrong again he won't be able to fix it."

Gran spied Thom in the doorway. "Ah, Thom ... the beans. Quick Will, go and shower." She ushered Grandpa away.

"What were you talking about?" asked Thom.

"Don't you worry about that, Grandpa will see to it all. Now, how about you help me prepare the beans?"

Thom knew better than to pester his grandmother, he hated being excluded from things, even if it was bad. He decided he would speak to Grandpa after supper when his Gran went to the Women's Institute meeting. It is what Gran did every Monday evening without fail, always clutching a home-made cake as she left the cottage to walk down the hill to the village hall. There she met the other ladies to talk about whatever ladies talked about when they got together – which he couldn't imagine was very exciting.

"So, what's the matter, boy?" Grandpa eyed Thom from his armchair by the window.

"Nothing."

"You've been fidgeting all through dinner and couldn't wait for Gran to leave the house. What's on your mind?"

"I overheard you and Gran talking about 'Bessie'."

Grandpa's face was stern. "That's not for you to worry about, my boy, I've all that in hand." Grandpa's tone stopped Thom in his tracks, he knew that it would not be a good idea to ask any further questions. When Grandpa sounded like that, you just didn't ask.

Instead, Thom changed the subject. "I found something today."

"On the island?"

"No, in the harbour. In fact it was almost as if it found me."

"What was it?"

7

"I'll go and get it." Thom went into the hall to retrieve the bottle.

Grandpa's face paled as Thom handed it to him.

"There's a message ... inside it ... for you."

Grandpa turned the bottle over in his hands and gently slipped the cork out. He pulled the leather thong and the message slipped out easily. He read it and let out a sigh. "So, the time has come."

"What does it mean? Is the 'boy' meant to be me? Why do I have to sail the high seas ... I already help with the fishing when I can."

"You read it?"

Thom felt his cheeks grow warm and nodded. "I didn't know it was for you until I'd opened it." He stared as his grandfather rolled the small piece of paper up and slipped it back into the bottle, which he continued to turn over and over in his hands.

After a few moments he said, "Sit down, boy, I've something to tell you, perhaps should have told you a long time ago."

Heart racing, Thom sat down on the sofa opposite his grandfather. Grandpa looked more troubled than he'd ever seen him before, which scared him. "What's wrong, Grandpa?"

"Thom, you're to go away to school -"

"But I already go to school in Ketchworth."

"This is a different school; a different *kind* of school."

"Where?"

There was a pause.

"Thom, before your parents died they left a request, in a letter, that if anything were to happen to them, when the time was right, you were to go to a special school."

"A private school?" Thom felt his heart sink. What about all his friends?

"Of sorts. Thom this is very difficult for me. Until now you've led a very ordinary life here with me and Gran, but you've a destiny that you know nothing about. I've never told you anything about it before, perhaps I should've."

Thom's heart thumped in his ears. "Tell me now."

Grandpa sighed and for the first time ever Thom saw him as an old man. "Your great-great-grandfather, Seamus Prow, as you do know, was rumoured to be a smuggler."

Thom nodded, was he finally going to hear the whole, exciting story?

"Well boy, he wasn't a smuggler he was ... a pirate."

"A pirate!" Thom couldn't believe his ears, weren't pirates just found in books and films?

Grandpa gazed at him. "He was an infamous pirate of his time, fierce, determined, dangerous, but fair. He treated his crew well, but

9

his brother-in-law and ship's mate, Stefan Teach, betrayed him and started a mutiny against him. Teach murdered him in cold blood and stole his ship. He also wanted his treasure."

"Crikey," said Thom, sitting up straighter.

"The treasure was well hidden by Seamus. Teach thought he knew where it was, but after he'd killed Seamus, he realised that he'd no idea – it wasn't where he thought it was. Seamus must've had his suspicions, to hide it in time. Teach was furious and swore he would never rest until he'd found the treasure. He never did though. To this day, we don't know where that treasure has been hidden. According to 'legend' there is a map that'll lead to the treasure, but nobody has ever found the map. The treasure, my boy, belongs to you. It's your rightful inheritance - if it can ever be found. However, you'd have to find the treasure map first and I hate to tell you this, but I think it's unlikely that you will, many have tried before ... and failed."

Thom stared at his grandfather. "But why do I have to go to a different school? What has that got to do with finding a treasure map?"

"It's a very particular kind of school, only the chosen can gain an education there; it will be a unique kind of learning to help you in your life's journey towards your career, your destiny."

"Grandpa, I'm only twelve, I don't know what I want to be yet. I thought maybe I'd be a fisherman like you."

"The fishing industry is not as strong as it used to be, my boy. You need another direction, a different vocation."

Grandpa, unhurriedly, got out of his chair, placed the bottle on the coffee table and sat down next to Thom. He took Thom's hand.

"Grandpa, where is the school?"

"It's in a place far away from here. It's called the School for Scoundrels."

"You mean it's a boarding school? And Scoundrels? Is it a school for naughty children? But Grandpa, I'm not that naughty and I promise I can be better behaved, please don't send me away."

Grandpa's face turned pink beneath his beard and he placed a firm hand on Thom's shoulder. "It is a boarding school, but no it's not for naughty children."

Thom felt his stomach flip and the realisation of the truth dawned on him like a dark shadow. "I don't want to go."

"You must," said Grandpa. "You have to prepare to become a pirate."

"What if I don't want to be a pirate?"

"It's your destiny."

Thom was silent; he felt an inner panic rising.

11

"I'm sorry, it's not what I would've wanted for you, but it's in our blood. You're the chosen one, it seems, chosen to search for and find the stolen treasure."

"But what if I don't want the treasure, what if I want to stay here with you and Gran?"

"Then somebody else may find it, somebody who doesn't deserve it. I'm guessing, from this note, that Captain Ginger, the Headteacher of the School for Scoundrels, is already afraid that somebody unworthy will discover it and that is why he has summoned you."

"But who else knows about it?"

"Pretty much everyone in the pirate world including your distant cousin, Stanley Teach, he is Greybeard's great-great-grandson. Stanley's two or three years older than you, he's already completed some years at the school; you cannot let him get to the treasure before you. You owe it to your great-great-grandfather, but also to your parents."

Thom frowned, his mouth went dry. "That's it! That's why mum and dad were diving that day, wasn't it? They were trying to find the treasure."

Grandpa shrugged and looked uncomfortable.

Thom felt as if he had been slapped. "You lied to me. You led me to believe that it was an accident at work."

"It was ... of sorts. Your father, as you know, was an underwater archaeologist and a fine one at that; your mother a great deep-sea diver. All we know is that they died tragically when their boat caught fire. I don't know if they were treasure hunting that day -" Grandpa's voice caught in his throat.

Thom felt himself grow cold, despite his grandfather's anguish. Grandpa had lied. Gran too.

"I can't believe you've lied to me all these years!" Thom snatched the bottle from off the coffee table. "I wish I'd never found this stupid bottle."

"Thom, we told you what we thought was best."

"Best for who?"

"Thom, come on -"

"Leave me alone!"

Thom slammed the front door as he left the house. He hurried down the hill towards the harbour, his feet carrying him away from what had just been revealed; his mind was a whirlpool of thoughts.

Much later, Thom sat on the harbour wall still grasping the bottle. He stared out across the silver sea, the moon, full and bright in the starry sky. Everything blurred as he let the silent tears fall down his cheeks. With as much effort as he could muster, through his anger, he took the bottle and hurled it as hard as he could back into the ocean.

Chapter 2
Kidnap

The next morning, Grandpa put his head round the door of Thom's bedroom as he did every morning they went out fishing together. "Are you ready, boy?"

Although he was awake, Thom dragged the duvet further up over his head. He didn't want to talk to Grandpa and he certainly didn't want to help him with the fishing. In fact, he doubted he ever wanted to help him again and who cared if the boat went wrong and he lost his fishing business? That would serve him right.

Later that morning, Thom heard the front door close and Gran leave the house. At eight o'clock she had come in with a cup of tea, but Thom had turned his back on her as she placed it on his bedside table. He had let the tea go cold.

The house, now empty, was eerily quiet. Thom walked straight to his grandparent's room where he phoned Sam. They arranged to meet at the harbour in half an hour.

As he was leaving the room, he spied the dark, wooden chest at the end of the double bed. Thom had always believed it stored blankets, but now he had his doubts – a box like that could hold many secrets. He opened the lid, it creaked on its hinges and he pulled out a couple of blankets. Hidden beneath was another smaller, wooden box, ornately carved. He placed it on the bed and opened it. He rifled through some old, yellowing papers until he found what he was looking for, an envelope addressed to 'Dad'.

Thom sat on the bed and pulled out the letter.

Dear Father,

I'm sorry that to this day I'm a disappointment to you. I'm sorry that I left the School for Scoundrels earlier than I should have done and that I didn't pass my Fully Qualified Pirate Finals Certificate. I realise now, with a son of my own, how much you want what's best for your children. That is why I want you to make me a promise ... if anything happens to me, or Violet, that you will see to it that Thomas graduates from the School for Scoundrels with his FQP certificate; nothing must stand in the way of this. I know now that I should have pursued my destiny and I'm sorry that I didn't. I don't regret marrying Violet, but I do regret not finishing school. Who knows, perhaps it would have helped me find the treasure.

There will come a time when Greybeard's great-great-grandson will be amongst the pupils there and that means he will know of the family's hidden treasure and it will be his aim to search for it while he's at the school too. All we know is that the secret to the hidden treasure lays within the School for Scoundrels *and if we are ever to have it returned it to its rightful owners (our side of the family) then Thomas* **must** *become a pupil of the school and do his best to recover the hidden treasure of the Prows.*

With love,

Ben

So, his father had been at the school, but had left because of his mother. Clearly his mother had been more important to him which made Thom feel warm inside. However, it seemed that his father would have liked to get the treasure that belonged to the Prows - at least he didn't want anyone *else* to get their hands on it.

Thom slipped the letter into the envelope and placed it back in the box. He closed the lid, left his grandparent's room and ran down the stairs. Grabbing his kite-surfing gear, he fought the spillage of tears all the way to the harbour where he had arranged to meet Sam.

It was already busy in the harbour area and Thom found it hard to meet anyone's eye that said a cheery 'good-morning'. He plonked his gear into the bottom of the row-boat and looked up to see Sam coming towards him.

"Wind's good this morning, should be great out there today," said Sam, as he approached and dumped his gear into the boat.

"Can't wait to get out there," said Thom, hating that his voice sounded unsteady.

The boys rowed out to Bos. The morning was bright and warm, and the wind was perfect for getting in the sails and driving them along.

"You're quiet," said Sam.

"Am I? Sorry, I was just thinking that I wish they'd bring kite-surfing into the school sports curriculum instead of football, I'm so much better at it."

"You are pretty rubbish at football, Thom, not very steady on your legs." Sam smiled at him. "Much better at balancing on your board though, you're a real natural."

"That'll be me sea-legs." Thom managed to smile in return and he felt his spirits lift a little as they got closer to the island.

Out on the waves, his kite hauling him at speed across the water, Thom felt his anger disperse into the moist, salty air. However, it wasn't long before he found himself thinking back to the look of misery on Grandpa's face, as he realised that Thom had just learned the truth about his parents' accident; the realisation that he had lied to his grandson. Thom's stomach shrank.

He should apologise.

Thom indicated to Sam that he was ready to go in. Sam's surprised face said it all.

"Sorry, I promised Grandpa I would be back in time to help him bring in the catch," Thom explained, as they packed away their gear.

"Oh ... all right. Same time tomorrow?"

"I'll have to let you know."

Thom could feel Sam's quizzical look following him down the sandy beach to the boat. He couldn't talk to Sam about this, not yet, maybe not ever.

Thom walked up the hill from the harbour. He just had time to take his gear back to the cottage, grab something to eat and meet Grandpa at 'Bessie'.

As he walked through the door, he could hear voices in the kitchen – had Grandpa returned already? Thom had been in such a rush to get back to the cottage he hadn't even registered if Grandpa's boat had been in the harbour or not.

Thom entered the kitchen and found Skipper and Gran talking in hushed voices. Gran's face was ashen and she was sat down in a chair, something that Gran never did unless it was mealtimes.

Gran's eyes widened at Skipper when she saw Thom in the doorway. Skipper turned, the look in his eyes immediately told Thom that something was wrong.

"What is it? What's happened?"

"It's -" started Gran, but her voice cracked.

"Thom," said Skipper. "I believe that your Grandfather told you about the School for Scoundrels last night?"

Thom nodded. "How do you know about it?"

"Your Gran's just told me about the message and how you're expected at the school tomorrow night."

"Yes, but what's that got to do with you?"

Skipper passed Thom a sheet of paper. "I found this on your grandfather's boat this morning. 'Bessie' was deserted and drifting out to sea, just like the *Mary Celeste*. There was no sign of your grandfather and I discovered this note stuck to the mast with a dagger. I had to tow 'Bessie' back in behind my boat."

Thom took the piece of paper. It felt dry and rough in his hands. He read and as he did so he felt a clutch of fear seize him.

We have William Prow. Give us the treasure map of the Prows or the old man's shark bait!

"Where've they taken him?"

"We don't know."

"Has the School for Scoundrel's taken him? Is it my fault because I threw the bottle back?" Thom felt his breath constrict his chest.

Skipper looked him directly in the eye. "Thom, you mustn't blame yourself. This feud has been going on for generations, but it seems it's coming to a head – something must've happened for it all to kick off again, but I doubt the School for Scoundrels is involved with William's disappearance."

"We have to do something," cried Thom.

Skipper sighed. "There's only one thing you can do to help, Thom."

"Anything, I'll do anything – I was so angry with him last night. I was so horrid to him. This is all my fault!" Thom started to cry.

Skipper took Thom's shoulders in his great hands and turned him to face him. "Thom, you must go. You must go and learn to be a pirate – learn what you can as quickly as you can. I will message Captain Ginger and tell him what's happened. He'll help you find your Grandfather – the school will not let you down, you're a Prow."

Thom sniffed hard and straightened his back. "Okay. I'll go."

"Grandpa will be so proud of you," said Gran, tearfully.

"I'll go and send a message immediately. I'll pick Thom and his luggage up tomorrow night about eleven and row him across to Bos as

21

requested. We must keep this to ourselves. Folk round here will start asking a lot of questions. When I towed William's boat back earlier, Fred asked me what had happened. I told him that William's boat needs fixing, so that he's taken the opportunity to go and visit his brother in Cornwall - while the boat is out of action."

"Did he believe you?" Gran's face was hopeful.

"I think so, but if he doesn't return soon then there'll be more questions."

"But what are we going to do about Grandpa?" asked Thom.

"I'll send a message to the kidnappers, there is a way. I'll explain that we don't know where the treasure map is, but that you're going away to school and that when you find it, you'll hand it over to them."

"No," cried Gran. "Will would never allow it."

"He's not here to argue, Ellie, and we must promise them something, otherwise we may never see William again."

The next morning, Thom felt the insects stampede around his stomach. His familiar room, the room that had once been his father's, would be empty once more. The trunk on the bed, that he and Gran had hauled out from under the stairs, was filled with clothes and books; biscuits and goodies baked by Gran.

Thom heard Gran rummaging around in her room whilst he was packing. She appeared a few minutes later with something wrapped up in a piece of red velvet. Thom now held a silver compass delicately between his fingers. It would come in useful whilst learning to be a pirate.

"Grandpa would want you to have this. Every pirate should have a compass, you won't ever get lost now. This belonged to Seamus Prow, so you look after it and it'll look after you."

Thom stared at the intricately carved outer casing of the silver compass; it was tarnished due to its age. Unclasping it, he revealed the mechanics of the compass within – a delicate pin which pointed north. It was beautiful.

"Thank you, Gran," said Thom, wrapping it up in the soft red, velvet pouch. "I'll take good care of it."

Gran nodded and stood beside him searching for something in the trunk. Finally, Thom heard a click and watched, fascinated, as a secret compartment sprung open in the side. Carefully, she took the red velvet package from him and placed it inside, clicking the flap shut again.

The old lady smiled at him sadly, patted him on the shoulder. "I'll leave you to it." Gran left the room and Thom heard her pause on the creaking stairs and blow her nose, he wanted to rush out and comfort her, but his own pain held him back.

Thom glanced at the photograph of his parents and himself as a toddler, he walked over to the windowsill and picked it up. The window was open and he heard a muffled noise below him in the garden; peering out he could see Gran standing very still on the patio, staring into space. A sinking sensation grew in him and he started to wonder if he had done the right thing in saying he would go. He gazed down at the photo in his hands ... his father's smiling face and dark eyes seemed to be reassuring him that he had made the right decision. A small gust of wind caught the curtain and it brushed against his cheek. *Be brave.* The woman's words were carried in on the breeze and away again.

Later that day, Thom was finalising his packing, when Gran called up the stairs that supper was ready.

The table was set with steaming plates of beef stew and dumplings, one of his favourites. There was an enormous chocolate cake on the side for pudding. A third place had been set, but the seat remained empty.

"Come on, Thom, eat up," said Gran, barely touching the food on her own plate. "Tell me how Sam and George took the news today?"

24

"They were shocked and said that they'd miss me, but Sam said we'll still have the holidays to catch up in. I just hope they won't forget all about me whilst I'm away!"

"Of course they won't and you'll soon make new friends too. Do you have everything packed?"

He nodded and took the large slice of chocolate cake that she handed him. Although he didn't feel hungry, he didn't want Gran to worry any more than necessary so ate his supper, having to swallow hard on a number of occasions so that the food would actually go down.

Gran was very quiet after supper. Thom knew that she was worried about Grandpa, but also about him going away to school – the timing couldn't have been worse. He tried to fill the silence by asking her what she knew about the school.

"Well, as you do know, Skipper will take you in the row-boat to the Isle of Bos, where you'll be collected and taken to your ship."

Thom's mouth went dry. "My ship?"

"Yes. The School for Scoundrels is a school positioned out in the oceans, it moves around the globe; the classrooms are not in buildings, but on ships."

"Wow! Classrooms on ships?"

Gran nodded, a slight movement towards a smile playing on her lips.

Thom tried to imagine what his new school would be like. Were English, Maths and Science all subjects that pirates would have to learn, or would it be sword-fighting and how to sail the ship? The more he learned about the unusualness of the school, the more his nerves turned to excitement.

"I remember when we visited your father, when he first went to study there. The ship he was on was called the 'Sudden Ghost', it has the same name as the ship your great-great-grandfather, Seamus Prow, was Captain of. They built a new ship after Greybeard destroyed it. I'm guessing that you'll be on the same ship too. The generations of families seem to study on the ship that their ancestors did before them, it is certainly true of your cousin, Stanley: he's aboard 'The Hades Rambler', appropriate name in my opinion. Their ship is the original vessel that his great-great-grandfather, Greybeard, became captain of after he destroyed the Sudden Ghost, the thieving ..."

"Do you think Stanley might be involved in Grandpa's kidnap?"

"I don't know. I just wish I knew he was all right." Gran's eyes were wet.

"He'll be okay, Gran, I'm sure of it. Skipper said they won't hurt him, he's too valuable to them." Thom tried to sound confident and grown up, but inside he wasn't so sure.

Thom was restless after dinner, unable to settle and watch the TV. He could tell that Gran was discreetly watching him from behind the ironing board. Thom knew that Gran needed to keep busy, but noticed that she took a long time over one of grandpa's pyjama shirts.

At eleven o'clock Skipper arrived.

Thom stood, his stomach dropping to his feet as he felt Gran's arms pull him closer to her and hold him in a tight embrace. She let out a sigh. "Have a great first term, Thom. I hope you enjoy the lessons and make us proud."

"I will, Gran. I'll write as soon as I can and I'll see you very soon." Although Thom realised that he had no idea when he would next see her.

Gran gave him another large squeeze then let him go and shuffled out of the room towards the front door. Holding the door open for Skipper, who was carrying Thom's trunk, she said: "Go and find Grandpa, bring him home, Thom."

Thom gave her one last hug. "Of course, Gran, he'll be home soon, I promise. Take care of yourself."

Gran gave him a small smile.

"I'll take care of her, Thom," said Skipper, as they left the house.

Thom turned round, at the end of the short garden pathway, and was surprised to see that Gran had already shut the door. How could he be leaving her now that Grandpa was missing? They walked in silence down the cobbled hill in the near darkness; a full moon was hidden beneath thick clouds. The rows of fishermen's cottages were all in shadows. A large, black cat sat on a wall and watched them stroll down to the harbour. Thom saw the cat's green eyes reflect in the torchlight, before it fled across the street and into another garden and away.

"Why do we have to leave at such an odd time?" Thom asked.

"We have to leave under the cover of night so we don't bring any attention to ourselves, or the ship. The general public, or landlubbers as Pirates call them, know nothing of the School for Scoundrels; it is a very different world out there on the oceans with its own adventures, some magic and all kinds of people and dangers."

"Did Grandpa, go to the School for Scoundrels as well as dad?"

"Didn't he tell you? Yes, he graduated and became a Fully Qualified Pirate, unlike me, I flunked all the exams. However, he fell in love with your Gran and wanted to stay on land. He still loves the sea – his fishing helps fulfil that side of his dreams, but he couldn't leave Ellie, same as your dad with Violet."

Thom wondered how you could love a girl so much that you would do anything for them, even give up the things you loved doing. He would never give up his kite-boarding, especially not for a girl.

It was as if Skipper had read his thoughts. "I know you find that hard to understand right now, but give it a few years," he chuckled.

The full moon had come out from behind the clouds and shone as they rowed out of the harbour towards the small Isle of Bos. As they passed the harbour walls, Thom felt a sudden panic, what if he couldn't find Grandpa or the map? He took a deep breath and tried to calm his rapid breathing.

The splish-splash sound of the oars was all they could hear, as they approached the island. It was a still and cool night.

"I hope I can find Grandpa. That's the only reason I'm going."

"Aye," said Skipper. "I know you'll do your best, Thom. I've known you since you were a little nipper. William's my best mate. I reckon he's okay."

"But what if I can't find the treasure map?"

"Then we'll find another way to get William back. He's a tough one you know."

The treasure map had seemed unimportant to Thom two days ago. Now, he knew he must discover it, not so that he could be rich, only so that he could take Grandpa safely home to Gran. Home. He wished he could be there now instead of hoisting a heavy trunk from a small row-boat onto the beach.

Thom glanced at his watch 23.57, still no sign ... had they forgotten him? Had throwing the bottle back revoked his right to attend the school? Thom was about to ask Skipper if there could have been a mistake, when he heard a rumbling sound. The beach beneath his feet began to tremble, ever so slightly at first, then more vigorously.

An earthquake. Thom grabbed hold of Skipper's arm - he glanced sideways at him, but he was stood calmly, looking out to sea, waiting.

The shuddering was followed by the sound of rushing water and Thom stood transfixed, as a way out from the beach, in deeper water, a huge surge of waves, illuminated by the light of the moon, began to rise up out of the ocean. The prow of a huge, wooden ship, unfurling sails billowing in the breeze, appeared from the depths of the ocean before them.

Thom clutched Skipper's arm and Skipper squeezed his hand reassuringly in return. "Your future, sonny, awaits you."

Thom stared at the wooden vessel before him on the surface of the sea. A ship that sailed under the water ... was this his new classroom? The ship had tall masts full of white sails on which Thom could see the crew members milling around like insects in a tree. How had they not drowned beneath the waves?

Thom and Skipper stood watching as the crew let down a small row-boat which had an oarsman seated in the middle. The man rowed to shore. Thom was rooted to the spot and was surprised when Skipper spoke to him. "I'll help you with the trunk onto the boat then I'll head back to the mainland."

Thom turned and looked at him. Suddenly, he felt very afraid and wished he could just climb back in the boat with Skipper and for his life to return to normal. Unfortunately, his life was not normal anymore and he wondered if it ever would be again.

A man's gruff voice cut through their silence. "Come on, I 'aven't got all night, I've others to collect too."

"Goodbye, Skipper. Please look after Gran."

"Of course, see you in a few weeks." Skipper helped him put the trunk into the row-boat then stood watching as Thom climbed aboard.

The oarsman was an ugly fellow with a scarred face; long, grey, wispy hair protruding from an almost-bald head and a patch over one eye. If Thom had not believed that he was going to a school for pirates before this moment, he did now.

"Take care of him," called Skipper, as the oarsman struggled to get the boat back into the water.

"Don't you worry, Kenneth Skipper, they'll be teaching 'im how to take care of hisself," growled the oarsman.

Thom sat still in the boat and watched the pirate with his strong arms and taut muscles in his back, as he leaned in and out with the rhythm of the oars. The pirate didn't speak and Thom didn't feel that he could engage him in conversation either. There was a rather unpleasant smell that seemed to exude from this tatty, old pirate and Thom tried to concentrate on the salty smell of the sea instead. Thom stared as Skipper's figure got smaller and smaller and the awaiting ship loomed larger and larger ahead of him.

Chapter 3
A Night Voyage

As they approached the ship, Thom could see silver writing on the side: Sudden Ghost. So, Gran had been right, his class would be aboard the same ship as his father and grandfathers' before him. The ship looked ancient, but Gran had said it wasn't the original; that had been destroyed during the mutiny on Seamus Prow's ship, but it had been re-built in the style of the earlier Sudden Ghost.

Up close, Thom could see the wooden planks that made up the ship's body. Great white sails were now pulled up on the tall masts, in order for the ship to remain still, which made the vessel seem skeletal; port holes lined both starboard and portside. Thom wondered if there were any canons ready to be pushed forward, loaded, lit and fired. Would that be a necessity while he was on board, he wondered; hoping not. Nevertheless, a shiver of excitement ran through him at the hint of adventure.

"Ahoy, there!" called a voice from above.

"Thomas Prow coming aboard," hollered the miserable oarsman.

"Climb aboard."

Thom looked up as a rope ladder uncoiled towards him and a couple of faces peered over the side of the ship. He hesitated for a moment then stood, trying not to make the boat sway too much. He grabbed hold of the wet, stiff rope and started to climb, but he slipped almost immediately. The youths above him sniggered. Red-faced, he continued to climb, carefully at first, then with more confidence. Thom daren't look down and realised, with a sinking feeling, it would be bad if he had to climb the rigging any time soon.

Reaching the top, his legs like jelly, he saw two faces gazing at him over what looked like an enormous banister rail from the staircase of a very large mansion - its polished wood gleamed in the light of the full moon. Two boys stood holding a lantern, its light dull. One of the faces was round with green eyes, framed by golden curls and a spattering of freckles across his nose; a black scarf struggled to tame the curls beneath it. The other boy was black-haired with much sharper, but handsome, features and chocolate-brown eyes. He held a black, three-point hat in his left hand. When Thom stepped on the last rung they smiled and hauled him aboard with outstretched hands.

He had just got his feet on the deck when he heard a shout.

"Look out!"

Thom felt himself thrown to the boards as a dagger sliced the air over his head.

"Watch it!" shouted the curly-haired lad as he helped Thom back to his feet.

34

Thom spied a group of youngsters with swords and daggers brawling on the deck above him; swords clashed and clinked, moonlight reflecting in their sharp blades. Forceful shouts of 'lunge and parry' carried towards him on the night air.

"Sorry about that. Night practise. You never know when you're going to be attacked and it's very different using a sword in the dark," the boy continued.

Thom nodded, his heart hammering against his ribs.

"Welcome aboard, me hearty," said the dark-haired youth, shaking Thom's hand enthusiastically.

"Hello," he replied, trying not to laugh at the greeting, he'd no idea that pirates actually spoke that way, although why should they be any different than in the stories he'd read? "I'm Thomas, Thomas Prow, but everyone calls me Thom."

"We know who you are," said the curly-haired boy, a mischievous glint in his eye.

Thom felt uncomfortable. How did they know who he was? Who had told them? *What* had they been told?

"I'm Angus and this is Roscoe," said the dark-haired boy, smiling broadly and nodding his head towards the curly-headed boy.

"Nice to meet you."

"You're to be our cabin-mate, we get to share our cabin with you," said Roscoe, grinning.

"Great," said Thom, although he had been hoping that he would have a room of his own; he wasn't used to sharing.

The old oarsman gave a yell from below.

"Heave-Ho," cried Roscoe.

Thom realised that he should have been helping to pull his trunk aboard, so joined in the tugging of the rope. Together they dragged the heavy trunk which landed with a loud thump on the deck of the ship.

"Blimey, what you got in there?" said Roscoe, having turned rather red in the face.

"Just some clothes, a few books ... oh, and goodies that Gran baked."

"Great, just in time for a midnight feast," suggested Roscoe, who evidently liked his food judging from the size of him.

"Sure, there's plenty there," agreed Thom, becoming aware of a lot of shouting below.

The boys stuck their heads over the side of the ship where the oarsman was bellowing at them. "Come on, I 'aven't got all night, you cretins. Haul me up will you?"

"Friendly, isn't he?" said Thom, as he helped the two boys haul the old pirate aboard.

"He's always like that, don't take it personally," said Angus. "His name's Windbags."

"Really?" asked Thom.

"Really," replied Angus, laughing.

Thom was a little unsure if Angus was telling the truth or not, so he decided he wouldn't call the old pirate 'Windbags' until he'd heard another pupil say it to his face. He didn't want to get into any trouble, certainly not on his first night aboard the Sudden Ghost.

When they had hauled Windbags onto the deck he went off with Thom's trunk muttering under his breath.

"Where's he taking my trunk?" asked Thom.

"To our cabin," replied Roscoe. "We've been told to take you straight to Captain Ginger."

"Oh?"

"He's the Headteacher of all the ships in the school."

"How many ships are there?"

"Three in total, unless you count the Elusive Wolf as well, of course."

"Elusive Wolf?"

"Yes, the ship comes and goes; nobody ever knows when or where it'll appear next," said Angus.

"Sounds very mysterious," said Thom.

"There's a lot that's mysterious around here," stated Angus. "You'll soon notice that not all is as it seems."

Thom felt a shiver run through him at Angus' now serious tone; he much preferred his humorous one.

Roscoe and Angus led Thom along the deck towards some double doors at the end. Angus knocked firmly. "Captain's cabin," he whispered to Thom.

"Don't worry, he can be quite nice at times," said Roscoe, grinning.

Thom felt cold.

"Enter," boomed a voice from within.

"We'll wait here," said Angus, taking a step backwards.

Thom hesitated before he turned the brass handle of the door and crept into a dark, lamp-lit room. Antique furniture cluttered the space, including a large, polished desk at one end. A huge bulk of a man sat behind the desk, his size overwhelming. As Thom approached him, he began to make out the Captain's features: an enormous, bright ginger beard; full red lips and bright blue eyes that looked out of red, weathered cheeks. Thom realised that he was being watched by a second pair of eyes – on the desk sat a sizeable, black cat, its green eyes staring unblinkingly at him. He swallowed.

"Thomas Prow," growled the Captain standing up, his height immense. He was holding out an enormous hand over the desk, which was covered in maps and papers; compasses and a brass spyglass.

"Good evening, Sir," replied Thom allowing his hand to be shook by the Captain's almighty paw-like hand. "I-I mean Captain."

"I'm Captain Ginger, this here's Storm ... mind her, she's a little feisty!"

Thom went to stroke the cat, but she hissed at him. Instantly, he pulled his hand away, afraid of being scratched or bitten.

"Good lad, good lad," said the Captain staring at Thom. "Well, well, William Prow's grandson, a pleasure to meet you, lad."

"Thank you, Captain. You knew my Grandfather?"

"Yes, very well, an exceptional pupil – I do hope that you will be an exceptional pupil, Shipmate Prow?"

Thom nodded. "Yes, of course, Captain." He was a little confused as to how Captain Ginger knew Grandpa was an excellent student. "Were you and Grandpa both pupils here at the same time?"

Captain Ginger laughed, showing a mouthful of rotting teeth. "No, no, he was one of me best students."

"Oh." Captain Ginger did look old, but his bright orange hair certainly belied his years.

"Welcome to the School for Scoundrels and your class-ship, Sudden Ghost. I expect my message came as a bit of a shock for you and your grandfather". He indicated for Thom to take a seat opposite him and slumped down in his chair. "We've had a little trouble recently with a suspected mutiny on one of the class-ships and knowing your family history, I thought I'd see if old Seamus Prow's great-great-grandson was ready for his quest."

"Quest?" asked Thom. "I thought I was coming here to learn to be a pirate."

"All part of it, my lad, all part of it. Now then, have you been introduced to any of your crewmates yet?"

"Yes, Captain, two so far called Roscoe and Angus."

He bellowed with laughter again. "Ah, yes, right couple of scoundrels those two, be good pirates one day, good to have aboard. I hope they made you feel welcome?"

"Thank you, Captain, they did."

All of a sudden, Thom was thrown forward in his seat and had to hold onto the desk to stop himself from falling to the floor. "What's happening?"

"We're setting sail," roared the Captain, his eyes shining mischievously.

"But it feels like we're falling."

"We're going under ... we've a couple more students to pick up tonight ready for the new term."

"U-under?"

"Yes, better hold your breath, Thomas Prow," he roared with laughter as he watched Thom take a deep breath. "I'm pulling your wooden leg, Thomas, we don't need to hold our breath; the magic of the Sudden Ghost will keep us safe."

Thom held on tight to the chair whilst the ship tilted forwards and sped into the depths of the ocean, down and down they went; Thom's heart in his mouth as if he were on a roller-coaster ride. Suddenly, they levelled off and Thom was thrown back violently in the chair. The Captain had laughed the whole way down and Thom was amazed that it didn't seem to bother him at all.

"You'll find your sea legs soon," he stated. "Now, we must get down to some serious business, Thom. Old Skipper sent me a message saying your grandfather's been kidnapped."

"Do you know where he is?"

The Captain shook his head. "I've some of my connections trying to figure out what's going on, but we don't have much to go on yet. Did your grandfather say anything to you before he went missing?"

"Only that I had to come to this school and that it was to do with my great-great-grandfather's treasure map. Since that red bottle arrived two days ago, everything has changed."

"Try to stay calm and focused, Thom. You'll need a clear head to try and solve these mysteries.

I'll help you all I can, but you must realise that the oceans are vast and can hide many secrets."

"I don't know what to do, or even where to start," sighed Thom.

"You can start by getting some sleep. The school will teach you what you need to know to become a successful pirate. In the meantime, we'll try and figure out what's happened to William." The Captain paused, but seemed to want to say something else.

"But?"

"Just one more thing ... *do* you know where the treasure map is?"

Thom felt surprised at the question. "I've no idea. I wish I did. I knew nothing about the pirates in our family until two days ago, let alone a long, lost map."

The Captain regarded him closely. "All right then, off you go. Roscoe and Angus will show you to your cabin. We'll speak more another day, just try and settle in, and the least said about any of this to anyone, the better – do you understand, Thom?"

"Yes, Captain," he replied, embarrassed to hear his voice tremble.

"I'll be seeing you, Shipmate Prow."

Thom walked towards the doors that would take him onto the deck where he hoped that Angus and Roscoe would be waiting for him. He turned to say goodbye to Captain Ginger and was stunned to see that the Captain was no longer in his quarters ... where had he gone? He looked briefly around for an additional door that might have led to a further room, but couldn't see any in the dark shadows of the office – only the green eyes of the cat glinting at him. He felt the skin on the back of his neck shrink.

Thom stepped out onto the deck. He was astonished to see that the moon-lit sky had been replaced by a midnight-blue ocean. The waters surrounded the ship on all sides, like a giant bubble, but did not touch the vessel. A strange luminous glow lit up the ocean around him and he watched in amazement as a group of brightly coloured fish swam past - all the colours of the rainbow. As they swam, they changed colour; first, yellow, then green, blue, purple, red - a chaos of colour beneath the surface.

A moment later, out of the corner of his eye, a large shape approached him overhead. The view reminded him of an underwater viewing gallery at a marine-life centre. He gave a shout as a shark bared its teeth at him, before swimming off into the dark depths.

"Was he in a good mood?" asked Roscoe, appearing at Thom's side.

"What, w-who – the shark?" asked Thom.

"Hey, you all right?" asked Angus, holding onto Thom's arm. "You're shaking."

Roscoe laughed, but Angus shot him an angry glare.

Thom tried to pull himself together, but didn't seem to be able to stop his legs from shaking beneath him. He was surprised as he had always had good sea-legs when on Grandpa's fishing boat, but then that had never gone under water where he'd come face to face with a shark.

"Come on, we'll take you to our cabin."

Roscoe and Angus held onto Thom's arms and led him steadily across the now deserted deck towards the stairs which led to the lower parts of the ship then down to the cabins. Many doors led off a long corridor where Thom imagined the pupils, and maybe even the teachers, slept.

Roscoe opened a door and led Thom inside. The cabin was fairly small. There were three desks, three chest of drawers and three hammocks that swayed with the motion of the current. One wall was lined with books, which were held in place by string pulled tightly across their spines. Thom noticed a couple of titles as they guided him to a chair at a desk and sat him down: How to Speak Mermaid and Swashbuckling for Beginners.

"I think he needs some R.U.M.," said Roscoe.

"Rum! Aren't we a little young to be drinking rum?" Thom asked.

It was Angus' turn to laugh. "It's not what you think. In fact it's not what anyone thinks.

Pirates are reported to drink Rum all the time, but in this school it's different. We do drink R.U.M., but it is just a mix of Rhubarb juice, a drop of an Unknown ingredient and Mango juice. The Unknown ingredient is supposed to have healing qualities, but the fruit is to help us against scurvy!"

"Sounds disgusting!"

"Tastes divine ... tastes like fruit chews, don't know how it works, but it does."

"Roscoe, go and wake cook, get him to make Thom some R.U.M."

"Do I have to? Won't he be angry if I wake him?"

"Possibly, but his growl is worse than his bite."

Reluctantly, Roscoe left the cabin.

"Look Thom, I think Roscoe forgets, we've been here for a year already, we've found our sea-legs and are getting used to the mysteriousness of the school and how it's run; the unusual magical element of it too."

"It's ok. It's rather different to my last school, nothing exciting ever happened there, just boring old subjects and stuffy old teachers – well some of them anyway."

There was another sudden jolt and the ship tipped to its prow and sped skywards; although Thom had to hold on tight, Angus stood still, hands on hips.

"How did you -"

"Just takes practice. We're picking up another new kid, but he's in a different cabin, we'll meet him tomorrow."

"How do you know it's a boy?"

"We're an all boys' school. Didn't you know that girl pirates aren't allowed?"

"I'm sure I read somewhere that there were female pirates. Grace O'Malley, wasn't she a pirate?"

"Ah yes, the infamous Grace, she is mentioned in our 'Ancestors' lessons quite frequently, but it is bad luck to have a woman aboard a ship."

"I don't mind there being no girls, they're normally trouble."

Angus laughed and at that moment Roscoe entered carrying a tankard full of a strange pink/orange liquid. He handed it to Thom. "Drink this, it will help you relax and get some sleep."

Thom took a small sip of the revolting looking drink, but was pleasantly surprised to discover that it did taste delicious, like fruit chews, although it was sweet it was thirst quenching too.

"Now, how about that midnight feast?" suggested Thom, reaching for the trunk.

"What you got?" asked Roscoe stepping towards Thom as he opened the lid.

"Plenty. There are cakes, sausage rolls, homemade cookies – they're the best."

"We'd better not eat it all," said Angus. "Save some for another day, ship's cook is ok, but not very adventurous sometimes. All right if you like fish, but he does come up with some rather unusual concoctions. Be warned."

"Hmmm, we had Squid sucker pie tonight, a bit, em, chewy to say the least!" laughed Roscoe.

"That sounds revolting," replied Thom, reluctantly handing over Gran's amazing triple chocolate chip cookies that melted in your mouth. He felt a glimmer of guilt as he thought about how Gran, despite what had happened, still managed to bake lots of delicious things for him to take away to school. He knew it helped her to be busy, keep her mind occupied.

"Oh wow, will she send you any more of these?" asked Roscoe, stuffing the crumbling cookie into his mouth in a disgusting fashion.

"I hope so, if she can figure out how to get them here."

Angus grinned. "She'll find a way. Probably won't fit in a bottle like the messages do, but other pupils receive parcels in all sorts of ways; mostly by Dolphin delivery. You see scientists believe that they will be able to communicate with dolphins in a few years. However, us Pirates know that dolphins can already communicate with us. Nevertheless, they choose not to speak to most humans because they are not as intelligent as the dolphins. Of course, scientists believe it is the other way round, but you are highly honoured if a dolphin speaks to you."

"Have you ever had a dolphin speak to you?" asked Thom.

"Yes," they both nodded, smiling.

"Wow."

The ship had been still for a while now and Thom heard voices outside in the corridor. He waited until they had passed by then turned the handle on the door. Peering out into the lantern-lit corridor he could see three boys: one was really tall and thin, the other two were more round and much shorter. Was that ... he squinted to see if he'd imagined it, but no, one did have a wooden leg. Thom wasn't quite sure if he was more surprised about the fact that some of the pirates were exactly as they'd been portrayed in his story books, or that they existed at all.

The ship took another downward tilt and Thom shut the door quickly to find something to hold onto. Unfortunately, he grabbed hold of Roscoe and they both ended up in a heap on the floor of the cabin. Thom apologised and tried to stand up, but found that he couldn't get up, let alone stand. He just continued to roll around on the cabin floor until Roscoe and Angus managed, through fits of laughter, to haul him to his feet enough to lay him horizontal into his hammock.

"Thanks, shipmates," he laughed.

"Anytime," they replied.

Roscoe was still laughing as he climbed into his hammock, the ship now on an even keel. Angus blew out the lanterns and Thom found himself in utter darkness. After a while he could hear the gentle snores of his cabin mates and his own eyes began to feel heavy.

As he was dropping off, his thoughts turned to Grandpa. Where was he? Was he going to be okay? Captain Ginger had promised they would do all they could to help him in his quest, but Thom knew that deep down he was their new hope – the one who hadn't yet started the search for the treasure map, the one they were now depending on. It felt like a very heavy responsibility, not one he felt ready for.

Chapter 4
First day of school

A loud clanging sound followed by shouts all around him roused Thom from his dreamless sleep. He tried to open his eyes, but he felt groggy and his eyelids were as heavy as lead. He was surprised by this, as he was used to being awoken early to go out on his grandfather's boat, but his whole body felt tired. He guessed it must have been all the excitement from the past few days, that and his late night. He lay for a moment feeling the gentle sway of the ship and felt a sudden pang of homesickness. He thought of Gran alone in the cosy cottage back home, eating her porridge and slurping her first cup of tea of the morning. He wondered where in the world he was and where Grandpa could be too.

"Come on, Thom, you don't wanna be late," called Roscoe, as he ran, barefoot, past Thom and out of the door.

"Where're we going?" he asked Angus who was slipping on his t-shirt.

"Breakfast, chores and then lessons."

Thom shifted himself out of his hammock and stepped unsteadily onto the wooden floor of the cabin. His trunk was open and he could see that Gran's goodies were all safe, although they had munched their way through most of the cookies the previous night.

"What's for breakfast?" Thom asked, as he followed Angus down the corridor. He could feel the roll of the ship was gentle this morning, perhaps they had docked somewhere overnight.

"We get a lot of choice, but choose carefully," Angus advised, screwing up his nose. "There's bacon, eggs, porridge, toast and sometimes kippers. But avoid the porridge."

They entered the dining deck where round tables were scattered about. Some boys were already sat eating and others were lining up to receive their food, plates in hand. Thom felt all eyes upon him and tried hard to keep his head high. He smiled at a few boys. Some just returned hard stares but a few smiled half-heartedly. Thom found himself behind the round boy with the wooden leg he'd seen the night before and tried hard not to stare at it, not wanting to offend him. However, the boy must have felt his gaze because he turned and glared at Thom.

"That's Silver," Angus whispered in his ear. "Great-great-grandson of Long John Silver."

"What? I thought he was a fictional character?" said Thom, frowning.

"Fictional to all landlubbers, but not us pirates," said Roscoe in a quiet voice. "You don't want to get on the wrong side of him."

"Thanks for the warning."

The queue for food went down quickly and Thom found himself face to face with a pirate wearing a chef's hat. His once-white uniform was now grey, with yellow patches down the front with orange-brown splatters in places. The man was very, very fat and his double-chin seemed to have doubled again, it wobbled as he stirred whatever was in the huge pan.

Thom knew he was staring, but he couldn't help it, this man was revolting and here he was offering Thom some very lumpy looking porridge. The pan was full of a gloopy, gooey, grey mass of liquid that nobody could pass off as porridge.

"Bacon and toast please," Thom stated firmly.

The ship's cook flung two slices of toast from the rack onto his plate then threw a couple of rashers of bacon on top. Thom went to the table and sat himself between Angus and Roscoe.

"This your new cabin mate?" asked a scrawny looking boy with bright red hair, sat at the same table.

"Yep, sure is, name's Thom, Thomas Prow," said Roscoe.

"Glad to meet yer, Thom Prow," said the boy, offering his grubby hand across the table. "I'm Rufus." He laughed showing lots of brown, crooked teeth. Thom wondered if he had never heard of a toothbrush, or a dentist before. Thom hoped his teeth wouldn't turn out like that.

"Where y' from?" asked Rufus.

"Devon coast," replied Thom, not wanting to give the exact location. "How about you?"

"Scotland."

"Cool," said Thom. He'd been to the Highlands of Scotland before with Gran and Grandpa, was impressed by its magnificent wildness and open spaces. The waves there would have been awesome for kite-surfing if it wasn't for the cold.

Thom chewed on his toast whilst listening to some of the conversations going on around him. They were mostly of what duties or chores the students had before lessons started at nine o'clock.

"This is going to take some getting used to," he whispered to Angus. "It'll take years for me to remember all the crews' names, let alone the teachers. What are the teachers like here? Are they all pirates too?"

Angus nodded. "They sure are, look over there."

Thom followed Angus' pointed finger to where a group of coarse-looking men were sat at a larger, round table. "That's the teacher's table."

Thom could see teachers of varying ages and in states of dress, devouring their breakfast.

"The older guy is Sir Walter (he always has breakfast here although he is part of the Loyal Trinity crew), you will always remember him because he wears a suit and a different colour bow-tie each day – he teaches History and Mythology. The one to his left is Pirate Notts he teaches Needlecraft, although he never calls it that, he calls it 'sail-mending'. He does knot-tying too."

Thom nodded, trying to take it all in.

"Sir Rupert, who takes his subject very seriously, teaches Navigation and Master Wainright, Weaponry. There are other teachers too, on the other ships. Sometimes they teach on their own ships, sometimes on others."

Thom gazed at the teachers. He didn't know how he would remember all their names. The most flamboyant at the table was definitely Master Wainright, with his purple velvet breeches, a white shirt and a crimson waistcoat that made his dark curls more prominent. Thom imagined him prancing around, light-footed on deck, giving instructions on how to use the weapons. The knowledge that they would be learning how to use real weaponry, made Thom's stomach tie up in knots.

After breakfast, they ascended to the upper deck. Thom found that they were met with blue skies, wispy clouds and the sun climbing higher into the sky - it was going to be a lovely day. The ocean was indigo and there was no land in sight. Thom glanced up at the masts and sails above him, which were so high that he felt dizzy. The white sails were tied up and looked like fancy icing on a wedding cake, the folds and rolls billowing in the light wind. The ship was anchored and Thom watched a group of boys climbing up the rigging, confidently leaping from the ropes like monkeys in a zoo. He would never be brave enough to do that, he thought to himself.

"Where are we?" Thom asked.

"The Bahamas," said Angus. "Beautiful isn't it? Real pirating waters these."

"Blimey, we got here quick," he said.

"That's the magic of subaqueous sailing," Angus replied.

"Come on, I've something to show you," said Roscoe, leading Thom starboard. Angus followed them.

"Look, over there." Roscoe pointed out across the sea. Thom's eyes followed.

A little way off, there was another ship identical to the Sudden Ghost except it had blue sails.

"What's it doing there?" Thom asked.

"That's one of the other classes in the school, there are four altogether as I explained last night, but you'll only see two others here today. Each ship has distinctive sails so that we know which one is which at a distance – the ships are all identical otherwise, except the crew of course, they're very different. The ship with blue sails is The Loyal Trinity. Come on, I've another one to show you."

56

Thom followed Roscoe and Angus to portside trying to avoid some miserable looking boys who were scrubbing the deck. One in particular, a boy with jet black hair and a small tattoo of a black rose on his cheek, looked particularly disgruntled. He saw Thom staring at him and snarled like a dog, bearing his teeth.

Thom quickened his pace. "Who's that?"

"That's Black Rose's son, known as 'Spike'. His mother is a fearsome female pirate who now lives in the Pirate World," stated Angus. "He's always in trouble, so is always scrubbing the decks."

"The Pirate World, aren't we in it?" asked Thom.

"No, you don't get to move on to the real Pirate World until you pass your F.Q.P. final exams. That's the whole point of them. We may visit from time to time if it's absolutely necessary, a matter of life or death, but otherwise you can't," said Angus.

"Where is it?"

"It's a parallel world to this one, but you can only get there through a vortex in the Bermuda Triangle. You may have heard of the *USS Cyclops*, a ship that disappeared sometime in the spring of 1918. There were three hundred and six crew and passengers on board, but they vanished without a trace," stated Roscoe. "The Bermuda Triangle is a very mysterious place, lots of planes and ships go missing there, or so the landlubbers think."

Thom could only nod. The mention of the missing crew reminded Thom sharply that his grandfather's boat 'Bessie' had been compared to the *Mary Celeste* the day he had been kidnapped.

"Look, there's the other ship," Angus interrupted, pointing out over the portside.

Thom looked out to sea again, this time he spotted a ship with black sails.

"That's the Hades Rambler. I believe you may know the Captain of that one," said Roscoe.

Thom shook his head. "I don't know anybody here at the school."

"Oh, I thought you knew Stanley Teach. Isn't he your cousin, did they tell us wrong about that then, Angus?"

Angus shrugged.

"Oh, yes of course, Stanley is my cousin, but I've never met him, or any of his family."

"He's your cousin and you've never met him?" asked Roscoe.

Thom hesitated. "No, I've never met him and I'm not sure I want to." Thom looked over at the ship with black sails, all seemed still and quiet, there was no movement on deck or up in the rigging. It was strange because the Loyal Trinity and the Sudden Ghost were busy with their pre-lesson duties.

"Well, you're going to have to at some point soon," said Angus.

"I know, but there's a family feud that's been going on for generations." Thom almost felt he could tell Angus and Roscoe the whole story, but something inside him was not quite ready to share that information with two boys he'd only just met. "Maybe I'll tell you about it sometime."

"Sure, shipmate, in your own time," said Angus, nudging Roscoe hard in the ribs as he was about to press for more information.

A bell tolled.

"Cripes," said Roscoe. "Time for lessons already."

"What about our duties?" asked Thom. "Weren't we supposed to do them beforehand?"

"Yes, but our duty was to show you round this morning and make sure you had breakfast, so we're done on that score. Now, what's our first lesson this morning?"

"I don't have a timetable," said Thom frowning. "I've no idea where I'm supposed to be."

"Don't worry," said Angus. "We're your guides for the first week. You should get your timetable from Long Harry soon and you'll most likely have your lessons with us too."

"Long Harry?" asked Thom.

"He's our Tutor, sometimes takes lessons too, if any of the teachers are ill or away. He's

Captain Ginger's great-grandson, I think, but he's okay."

"Right, then," said Roscoe. "History first, followed by break-time, then Mythology."

"Slightly different to Maths and English, but sounds far more exciting!" said Thom.

As Thom trailed behind Angus and Rosco to his first lesson, he could feel his heart thumping inside his chest. They led him to a large room on a lower deck that was filled with books. Many were ancient leather-bound texts, some more modern. Individual wooden desks were scattered around the room facing a desk and whiteboard at the front. Maps and portraits of fierce-looking pirates adorned the walls. Amongst these were paintings of very strange looking mythological beasts as well as whales, dolphins and other ordinary sea creatures.

The students, who were already there, were chatting noisily just as they would have been at Thom's previous school. However, when a tall, skinny, blond young man of about twenty-five walked into the room, they all stood up straight behind their chairs and fell silent.

"Aye, Aye," said the young man.

"Aye, Aye, chorused the boys then took their seats.

Thom followed the others in sitting still at his desk as the young man continued to speak.

"Pleased to see all duties complete this morning and all ship-shape, shipmates," he said looking round the room at the other crew members. He had blue eyes like his grandfather, but that's where the similarity ended. "Today, we must welcome our new shipmates on board ... busy night collecting the three of them. Old Windbags was in a foul mood when I saw him earlier." He paused while a snigger went round the room.

"In a few minutes, I'll introduce each of the new students in turn and then you can stand up and tell us a bit about yourselves. I'll start us off. However, first we must ask our new recruits to swear an oath to the Pirate Code."

"What's the Pirate Code?" Thom whispered to Angus who was sat at the next desk.

"It's the rules by which all pirates must live – just agree to everything and you'll be fine," Angus replied with a wink.

"Right O', let's have all new students up here at the front," called Long Harry.

Thom hesitated, but as soon as he saw a young, timid-looking boy rise from his seat he followed him along with another boy to the front of the room. With their backs to the class they faced Long Harry.

"Raise your left hands," he said.

The boys did as they were told.

"Repeat after me. I ... then give your name ... swear upon my honour as a pirate to follow the pirate code."

The boys repeated his words.

"I swear that I will never:

Raise a Mutiny.

Steal from another Pirate, something that does not belong to me.

Murder a Pirate."

Thom repeated the words and felt a growing sense of pride. He'd never sworn an oath before and it felt good to promise something, especially as he could never imagine doing any of the things he had agreed not to.

"Well done, crew," said Long Harry, smiling. "Go back to your seats and we'll get these introductions done."

Thom felt his cheeks burn, he hated standing up in front of the class, but it seemed he had no choice; at least he could sit down for the time being.

"I'm your Tutor, Long Harry. You would have met my Grandfather, Captain Ginger, last night - he is the overall captain of the school, a Headteacher of sorts. However, I'm the Tutor on this ship and everything I say, goes too. I've been a Tutor for the past four years and I like a tidy, loyal crew. If you're loyal and obedient to me, then you will find me a fair pirate. Any getting out of line

..." Here he stared at Spike who just looked into space, avoiding Long Harry's eyes. "... you will reap the punishments, some of them severe."

Thom liked Long Harry immediately. He was forthright, with kind eyes. Although there was no doubt that Long Harry would not stand for any nonsense (however much you scowl) he thought, taking a quick peek at Spike who was now driving a small dagger into the top of his wooden desk.

"I'm your first port of call if you're in danger, worried or just need a chat. I'll take some of your lessons as well if a teacher is unable to. I will be taking History and Mythology today for Sir Walter who is feeling rather unwell following breakfast - I believe it might have been the porridge, he does insist on having the revolting stuff."

A laugh rolled around the room.

"Right-O. First, I'd like to welcome aboard, Master Tim Stone."

A small, thin boy stood up, his face pinched with terror as the whole class looked at him. "I-I'm Tim, I come from a family who live near London. I was rather surprised when the ship arrived to collect me from the River Thames; it was amazing how it glided up the estuary like a ghost ship out of a storybook. I still can't believe I'm here."

"Thank you, Tim," said Long Harry.

Angus whispered in Thom's ear, "He needs to toughen up, or he won't last a week, let alone the first term."

Thom swallowed the lump in his throat as Long Harry introduced the next new recruit.

"Welcome aboard, Lucifer Kidd."

This time a large, broad boy with a stony expression stood. He towered above Tim which made Tim visibly tremble from head to toe. He had a deep voice as he introduced himself to the class. "I'm Lucifer. I've always lived aboard ships me whole life, my parents thought a little discipline from the School for Scoundrels might see me right, I think they're wrong. I'm already a scoundrel." He glared at Tim who sat down into his chair with a bump, as pale as a full moon. Lucifer laughed.

"Always room for improvement, Lucifer," said Long Harry.

It was Roscoe's turn to whisper to Thom. "We're gonna have trouble with that one."

"Finally, we have Thomas Prow," Long Harry announced, his eyes watching Thom closely.

Thom stood and a sea of faces stared up at him, he felt his knees go weak; perhaps the sea was getting rougher. "Hi. I'm Thom, I come from the Devon coast and my ancestors were all pirates. My father wanted me to be educated at the School for Scoundrels the same as himself and his father before him."

"Do you always do what Daddy says," sneered a dark eyed boy from near the front.

"His father's dead," stated Spike, his mouth in a cruel smirk.

A whisper went round the room. Thom felt an unease wash over him and he stared at Long Harry.

Thankfully Long Harry came to his rescue. "Sadly, Thom's father and mother were both killed when Thom was very young; it is admirable that he wishes to follow in the footsteps of his ancestors, as do many of you others."

"His great-great-grandfather was Seamus Prow," said Spike, a cruel spark in his eyes.

Another whisper rang round the room.

"He was murdered by his own family and crew," continued Spike.

A gasp came from Tim who now sat wide-eyed. "I-I've heard that story."

Thom noticed a few nods amongst the pupils and the excited chatter grew louder. At that moment, he wished he could go back home to Grandpa and Gran and for life to return to what it had been. What was he doing here amongst this rough lot? He wanted the warmth and security of home, to row freely around the harbour and out onto the Isle of Bos where he could feel the wind take his kite and lift his board into the air, that feeling of flying, of being free ...

Long Harry rang a bell on his desk and the whole class soon settled, except a small snigger from Spike.

Thom sat down. Angus placed a reassuring hand on his arm, but this did not stop the feeling of dread that had begun to grow within him.

"It's a story you'll be covering later this term, in History, but for now we're going to talk about Grace O'Malley, a female pirate that commandeered three ships in her time. Roscoe, Angus - books please."

Angus and Roscoe jumped to their feet and headed for the bookshelves. Thom watched as Spike positioned his foot purposely and tripped Roscoe up as he went past. Roscoe glared at him, but Spike was unbothered and smirked as Roscoe went away rubbing his ankle.

Long Harry put the students into groups and asked them to research what they could about the feisty, female pirate of the 1500s. After discovering some interesting facts about her, the groups then had to give a presentation to the class.

A while later, Angus, Roscoe, Rufus and Thom presented the class with their findings.

Roscoe stood up and was spokesperson for their group. "Young Grace O'Malley begged her parents to let her go to sea, but they refused. Not to give up easily, she cut off her hair and disguised herself as a boy in order to go aboard her father's ship. O'Malley saved her father's life one day when she was watching a battle from the rigging and saw a man try to stab her father in the back. She jumped on the man's back and in doing so saved their ship as well as her father".

"Great effort, excellent detail," said Long Harry above the applause from the other boys.

Spike's group, which included Lucifer, Spike and another tall, lanky boy called Fergus were not so well praised.

Spike's only conclusion was, "Female pirates are not pirates, however they dress, and whatever weapons they hold. A woman is bad luck aboard a ship and under no circumstances should one be called a pirate."

"Your mother's a pirate," said Sonny Boy whose name was unlike his physique and disposition of a moody pirate.

"She ain't now ... like I says, not the place for a woman, or a girl."

"That's a bit harsh," said Angus. "I think some girls would be great pirates, better than some boys." He held Spike's gaze.

"There's only one reason you'd want girls on board, Angus, so you could kiss them," Spike sneered at him.

Angus stood and scowled at Spike.

"Sit down, Angus," said Long Harry.

"I've a cousin, Sir, she's as good a swordsman as any of these scallywags," stated Angus, his eyes fierce.

"I'm sure she is," said Long Harry. "However, the fact remains that no girls should be educated at the School for Scoundrels it's an ancient rule – apparently women do bring bad luck on board ships."

"Do you really believe that, Sir?" asked Roscoe.

"It's not for me to say, I follow the rules of the ship as everyone else should. The rules have been the same since the school began in 1642."

"Well, I think some rules should be changed," called Rufus. "Bring it up to date. In fact my Aunt has been rallying for girls to be allowed aboard for years – calls it the 'Girls Aboard Campaign'. My sisters would make fantastically fierce pirates."

"Yes, Rufus, we're quite aware of your Aunt Petra and her ideas on getting girls on board."

Roscoe whispered in Thom's ear: "Aunt Petra also disguised herself as a boy so that she could come to the School for Scoundrels, but she was discovered after six months and made to walk the plank. Amazingly, she survived the shark attack and lives on to fight for her cause of female pirates. She has a nasty, jagged scar on her left cheek, but she carries it with pride."

"She managed six months before she was caught?" Thom felt a sense of admiration for Aunt Petra.

Above them a bell tolled.

"Break time," yelled Spike leaping out of his chair, knocking it backwards onto the floor and making no attempt to pick it up.

"SIT!" bellowed Long Harry. It was the first time Thom had heard him raise his voice.

Spike responded reluctantly and Long Harry continued. "Right, shipmates, you may go, except Spike who can put the books away – in the correct place – before he goes."

The boys jostled each other out through the doorway and headed for the upper deck where oranges and water were being given out to each in turn.

Thom was relieved that the first lesson and the introductions were over, so that the attention could be shifted away from him and his family connections.

Chapter 5
Welcome Aboard

Roscoe, Rufus, Angus and Thom leant against the gunwale and looked out to sea. The Loyal Trinity was on break too as some of the pirates on deck waved to them in a friendly manner, oranges in hands.

"So, that's your secret family feud then," said Roscoe.

"Sorry?" replied Thom, turning to look at him.

"You're the great-great-grandson of Seamus Prow, the famous Pirate whose brother-in-law *murdered* him and tried to steal the family treasure."

"Yes, but I didn't even know myself until three days ago," Thom stated. His secret was already common knowledge, thanks to Spike. He hated Spike.

"Spike's not a nice kid," said Angus, as if reading his thoughts. "He's Captain's mate and as likely to cause a mutiny as your great-great-uncle."

"He's Captain's mate?"

"He has the position because of who his father is." Roscoe's face was twisted in anger.

"Who *is* his father?"

"He's part of O.U.S.T.Ed." replied Angus.

71

Thom frowned.

"Stands for: Office of Useless Scoundrels & Traitors of Education," chorused Angus, Roscoe and Rufus together.

"What do they do?"

"Cause as much chaos as possible. They come on board unannounced and inspect the staff and pupils to see if they are doing a first-class job. If anyone is found to be falling short of their expectations, the teachers have to walk the plank and the pupils are expelled," explained Angus. "It could be the end of the school altogether if we fail an inspection."

"What do they inspect?"

Angus' expression was one of displeasure. "Whatever they feel like on the day of inspection it seems. They're forever changing the guidelines and grade boundaries of the F.Q.P. finals too. I know Captain Ginger is always very irritable when they're expected, so are the rest of the staff. Last time, even the pupils were having sleepless nights."

"Who makes all the changes then, O.U.S.T.Ed?" asked Thom.

Roscoe shook his head. "The Minister Pirate Education, Maximilian Graves. He has nothing better to do all day 'cept to make us all jump through hoops. Apparently he knows nothing about education or pirates, so how he can make the rules is beyond me."

Rufus sighed and interrupted them, "Come on guys let's talk about something else ... I've heard enough about those useless scoundrels for one day."

Angus nodded in agreement. "Break's almost over, we've got Mythology next."

"What do we study in Mythology?" asked Thom.

"*Mythological* creatures," said Angus.

"Are they mythical then?" asked Thom.

Angus and Roscoe stared at him.

"What do you think, Thom?" said Roscoe, grinning.

"I guess not then, only to landlubbers?"

The other boys nodded.

"Yes, the creatures landlubbers read about in books and encounter in films, some of them are real, but rare, and only seen on few occasions," said Angus before hurrying across the boards and down the steps to the deck below.

Long Harry was already in the classroom waiting. He smiled at Thom as the four boys entered. "Enjoying your first day, Prow?"

"Yes, thank you, Sir. Think it might take a little getting used to though."

Long Harry laughed. "Not your usual kind of school is it?"

Thom shook his head.

"Well, you know where I am if you need a chat, about anything ... and Prow ... take no notice of Spike, he's just trouble."

"Isn't that what pirates are supposed to be?"

Long Harry grinned and nodded his head. "I guess so, but there will always be some real good and some real bad ones, even amongst pirates."

As the class settled, Long Harry turned on an old-fashioned gramophone that sat on his desk – its speaker in the shape of a large conch shell. Then, surprisingly, he took from his pockets some ear-plugs and put them into his ears.

A melodious singing, filtered around the class. One by one, the boys became transfixed. Thom began to feel the effects of the tune, it washed over him in waves and he felt himself in that state between wakefulness and sleep ...

He woke with a start.

As he looked around, the other boys looked bemused and sleepy, as if waking from a deep sleep.

He turned to Angus. "What's going on?" He noticed the music had stopped.

"I don't know," replied Angus, yawning.

Sonny Boy fell of his chair and a roar of sleepy laughter rang around the room. "What's up?" he asked, bewildered and confused, trying to pull himself back up into his seat.

"What's happening?" called Roscoe.

Long Harry removed his ear-plugs. "That, shipmates, is one of our most sinister enemies on the high seas, one that can come out of nowhere and lure you into a brutal death. These creatures, called Sirens, are a curse to all who sail the oceans."

"Sirens?" the boys chorused together.

Long Harry nodded. "They are beautiful sea-nymphs who charm sailors with alluring songs. Odysseus, a Greek leader and King of Ithaca, was aware of them too. On one of his voyages, he plugged up his own ears and those of his crew with wax, so that they couldn't hear the Sirens' singing. He then bound himself to a mast, so he couldn't leave the ship and go to them. If the crew were to hear the Sirens they hypnotically sail towards the singing not realising they are heading for perilous coasts where their ships will become wrecks upon jagged rocks."

"Wow," said Rufus. "I think I'll keep ear plugs in my pockets from now on."

"Funny you should say that, Rufus," said Long Harry, picking up a basket from the desk in front of him; it was full of ear plugs. "You can hand them out to everyone - you never know when you might need them."

"How long were we asleep, Sir," asked Thom.

"Nearly an hour, the bell for lunch will sound any moment. Today we've been invited aboard the Loyal Trinity for lunch and tomorrow night, the Hades Rambler. Captain Teach has kindly offered us dinner, shark steaks, no less." Long Harry's eyes fell on Thom and at that moment he realised that he would be meeting his cousin very soon - his stomach tightened at the thought.

The boys took their small packs of ear plugs and stowed them away in their pockets.

"I can't imagine we'll need these anytime soon," said Roscoe.

Angus shook his head. "No, can't say I've ever heard any Sirens on our travels so far."

"Perhaps they know something we don't," suggested Thom.

Roscoe, Rufus and Angus all looked at him blankly.

"What I mean is, perhaps they are expecting us to sail through dangerous waters in the coming days or weeks."

"That sounds a bit adventurous ... even for a pirate school," said Roscoe, glumly.

"Oh," said Thom. However, he knew differently. If he was going to find his grandfather and the treasure map it wouldn't do any good just staying anchored in one position, no matter how beautiful and balmy it was. They would need to search the seas and Thom didn't care how much hunting or sailing they did as long as they found Grandpa, and soon.

Thom followed his shipmates to the upper deck where the boys were jumping and diving over the side into the clear sea below. A cacophony of screams, shouts of laughter and infectious excitement grew amongst the crew as they launched themselves into the warm waters.

"Come on, they always do an amazing lunch," called Roscoe running to the gunwale and vaulting himself over, it was followed a few moments later by a loud splash.

Thom peered at the clear waters below and felt a wave of nausea sweep over him - it was a long way down.

Angus looked at him. "You all right?"

Thom nodded. "I'm fine, you go. I'll catch you up."

"You *can* swim, can't you?"

"Of course. I do – did - a lot of kite-boarding and swimming before I came aboard here. I've just never done much diving from great heights before."

"Ah, just close your eyes, take a deep breath, and jump. You'll love it."

Thom climbed up on to the rail, his bare feet feeling the warmth of the wood, but his head was spinning. He took a deep breath and before he could change his mind, jumped.

He hit the water hard and felt himself going deeper and deeper. How would he continue to hold his breath long enough? What if he just kept going down and down? He started to kick his legs and found that his breath was fast running out; the pain in his chest and throat were becoming unbearable. When he felt as if he could no longer hold his breath, something hard hit him from beneath. Suddenly, he felt himself being pushed upwards towards the surface at high speed; something was pushing him, helping him.

As soon as he surfaced he took an enormous breath of air, coughing and spluttering. He looked around, trying to get his bearings. The Loyal Trinity was a few metres ahead of him and boys could be seen climbing up the rope ladders that had been lowered to let the guests aboard.

"You ok?" asked a voice beside him.

He turned and to his amazement saw a bottle-nosed dolphin beside him. "Er, yes ..."

"Could see you were having a bit of trouble, so thought I'd help ... first time?"

Thom couldn't believe his eyes, or ears - the dolphin was talking to him. It was a high-pitched voice that sounded a bit like a dolphin did when it spoke its own kind of language, but he could understand what it was saying.

"Thank you, that was very kind." Thom continued treading water, thankful he could now breathe freely, his heart rate returning to normal.

"No problem, been doing this for years now ... you're certainly not the first and you won't be the last ... just takes a bit of getting used to. I'll be here again, if needed."

"Thank you."

"What's your name?"

"Thomas Prow," he replied.

"Ah, one of the Prow crew, nice to meet you. Be seeing you." In an instant the dolphin was gone, its dark shadow disappearing into the depths of the ocean.

Even the dolphin had heard of his name.

Thom shook his head then swam the few metres to the Loyal Trinity. He climbed the rough rope to the upper deck.

Roscoe, Rufus and Angus were all stood together holding hot-dogs that were being handed round by the boys of the ship, all of whom wore dark blue headscarves the same shade as the sails.

"What took you so long?" asked Rufus.

"I was enjoying the swim," he lied, avoiding eye contact. "There was a dolphin and I wanted to watch him. I've never been that close to one before."

Roscoe started to laugh. "Ha, of course, you're new to all this. I had a dolphin on my first jump too, jolly useful he was."

Angus passed Thom a hotdog smeared with ketchup. He was ravenous and took a huge bite. Immediately, he spat it out.

"Yuk! What is *that*?"

"It's eel."

"Cripes, I thought it was a hotdog ... how very disappointing. I thought you said they did good food?"

The other boys laughed and Thom felt his face flush red.

Angus put his arm around his shoulders. "Come on, let's get you some lime-juice, it's delicious, take away that awful taste."

"But you're all eating them."

"Yes, the ketchup helps but they are disgusting, takes a lot of getting used to," said Rufus, having difficulty swallowing.

The boys all took a glass of lime-juice from a boy that passed by, holding a tray full of bright-green drinks. Although it was sharp, it was refreshing and delicious; it reminded Thom of Gran's home-made lemonade.

Thom noticed a figure dressed in casual, almost stereo-typical, pirate attire. The man wore breeches, a loose white shirt, a yellow waistcoat and the same blue scarf wrapped around his head as the younger members of the crew. He was holding a book in which he had thrust his head and was muttering away to himself.

"Who's that, Angus?"

Angus looked to where Thom was watching the man sauntering around the deck, oblivious to anyone else it seemed.

"That's Captain Blake, he's Captain of the Loyal Trinity. He'll be teaching us Literature and

Message Writing. The Captains of the other ships all teach, except Captain Ginger of course."

"Captain Blake seems a little odd," said Thom.

"Yes, rather ... eccentric ... I think they call it."

Just then, another boy walked past with trays of delicious-looking cakes. He wore the blue scarf tightly on his head, but his black curls were struggling to escape. On the tray there was chocolate cake, Victoria sandwich, carrot cake, flap-jack and coffee and walnut cake.

"Are those normal cakes?" Thom asked, eyeing them suspiciously.

Roscoe nodded. "Yes, these cakes are superb, for some reason the Loyal Trinity makes the best cakes in the school. The chocolate and the carrot are most excellent in my opinion." Roscoe grabbed both cakes and started stuffing one in his mouth in a way that Gran would have scolded Thom for.

Thom helped himself to a slice of carrot cake and smiled at the boy who was carrying the tray. The boy stared at him.

"You one of the new shipmates?"

Thom nodded; his mouth full of cake.

Angus spoke for him, "This is Thom Prow."

"Pleased to meet you, shipmate Prow." The boy extended his hand, balancing the tray of cakes precariously in the other. "I'm Arabia." His voice was soft, but confident.

"You too, Arabia. Great cake by the way."

"Thanks. Sorry about the eel," Arabia said with a chuckle. "We have a trainee cook." He smiled then wandered off amongst the crowds of boys who were swiping pieces of cake, like vultures, from the tray as he passed by.

"So, tomorrow night you're going to meet your long, lost cousin, Stanley Teach," said Roscoe his eyes glinting.

Thom nodded. "I guess so, unless I can get out of it somehow."

"Would look a bit obvious," stated Angus. "Not particularly courageous."

"So, it was his great-great-grandfather that murdered yours then?" asked Roscoe.

Thom felt very uncomfortable, he hardly knew any of the facts himself and he'd only learned them a few days before. He wished that the others would let it go, but he replied, "Yes, his ancestor killed mine. I believe it was over some treasure."

"Is it true that there's a map somewhere that shows where the treasure is buried?" asked Roscoe.

"There's supposed to be."

"Where is it? Do you know?"

Thom shook his head firmly. "I haven't got a clue."

"Perhaps we should talk about something else?" said Angus.

Rufus ignored him. "It wasn't Stanley's fault I suppose. Although, if he has an idea of where the map might be, he should hand it over to you ... the treasure is rightly yours, according to legend anyway."

Thom didn't know what to say. His great-great-grandfather had been murdered, his ship taken over and his treasure stolen. Even if Stanley didn't have anything to do with it, he still wasn't sure how he felt about this cousin whose ancestors had ruined the lives of his own. If the treasure had stayed in its rightful place, perhaps his parents would still be alive and maybe Grandpa would be safe at home?

Thom needed to get away. "I'll see you back on the Sudden Ghost," he said and walked away from the other boys, but not without‑ hearing Angus having a go at the other two for being so insensitive.

Thom lowered himself down the rope ladder from the upper deck, rather than jumping. He thought he wouldn't go as deep into the ocean if he didn't jump from such a great height as earlier. As friendly as the dolphin was, Thom needed to be alone. The water was cool, but refreshing and he swam back to the Sudden Ghost with strength and speed, but feeling low.

Climbing aboard he saw Captain Ginger go into his cabin - he was still aboard then? He thought about following him and asking him if he'd heard any news of Grandpa, but the thought of knocking on his door sent a cold shiver down his spine. No, he just needed some time to himself, to collect his thoughts. This new life was going to take some getting used to and it wasn't going to happen quickly, he feared.

Thom walked down the corridor towards his cabin. As he turned the corner he spotted Spike a bit further down the lantern-lit passage. It looked as if he had just come out of Thom's cabin. What was he doing in there? He watched as Spike ran in the opposite direction; he hadn't seen him.

Thom opened the door to his cabin and looked around. Roscoe and Angus' things were all shipshape, but Thom's trunk was open and his things were spilling out – he knew he had left it tidy. He searched for the hidden drawer and pulled it open. The compass was still safely inside; he let out a sigh of relief. Spike had been in their cabin and he was obviously searching for something ... the treasure map?

Thom tidied his things back into his trunk and helped himself to one of Gran's flapjack. Then he lowered himself into his hammock and let it sway gently to and fro. As he munched on the flapjack, a wave of homesickness swept over him.

He forced his thoughts to the boys he had met: Angus, Roscoe and Rufus seemed great. Roscoe a little outspoken and Rufus a bit rough, but they were learning to be pirates after all. What if he couldn't do it? What if he was useless as a pirate? He couldn't even jump off the upper deck without feeling terrified and the idea of climbing the rigging sent him into a cold sweat.

He thought of his grandparents. The look of hope and pride in Gran's eyes as she had said goodbye; his grandfather's look of shame as he'd spoken the truth about his parents ... his father's dream of him completing his schooling at the School for Scoundrels.

It was his first day. Had he really given it a chance yet? He heard the words he knew that Grandpa would have spoken to him, had he been there, and decided that he had to give it more time. Perhaps this afternoon would be better and who knew what would happen tomorrow night on board the Hades Rambler when he finally met his cousin Stanley?

The ship was rocking furiously, the waves must be enormous. Was there a storm? Thom opened his eyes which felt heavy with sleep and realised that it wasn't the ship at all, but his hammock that was swaying back and forth at high speed. Roscoe's mischievous laugh could be heard beneath him. Thom looked under his hammock and saw his new friend lying on the ground beneath him, swinging his hammock as high as he could.

"Come on, wake up! You're going to miss knot-tying."

"Having spent many times on my grandfather's fishing boat I've learnt how to tie a few already."

Roscoe interrupted. "There are many more to learn, I can assure you. Pirate Notts knows his stuff."

"Cool, let's go then," said Thom, eager to face the challenge of discovering more knots that he could then teach Grandpa when he had been rescued and everything could return to normal.

As he followed Roscoe to class, where the others were all waiting for him, he was glad that his excitement had returned. Perhaps earlier he had been tired and a little upset about all the talk of his ancestors. The thought of meeting Stanley Teach did not seem as overwhelming now as it had done previously. Who knew, perhaps they could even become friends and that was why they were destined to meet? Perhaps it was to put right all the wrongs from the past and unite their families again? Perhaps.

Thom realised his naïvety about knot-tying almost straight away. The classroom desks were covered in ropes of different sizes and lengths; a poster of 'how to tie knots' was hung over the board at the front, where the bent figure of a scruffy, wrinkly-faced, old pirate with a large, hooked nose stood fiddling with some rope. Thom felt unnerved as Pirate Notts looked directly at him, a cold look in his eyes.

"Right then, first knot of the lesson: let's see you all do a round turn and two half hitches."

Thom looked at Angus and frowned. "I've never heard of one of those before."

Angus whispered, "He does this every lesson when there are new kids. He knows nobody will know how to do it."

"Problem Prow?" sniggered Notts, as he shuffled over to Thom's desk. He watched as Thom twisted and tied the rope hopelessly into a messy knot, nothing like the one Pirate Notts was holding in his hands. "Call yourself a fisherman's son. Here watch this."

Thom didn't feel he could correct the teacher about his father and watched as Pirate Notts untied, then retied the rope, as quick as lightening, resulting in a perfect round turn and two half hitches.

"Now you try," he said, holding out the rope to Thom.

Thom tried again, but failed to get it to look like the knot that his teacher had made. Spike laughed loudly from the desk in front of him and Thom felt his cheeks grow warm.

"Angus, show the boy how it's done," scoffed Notts.

"Yes, Sir," replied Angus, taking the rope from Thom and slowly showing him how to tie the desired knot.

"Pay attention, Prow," said Notts as he wandered back to the front of the class, whacking Spike around the back of the head with his knotted rope as he passed him by.

"A good knot could save your life," he murmured. "A bad knot could be the death of you!"

Chapter 6
The Unusual Crew

Towards the end of the lesson, Thom was summoned to Captain Ginger's cabin. He walked, dry-mouthed, behind Windbags wondering why he had been called out of his lesson. Notts had been clearly disapproving by the stern glare he shot at Windbags when he had asked for Thom to be excused.

Outside Captain Ginger's cabin, Thom took a deep breath and knocked.

"Enter," boomed Captain Ginger.

"You wanted to see me, Captain."

"Prow. Yes, come in. A message has just arrived ... from your grandfather."

"Grandpa, is he okay? Has he been found?"

Captain Ginger shook his head. "I'm sorry, Prow, he's still being held captive, but he says he's okay and they are treating him fairly well, for now."

"But where are they holding him? Who's got him?"

"I don't know. There are no clues to his whereabouts or who's taken him."

Thom felt lightheaded.

"It'll be all right. William's a strong man. I'm doing my best to find him. I just wanted you to see his note, thought it might reassure you that he's all right." The captain extracted the message from the red bottle.

Thomas Prow, Sudden Ghost.
Hello boy - Although I'm being held captive, I'm being treated fairly well. I don't think they will be patient for long though. Send Gran my love.
Grandpa

Thom stared at the note. "What can I do, Captain? I feel so helpless."

"Be patient, that's all you can do at the moment," said the Captain looking sympathetically at Thom. "I still have my spies on the lookout. Hopefully they will discover something soon."

Thom slipped the bottle into his pocket and left the Captain's cabin, feeling weary.

Unable to face going back to class straight away, Thom went to his cabin to hide the message in his trunk. He didn't want anyone else seeing it, so he placed it along with the compass in the secret compartment.

He was making his way back up to the top deck when he passed a door which had 'Navigation' written on it. He glanced inside. There was nobody in the room. The walls were lined with maps; the bookshelves full of atlases and the desks were full of open maps and discarded compasses.

Thom sidled into the room, glancing round, making doubly sure there was nobody about. He was looking for a map, a map that would lead him to the treasure map of the Prows. This was the perfect opportunity to have a look and see if there was anything that could possibly be the one he was looking for.

Searching the maps on the walls first, Thom could see many curious places. There were numerous maps of all sorts of strange and unusual lands. One was of an island which stuck out of the sea like a giant crab; its claws in an open position, making two natural harbours for ships to take shelter. The beaches had orange/pink sand and the contour lines denoted that the cliffs above them were sheer and steep.

A noise outside the door startled him. Thom searched for somewhere to hide, but there was nowhere to go. He stood and waited; his pulse fast in his neck. A man with neatly cut greying hair, wearing cropped trousers above bare feet and a smart tweed jacket, entered. Seeing Thom he frowned.

"Are you one of the new boys?" he asked gruffly.

"Aye, Sir. Thomas Prow." Thom recognised him from breakfast, but couldn't remember his name.

"What are you doing in here?"

"I got lost, Sir."

"Hmmm. Well, you won't find no treasure map in here – these boards have been searched numerous times before, by various folk."

"I wasn't -"

"They ain't here, Prow, I know."

"No, Sir. Sorry, Sir," replied Thom scuttling out of the room and away from the teacher's accusing glare.

How could he have been so stupid as to assume he only had to walk into a room full of maps and the map to find the treasure map would just jump out at him? With his head low, he made his way back to the top deck to find Angus.

The following evening, Thom had written the last few lines of a letter to his Gran, before making his way to the mid-deck common room where, of an evening, the young pirates could meet up and play games, do homework, or just sit and chat. As he walked along the dimly-lit corridor, clutching the letter (unsure of how he was going to get it delivered) he felt his anxiety about the forthcoming evening grow. What would he say to his cousin, Stanley Teach? "Hey, I hear your great-great-grandfather killed mine – where's the treasure map that belongs to my family?"

Thom smiled grimly to himself. What would Stanley say to him? Did he even know he was aboard the Sudden Ghost? He suspected that he probably did.

A noise behind him made him turn. Spike was hurrying towards him, a look of spite in his eyes. He barged past Thom making him drop his letter.

"Teach can't wait to meet you," he spat.

"What do you mean?" asked Thom, his mouth dry. He wished Angus was by his side.

Spike ran off, his laugh echoing down the corridor.

Thom felt the butterflies in his stomach take flight again. He turned back towards his cabin. Nobody could make him go to the Hades Rambler not tonight, not any night.

"Thom. Where're you going?" It was Angus.

"I, em ... I ..."

"I just saw Spike – what did he say to you?"

"He said that Stanley couldn't wait to meet me."

"Well, that's great – isn't it?" asked Angus, frowning.

"It was the way he said it," replied Thom.

"Come on, Spike's just trying to wind you up."

Thom reluctantly let Angus lead him, by the arm, back towards the upper deck.

"I need to send this letter to Gran," said Thom. "I promised to send one once I was settled, but I don't know how to get it delivered."

"Come on, I'll show you – it's easy."

Thom tagged behind Angus up the steps to the top deck, but instead of going towards the group of boys being lowered in small boats, he veered away to the stern of the ship. Angus stopped next to a huge barrel which was full of coloured, glass bottles. There were red, yellow, green and blue.

"Here, just roll it up, put it in one of the bottles – what colour do you want? It's blue for a slow delivery, green for quite important, yellow for quick, but red for emergency?"

"Will it get there?"

"Of course, didn't you get called to school by a message in a bottle?"

Thom nodded. "But how does it know where to go?"

Angus shrugged. "Don't know, but all of my letters get home."

Thom rolled the letter up and placed it into a yellow, glass bottle. He then raised his arm, but hesitated and looked at Angus.

"Go on, throw it in! We're going to be late, the last boat's going."

Thom threw the bottle over the gunwale and watched it grow smaller as it dropped towards the sea. As it landed it sent ripples outwards. The bottle floated to the surface and then bobbed along, away from the ship.

He hoped that Gran would get his letter. He had told her that he was settling in well and that he was making some good friends. He decided not to tell her about the forthcoming meeting with Teach until he had something to report. He finished off by saying that he had heard from Grandpa and that she could count on him. He would find Grandpa soon, he promised.

The two boys sprinted across the deck towards Windbags who was lowering the last boat over the side to the choppy water below.

"I thought you two were going to miss the boat," shouted Roscoe as they approached.

"Get a move on boys," sneered Windbags. The odd smell that Thom always got a whiff of when he was near Windbags seemed stronger than ever.

Thom followed Angus' lead and climbed into the swinging boat and almost fell on top of Roscoe and Lucifer who were already seated.

"Watch it!" cried Lucifer, his face screwed in anger.

"Sorry," said Thom.

The sea was now the colour of red-hot lava. The sun, a crimson globe, seemed to be melting into the sea – setting the water on fire.

The other boats were quite a way ahead of them, getting ever nearer to the Hades Rambler. However, on board the ship there seemed, once more, to be no sign of life. The black sails were tatty, the breeze made no sign of movement amongst them. In contrast, the Loyal Trinity was alive with action, young pirates giving shouts of delight as they dive-bombed into the sea, but the Hades Rambler ... nothing, nobody.

Thom grew colder, despite the warmth of the setting sun, when he caught a glimpse of the Hades Rambler's figurehead. It was an enormous skeleton carved from ebony, dark, sinister - it appeared to be laughing a silent, cruel and evil laugh.

As the closer boats approached the portside, a black figure, tall and lean, appeared on deck. He wore a beetle-green, iridescent cloak, which swelled in the breeze. A three-point black hat was perched on his head. With bony fingers, the man let down the rope ladder and Thom watched as the boys started to climb aboard.

Soon enough, Thom's boat was at the bilge of the Hades Rambler. He followed the others and climbed the unsteady rope ladder. Reaching the top, he drew in a sharp breath as the dark pirate (who had let down the ladder) turned to him and smiled.

Ordinarily, a smile would seem welcoming, but beneath the triangular hat, was not the face of a man – but that of a skinless skull. Blood-red, bare muscle and tendons covered parts of the bone of the face; the eyeballs were there, staring, but there were no features as would be expected - the mouth not a smile as Thom had first thought, but a grimace of rotting teeth. Only a wisp of a beard and thin strands of black hair stuck out from beneath the hat.

"He looks worse than he is," Angus reassured. "Don't be surprised, the whole crew are rather, em, ugly!"

Thom stared around him. Where were the rest of the crew? They weren't very welcoming, not like the Loyal Trinity. "Where is everyone?" he asked Roscoe.

"Below deck, I expect. The crew of the Hades Rambler are unlike the rest of the students," Roscoe replied.

"In what way?"

"You'll see." Angus raised his eyebrows.

Thom looked around, the ship's deck was dirty, un-scrubbed; the sails were torn and tattered – the huge ship's wheel moved on its own accord, just slightly one way then the other, keeping the ship still. An awful smell, emanated from the deck below as they descended the steps; Thom hoped it wasn't their dinner. He felt another sudden pang of homesickness for Gran's cooking.

Below deck the ship was dark, the odd flickering candle cast shadows along the corridors and everything was quiet except for the voices of their own shipmates and the creaking of the ship as it swayed gently on the ocean. The ship's layout was almost identical to theirs, but its atmosphere was very different. Thom felt goosebumps on his arms.

The boys made their way through the corridors; most seemed to know where they were going and there was much chatter about what delicious things they would have for dinner. After a while, there came a noise ahead of them, a sound that was muffled as if behind closed doors.

"We're nearly there," said Angus.

Thom swallowed the lump in his throat.

Spike was at the front of the line and as he got closer to some double doors he sped up as if impatient to get through them. When he did, he ripped them open and a sound exploded into the corridor almost knocking Thom off his feet. There was music, shouting and fighting resounding from the common cabin in which, the whole crew of the Hades Rambler, were congregated. When the doors were opened and the crew of the Sudden Ghost assembled at the doorway, the commotion stopped, everyone stared for a matter of moments and then the hullabaloo started all over again as if the interruption hadn't happened. The stale odour, Thom had smelt earlier, seeped out of the room.

Suddenly, a voice bellowed out over the din. "Quiet you scoundrels, our guests are here." A tall, broad-shouldered, young pirate with short, dark, curly hair seemed to dominate the room and all the boys grew silent. The crew of the Hades Rambler glared at the crew of the Sudden Ghost who glowered back at the ugly faces that stood before them. For, in fact, they were ugly. All of their faces were either, badly scarred, deathly white or, like the pirate on top deck, had skinless muscle-covered skulls instead of normal faces.

"Cripes," whispered Thom. "They're really grotesque!"

"Shhh," whispered Roscoe.

One boy's skin hung loosely down one side of his face, his left eye stood from its socket, making it look like it would pop out any moment. Another had no nose, only the nasal passages of the skull and a small, skinny boy smiled through a lip-less mouth with black teeth.

"Welcome aboard me hearties, welcome to the Hades Rambler. I hope you'll have a great adventure whilst on board me ship. I'm Stanley Teach - your host." He scanned the sea of faces before him, coming to rest upon Thom.

Thom felt himself grow warm.

Stanley looked at Thom with an unreadable expression then walked towards him, smiling. Considering the other crew members ugliness, Stanley was a handsome young man. However, as he came closer, Thom could see there was a purple burn down one side of his whole face in the shape of a giant octopus.

"The mark of the Kraken," explained Angus in a whisper, as if reading Thom's thoughts.

"What does that mean?" asked Thom.

Angus didn't get a chance to reply.

Stanley's eyes moved away from Thom's face and searched out Spike. "Well, Spike, old mate, aren't you goin' to introduce me to my long, lost cousin?"

"Of course, Stan," said Spike, turning and dragging Thom, by the arm, to the front of the crowd.

Stanley walked forwards, his expression still unreadable.

Unexpectedly, he grabbed Thom and embraced him. "Welcome aboard, cousin," he said, squeezing him tightly. "So you're Thomas Prow, very pleased to meet you." He let Thom go and the two boys regarded each other. Stanley was smiling.

Thom felt his anxiety lift a little. "Pleased to meet you too," he said, not quite trusting the smile on his cousin's face, it didn't extend to his eyes.

"Come on chaps, time for grub," shouted Stanley.

The boys all cheered and scrambled towards the doors, pushing and shoving each other out of the way, their ugly faces made worse by sneers in their rush to get their dinner. The crew of the Sudden Ghost followed in a slightly more orderly fashion, but fuelled by the excitement of the others they too became more rowdy.

Stanley put his arm around Thom's shoulders and walked him towards the dining deck. "You're on captain's table tonight – our guest of honour," he said.

"Thank you," said Thom, not altogether comfortable with the tight grip Stanley had on him, or the dark and gloomy dining hall they entered that seemed to have a century's worth of cobwebs and giant spiders hanging from the beams.

Thom saw a feast fit for a king spread out on the trestle tables. There were foods of all sorts: roast meats; shark steaks and giant king prawns; delicious looking vegetables – bright and tempting (if vegetables could ever be such a thing); cheeses in varying sizes and colours; breads of different shapes and lengths too. Thom's mouth began to water, no wonder the others who had been here before were looking forward to dinner - not the company so much perhaps, but certainly the feast! Thom wished that their cook was half as good as this one.

The crew of the Hades Rambler scrambled to their seats, picking up the food and gorging themselves like pigs in a pen. Their manners were atrocious; using their hands instead of the knives and forks resting beside their plates. Gran would have had a fit if she'd seen the way they behaved during dinner.

"Don't mind them," said Stanley. "It's always like this on my ship. When we go aboard the other ships for dinner I make 'em mind their manners though." Stanley kicked a chair out from the table at the head of the room, and almost pushed Thom into it. "Fill yer boots."

"Thanks," said Thom. The other pirates at the table were greedily tucking in, but eyed Thom suspiciously as he took his seat at their table and reached for some succulent king prawns.

"These are two of me best buddies, Bart and Gunn," Teach introduced two mean looking pirates. "Boys, say hello to Thom."

Gunn snarled, showing black teeth full of bits of food and raised his tankard. Bart nodded a head full of thick, auburn curls towards him; he had one blue eye and one hazel, which was half closed and swollen; Thom wondered if he'd been in a recent fight or if his eye was always like that.

Thom took a selection of food and tucked in hungrily, it was much better than their own ship's grub. "So, you're Captain's mate of the Hades Rambler then?"

"Uh huh," replied Stanley through a mouthful of meat. "This 'ere is Captain Callow."

A tall, muscular man stood next to the table; his over-sized mouth was full of black and gold teeth. Unlike the other pirates his hair was short-cropped, but his beard was blond and bushy.

"Pleased to meet you, Captain," Thom stood and held out his hand, but Captain Callow only stared. His eyes were so crossed that Thom wasn't sure where he was looking and he groped around trying to find Thom's hand until he gave up and just nodded instead.

"Thomas Prow, I see – you look like your mother, Thom. I knew your mother years ago." He laughed loudly and the others around the table laughed too.

Thom felt his cheeks grow warm and he looked around to see if he could see Angus and Roscoe. They were on a table amongst other pirates from the Hades Rambler, who were greedily tucking into the feast snarling at each other, fighting over the food. It surprised Thom that the crews seemed to hate each other, yet were happy to host dinners together – why was that?

"Where are the other teachers?" asked Thom as Captain Callow sat down at the table with a plate full of food, his drink over-spilling as the tankard was so full.

"That's Surgeon Swale," replied Stanley, pointing at a huge, sweaty and dirty looking man with a shaved head on top of a fleshy, muscled face. He was decorated with brightly-coloured tattoos. "He's our surgeon, so if you lose a limb, he will give you a wooden one to replace it - if he can't save it that is."

Bart and Gunn roared with laughter.

"And that one over there is Pirate Cooper, he teaches carpentry."

"Carpentry?" asked Thom staring at the broad-shouldered, miserable looking man with barely any flesh at all upon his skeletal face.

"Yes, if the ship gets any holes, or barrels need making or mending," said Gunn, ripping into a juicy looking rack-of-ribs. "He's your man."

"I see," said Thom thinking how different the teachers in the School for Scoundrels were, compared to the ones in his previous school.

"So, you've enjoyed your first few days here then?" Stanley asked Thom.

"Yes, takes a bit of getting used to, it's nothing like my old school." Thom picked up a tankard by his plate and drank ... it was R.U.M. again, delicious and sweet, but thirst quenching too.

"You like the R.U.M.?" asked Stanley, watching him closely.

"What's not to like?" he laughed.

Stanley's next question caught him off-guard. "How are your grandparents – still alive?"

"They're fine," he replied, feeling protective. Did Stanley know where Grandpa was?

"Still living in that tiny cottage by the sea?"

Thom slowly nodded. "Where do your parents live? I didn't even know any of you existed until a few days ago -"

"Really? I've known about you and your family ever since I can remember."

"Oh."

Stanley regarded him for a moment before replying. "Mum and Dad live in Greece now. They have a mansion, in the Roman style, on the coast. Dad likes to keep an eye on the ocean and all its secrets."

"Its secrets?"

"Oh yes, the ocean has many, many secrets."

"How can they be secrets if you know about them?"

"Some of us know more than others. We have great teachers aboard the Hades Rambler, they may not look much, but don't underestimate them."

The two boys turned and stared as Pirate Cooper and Surgeon Swale grabbed at the last chicken drumstick and grappled with it on the floor amongst the tables and chairs.

Without warning, Stanley was on his feet banging a spoon against his tankard. "SILENCE."

The cabin went quiet, but Spike let out an enormous belch. The boys from the Sudden Ghost glared at him, but the ugly pirates bellowed with laughter as did the teachers who were now just sat on the floor, gnawing at chicken bones. Surgeon Swale was stuffing chicken into his mouth, his bare jaw-bone chomping his food, his wet tongue slid around his mouth, which was visible through the spaces where the skin should have been.

"Just showing my appreciation of the good food," said Spike, his eyes sparkling with mischief and malice.

"I'd like to welcome aboard the crew of the Sudden Ghost," called Stanley.

Tankards were raised. A cheer went up.

"I would especially like to welcome, my cousin, Thomas Prow," he continued.

Another cheer went round the deck and all eyes fell on Thom.

"I'd like it known that although our great-great-grandfathers were always fighting, I do not wish to continue this feud with my cousin – he and I will be great friends. We will have great adventures together. Let's raise our tankards in toast of ... family."

"Family."

The cheer went up and tankards clanked, R.U.M. was spilt.

Stanley pulled Thom to his feet and gave his shoulders a squeeze and they raised their tankards together arm in arm. Thom felt himself blush, his instincts told him to be wary.

Stanley sat back down in his seat and emptied his tankard of R.U.M. He smiled at his cousin. Again, the smile didn't quite seem to reach his eyes; it was a smile of satisfaction nonetheless. "Enjoy your pudding, Thom. I've someone I must speak to, but I'll be right back."

Thom returned his smile, hoping his was more convincing.

As Stanley walked away, taking Spike with him, Thom saw Angus approach. "Hey, this is great, isn't it?"

"Dinner's amazing," replied Thom.

"I didn't mean the dinner, although it is delicious, I meant your cousin he seems pleased you're here."

"I'm not so sure."

Angus frowned. "Why not?"

"It's just something. I'm not sure what."

"Ah, come on, Thom. He wants to be friends ... he's made that perfectly clear to everyone here."

Thom sighed. "Yes, yes, you're right. You'll have to excuse me though, I need the loo, be back in a minute." He got up from the Captain's table and made his way back the way they'd come. He had passed a toilet - known on board as the 'head' - on the way to dinner, just down the corridor – he was feeling a little queasy.

Having been to the head and now feeling less nauseous after taking a few deep breaths, Thom made his way back to the dining deck. As he passed a closed door, he heard raised voices from within. It was Stanley and Spike. He stopped to listen, his heart in his mouth.

"I don't care what it takes -" he heard Stanley say viciously.

"But do you have to be so nice to him?" remarked Spike. "It's so unlike you, he'll smell a rat if you're not careful or someone else will."

"He's going to be popular amongst the crew of the Sudden Ghost, I need to keep him close," said Stanley.

Spike grunted.

"If I'm going to find this lost treasure map, then he may be able to help me."

"But what if he doesn't know anything?"

"If he doesn't know anything now, I think he soon will – I'm sure there's a greater plan afoot than any of us realise. I think that's why he's here."

Thom felt a sneeze growing in his nose. He had to get away ... quick before the sneeze escaped and gave away his eavesdropping. Holding his finger under his nose, he walked quietly, but with speed, away from the door; he'd heard enough anyway.

So, that was it, he had been right not to trust Stanley – he was as deceitful as his great-great-grandfather, Greybeard. Well, curse him. Two could play at that game.

Chapter 7
Lessons to Learn

Thom took a deep breath and hurried back to the Captain's table before Stanley realised he had been absent.

"You okay?" Angus asked, taking a seat next to his.

Thom nodded. He couldn't confide in Angus, not yet anyway. He must keep this to himself. He grabbed a slice of apple pie and covered it in thick custard. If he filled his mouth with food he would be unable to say anything.

Thom was taking the last mouthfuls of the pie when Stanley and Spike returned, all smiles.

"How's the grub?" Stanley asked, placing a hand on Thom's shoulder.

"Delicious, thank you," replied Thom, feeling himself shrink from Stanley's touch.

"Lovely," said Angus.

"Great. I think everyone's finished eating so let's retire to the games cabin."

The boys returned to the cabin where they had first come across the unusual crew of the Hades Rambler. Some of the gang had already returned there, heavy rock music was playing from an old juke box in the corner and loud laughter filled the room. A few pirates were playing cards; others just lounging around drinking R.U.M. A group were huddled together involved in some kind of board game, on which there was a picture of a Kraken pulling a ship beneath the waves. Thom thought it looked quite good and was about to ask if he and Angus could join in when Stanley entered and kicked the table over – the board and pieces went everywhere.

"I've told you before. Nobody plays that game," he bellowed.

"It's only a game -" said one of the crew who had been playing it.

Stanley spat at the boys. "Get rid of it! Put them in the hold for a week. I never want to see that game again, got it?" he said, and with a red face, stormed off without even a glance at his cousin.

"What's up with him?" asked Thom in a hushed voice.

"He doesn't like anything to do with the Kraken," Roscoe whispered.

"Come on, time to go." Angus pulled on Thom's arm. "I'll tell you more later ... not here."

Thom, Angus and Roscoe ascended the wooden stairs to the top deck. The mood aboard the Hades Rambler was now sombre and everyone began to disperse. Aboard the boats, that returned the crew of the Sudden Ghost back to their ship, everyone was subdued. There was only the rhythmic sound of the oars splashing in and out of the water – the earlier chatter and excitement of the boys replaced by tired eyes. Thom couldn't figure out why everything had changed so quickly after Stanley had kicked over the game. The look on Angus' face had confirmed that there was more to it than a brief burst of anger – but what, Thom couldn't guess.

The whole evening had been loud and raucous aboard the Hades Rambler. Stanley had been pleasant and welcoming to his face, but there was no mistaking the conversation that Thom had overheard between Stanley and Spike. It was disappointing, but not surprising.

Greybeard had murdered Seamus Prow, in cold blood, tried to steal his family's treasure, but since that day the treasure hadn't been rediscovered. It continued to stay hidden, concealed from everyone. Had Seamus Prow meant his family to rediscover it? Thom thought he surely had, which meant there had to be a map, as rumoured, which showed where the treasure map was ... so where was that map now? If it wasn't on board the Sudden Ghost, where was it? Or, had the Navigation teacher told him a lie? If he could find the map, then maybe, just maybe, he could find the treasure too, but the thought of returning to the Navigation room filled him with dread – there were so many maps in there; he feared he may never find it. If he couldn't find the map, then what would happen to Grandpa? He couldn't bear the thought.

Back in their cabin, the boys lay in their hammocks in darkness, the gentle creaking of the ship, like old men's voices, lulled them.

"So, tell me why Stanley lost it like that?" asked Thom.

Angus sighed. "It's because of his burn, the one shaped like the Kraken. When he was about ten, he and his grandfather were out on his grandfather's boat and the Kraken tried to pull them under. Stanley tried to stop the beast by setting off a rocket-flare, but the boat caught fire. Stanley's grandfather was taken by the Kraken and never seen again. Stanley escaped, but with a large burn on his cheek. When the dressings were removed the burn was in the shape of a Kraken. It's a cruel and constant reminder that he couldn't save his grandfather. After that, he swore that he would one day have his revenge and kill the Kraken that killed his grandfather."

"That's some story," said Thom. "I almost feel sorry for him, but I'm too tired."

"Almost?" asked Angus.

"Hmmm," replied Thom.

"Aren't you glad that Stanley wants to be friends?" said Angus.

"Yes ... yes I am," replied Thom firmly, afraid he would give away too much if he continued to be negative about his cousin.

However, much later as he listened to Angus' and Roscoe's snores, he felt very alone and wished he had somebody to talk to. He didn't know his cabin mates well enough yet to confide in them. Spike was supposed to be part of the crew of the Sudden Ghost, but he was very close to Stanley and seemed more at home aboard the dark boards and gloomy corridors of the Hades Rambler than on his own ship. He certainly was not to be trusted, but what about Angus and Roscoe - could he trust them?

Unable to sleep, Thom grabbed his torch, got out of his hammock and made his way to the galley; he needed a glass of milk after all that rich food. Reaching for the milk bottle in the fridge, he almost dropped it as he felt something move against his legs.

"What the -?"

He looked down into the darkness, but couldn't see anything.

He felt it again.

Fumbling for his torch, on the side where he had left it, he shone the beam towards his feet. Two green, unblinking eyes stared back at him.

"Storm!" he said, his heart thumping in his chest.

The cat mewed and flicked her thick, black tail.

"Would you like some milk?" He poured some into a bowl and watched as Storm purred her way through the bowlful and then looked up at him, a small beard of milk on her chin. Thom laughed and she rubbed around his legs again.

"More?" he asked, pouring a little extra into the bowl. As she drank it, he bent down tentatively to stroke her, remembering the way she had hissed at him last time. "I hope you remember me giving you this milk and not try to bite or scratch me next time I see you."

Thom stroked Storm gently then made his way back towards the cabin. He felt exhausted and hoped now that he would be able to sleep. As he opened the door to the cabin he could hear the heavy breathing of the other two boys. Storm pattered past him. Thom watched as she jumped onto his hammock. She looked at him expectantly.

"You want to sleep in my hammock now, do you?" he asked.

The green eyes stared.

"Ok, but if you disturb me, or bite me, you're out."

He climbed into the hammock and Storm circled a few times before settling at his feet. The purring of the cat somehow soothed him and before long, he was asleep.

During the night Thom was awoken by the feeling of going speedily in a downward position and knew immediately that the school was on the move —

where would they be when they awoke the next day? Didn't Captain Ginger ever sleep?

Sunlight was streaming through the port-hole into the cabin when he woke the next morning. Through the round aspect Thom spied sapphire seas and forest-covered, jagged mountains rising up out of them into a cloudless sky. Roscoe was still asleep, but Angus was reading a book in his hammock.

"What are you reading?" asked Thom, noticing that Storm was no longer at his feet.

"Treasure Island," he replied.

Thom laughed.

"What's so funny? You need to read it too, it will be on your reading list."

Thom felt his heart sink. "You mean we still have to do English?"

"We do Literature with Captain Blake. He's Captain of the Loyal Trinity as you know and we have to read a lot, poetry too, but at least it's all about pirates and adventures on the high seas. We'll be studying the 'Ancient Mariner' too very soon, thankfully only in extracts. It would take years to read the whole thing."

"Actually, I know the story already," said Thom. "It's my Grandfather's favourite book; he has an abridged child's version with amazing illustrations – it's ancient and was given to him by his grandfather. I believe it belonged to his grandfather too, possibly ..."

"My Pops always read *Treasure Island* with me too, so I do know the story, but we've been told to read it and it's quite good."

"I don't hate reading, but I'd much rather be outside doing something active like kite-boarding. To feel the salt and sun upon me ... I rather miss it."

"Sounds like a lot of fun, perhaps you could teach me sometime?"

"Sure," said Thom. He was tempted to talk about Angus coming home with him one weekend, when it was his turn to have shore-leave, but realised that home was not the same as it had been. Nothing in his life was.

"Morning," said Roscoe, stretching and yawning. "Is it time to get up already?"

"Yep," said Angus, putting down his book and climbing out of his hammock.

"We're on rigging duty this morning," said Roscoe.

Thom thought about the high ropes and sails that swung loosely above the deck of the ship and swallowed hard. "W-what do we have to do?"

"Oh, just climb up them and make sure all the ropes are secure and rigging is safe," stated Angus. "Check for damaged sails; that type of thing."

"Oh, okay."

116

"Then we have Mythology, followed by Weaponry this afternoon," said Roscoe. "Swashbuckling is my favourite."

"Sounds brilliant," said Thom, brightening a little at the thought of having consent to wield a sword around. That would never have been allowed at his previous school – the risk assessment alone would have turned the Head's hair grey in the course of an afternoon.

After a breakfast of toast and smoked fish, which was deliciously fresh due to the location of the School for Scoundrels that morning, Thom followed Roscoe and Angus up onto deck. The sky was still blue, the wind was cold and strong – land could be seen a few miles in the distance. Huge mountains lay like giant sleeping trolls. Thom couldn't help but think it was a perfect day for kite-boarding. Above him, the raised sails flapped in the wind and the pulleys clanked loudly.

"Where are we?" Thom asked.

"Northern Orkneys, Scotland. Home," said Angus.

"No wonder it's cold," said Thom.

"Right, let's get this done," said Roscoe beginning to climb. "Oh darn it, I haven't finished my I.L.T. yet and I don't want to get behind. Captain don't like it if we get behind."

"What's I.L.T.?" asked Thom, watching as Roscoe leapt up the ropes.

"Independent Learning Tasks."

"Huh?"

"In ordinary schools it's called Homework," said Angus, as he too started to climb.

Thom looked up at his cabin mates as they climbed, as agile as monkeys, up the ropes towards the crow's nest at the top.

"Come on," called Roscoe. "You just need to check that there are no fraying ropes, loose knots or jammed pulleys."

"Erm ... okay. I'm on my way." Thom started to climb. "One foot above the other, just one foot above the other, keep reaching up," he chanted quietly to himself as he followed his mates up the rigging. "You can do this ..."

Roscoe was already near the top. How did he get there that quickly? Angus was not far behind him. "Don't look down ..."

"You're takin' your time, Thom," called Roscoe, now standing in the crow's nest. "You're not even half way."

"Aren't I?" asked Thom, looking down and immediately regretting it. His head swam, his legs turned to jelly and he felt a wave of sickness pass over him - he had to get down, but he was stuck fast – he couldn't move - either up or down.

"You all right?" asked Angus who had stopped about three-quarters of the way up and was now looking down at Thom.

"I-I'm fine," lied Thom. "Be with you in a minute."

In a moment, Roscoe and Angus were back beside him.

"You're scared of heights!" laughed Roscoe.

"Don't be unkind, Roscoe," said Angus, but a smile played on his lips nonetheless.

"Never heard of a pirate being scared of heights before!" continued Roscoe.

"Come on, I'll help you down," suggested Angus.

"I can't move," stated Thom. His fingers gripped the ropes tightly.

"Sure you can ... you must have been up high before," Angus tried to reassure him.

"Only when I'm on my kite-board."

"Well, imagine that's what you're doing. Take a deep breath, and feel the wind and sun on your face. Now, let go of the rope with one hand."

Thom felt Angus' hand on his, gently uncurling his fingers from the rope, he took a deep breath and felt his stomach relax a tiny bit.

"Wow. You are scared," said Roscoe.

Letting go of the rope, ever so slowly, Thom moved his hand down, followed by his foot.

"That's it!" said Angus. "Keep coming. Three points of contact at all times."

Thom continued to place one foot and hand below the other until he was back on the deck. He was still shaking and could feel the heat in his face; he was mortified to feel tears prick his eyes. He couldn't bear to look around to see if anyone else was about and had noticed him being such a coward.

"Roscoe. R.U.M.," ordered Angus.

Roscoe nodded and ran off towards the galley.

"S-sorry, I should have said I was scared of heights, but didn't want to look stupid," said Thom, his eyes cast downwards.

"Better to say, mate, otherwise you're gonna put us all in danger. If we're to be a crew, we need to know and trust each other, work as a team."

"Of course." Thom nodded.

"Come on, sit down," suggested Angus, pointing at a barrel at the side of the deck.

"I've always hated heights, looks like I need to get used to them though ... any suggestions?"

"Yes, practice. Just keep practising - go a little higher each time, until you can get to the top."

Thom sighed.

"Here's some R.U.M.," said Roscoe appearing and handing Thom a tankard.

Thom tasted it and immediately began to feel much better. Whatever the Unknown ingredient was, it seemed to help in times of need.

The bell tolled.

"Great, more Mythology," said Angus. "I wonder if we've got Sir Walter back today?"

As they entered the classroom, Thom was surprised to see that an elderly man, smartly dressed, including a bright pink bow-tie with yellow spots, was stood in front of a whiteboard. Long Harry was sat at the front of the class too.

"You're late!" the old man growled, glaring through round, wire-rimmed spectacles.

"Sorry, Sir," the boys replied, as they sat at their desks.

Sir Walter twisted his bow-tie and turned on an overhead-projector. He inserted a picture on the glass. It was of a great sea-snake; its scales were purple and black; it had red eyes and a serpent's tongue.

"This is the sea-serpent," said Sir Walter, pointing at the enormous snake-like creature which had wrapped itself around a large ship, not unlike the Sudden Ghost. "Throughout history there have been many sightings of this creature and reports of ships having been sunk by its enormous bulk."

"Not sure our swords would help kill that big beastie," whispered Rufus, his eyes full of alarm.

"Quiet, Rufus," said Sir Walter, glaring at him. "Some legends have it that the sea-serpent can grow to the size of the circumference of the earth."

"What's a circumference?" asked Fergus.

"It means a measurement round the outside," said Tim in a small voice.

"You tellin' me that this monster could wrap itself round the whole world?" sneered Lucifer. "I don't believe that."

"Apparently so, although I haven't ever seen one that big myself," said Sir Walter.

"Have you seen one then, Sir?" asked Fergus, his eyes wide.

"Sure have. When I was travelling by ship with my son and my brother last summer, there was a tremendous storm and this creature appeared in the middle of it."

"What happened?" asked Roscoe.

"My son shot it with a harpoon and injured it. We thought it was going to kill us, but it went back below the surface. My brother had to cut the rope before it took us down too. Amazing adventure."

A noise at the doorway made everyone turn.

Spike sidled in looking disheveled.

"Where've you been?" Sir Walter asked. "You're late."

"I-I had to finish a chore -"

"Chores do not take precedence over lessons, Rose. Make sure you finish them before class in future."

Laughter rang around the room. Sir Walter scowled.

Spike sat down heavily in his chair and huffed.

Thom wondered if he had been looking through his things again. He couldn't wait to go and check, but the lesson had only just begun, he couldn't ask to be excused already.

Sir Walter began talking again. "Now, before I show you the video I would like you to put on these 3D glasses. Silver, you can hand them out."

Silver mumbled something and took the box of dark glasses from Sir Walter. He threw a pair at each of the boys as he hobbled around the class. One by one the boys put on the dark, large rimmed glasses - a few sniggers flew around the room. The boys taunted each other about how silly they looked.

A television was wheeled across from the side of the room and Sir Walter turned it on – a small white box in the centre grew larger and larger until a picture appeared on the screen. Sir Walter pressed play on the video player - there was an aerial film of a large chain of mountainous islands, not dissimilar to those they were anchored close by to. A ridge ran through the middle of a large green/black landscape, sparse of any trees and shrubs, a bleak place. Suddenly, the island began to shudder and the boys sat back in terror as the island moved fully round and an enormous serpent's head sprang out of the screen at them:

saliva and fangs snapping in their direction. Tim fell off his chair and started to cry. Thom felt his heart jump into his mouth and heard Roscoe yell, then start laughing. Long Harry was amused too.

"Shiver me timbers!" said Lucifer. "That's amazing. Is it real footage?"

"Yes, it was taken from an aeroplane above the ocean near the Bahamas," said Sir Walter, his tone now more serious. "It seems that the sea-serpent likes to disguise itself as an island in some cases, so be aware out there on the seas."

"My great-grandfather killed one. Its skeleton is still on display in a museum in the Bahamas," boasted Spike. "I reckon I could kill one too."

"If you do better in swashbuckling than you did last week," taunted Roscoe.

Spike stood up and glared at Roscoe, clenching his fists.

"Sit down!" roared Sir Walter then straightened his already straight bow-tie.

"What happened in swashbuckling?" Thom whispered to Angus.

"Sonny Boy nearly had his hand off," replied Angus.

"Really?"

"If it hadn't been for Long Harry, Spike would have lost more than his hand too."

"Whoa," said Thom, now feeling a little unnerved about his afternoon lesson with real weapons. It was going to be so much fun, but dangerous too – how thrilling.

Thom's stomach was rumbling when the bell rang for lunch. The boys were making their way up to the top deck chattering about the sea-serpent lesson.

"Do we have any lunch guests today?" he asked, fearing that the crew of the Hades Rambler might be joining them.

"Yes, the Loyal Trinity are coming over," said Angus.

"Great," said Thom, feeling relieved that he wouldn't have to face Stanley again just yet.

"Yes, they'll be joining us for rigging-racing in a few days, so they're probably wanting to suss us out."

"Rigging-racing?"

"Yes," said Roscoe. "We're all put in groups and then we race each other up and down the rigging. It's great fun!"

"Yes ... sounds great ..." Thom felt his heart sink. How was he going to get out of that?

Lunchtime was relaxed. Thankfully the Loyal Trinity crew had brought some of their delicious cakes with them, which took away the taste of the fish-paste sandwiches that cook had made. The members of both crews sat in groups up on deck in the sunshine chatting away about their morning's lessons. Thom sat amongst Rufus, Roscoe and Angus with Arabia and some of the other boys from the Loyal Trinity he had not yet met properly.

"How come you guys know how to make such amazing cakes?" asked Angus.

A scruffy, dirty-faced young boy called Tan replied, "Well the food was so disgusting we had to do something and I can't cook so I got my Gran to teach me last holidays. The food during the first term was so awful I couldn't bear the thought of coming back. Nesta had stayed with me during the holidays as his parents were away with mine, so Gran got us into making cakes."

Thom peered at Nesta who wore a serious expression and was whittling a piece of wood with a dagger. "It's quite simple," he said.

"Thom's Gran makes great cakes too. Perhaps she could get you, Thom, to learn how to make 'em then we could have more delicious cakes on board the Sudden Ghost?" suggested Roscoe.

Arabia glanced at Thom and smiled. "That's a great idea, nothing wrong with having some good cooks about; in fact I think that it should be encouraged."

Thom found himself wanting to impress the dark, mysterious Arabia. It was as if his dark eyes held some mystery; he seemed exotic in his blue, velvet trousers and loose, black shirt with a ruby red waistcoat. His dark curls were partially hidden beneath a dark blue headscarf.

"Come on," said Roscoe. "I'm going to practise for the rigging-race, anyone else?"

Everyone except Thom and Arabia got up.

"I'll practise another time," said Thom, not looking up at the others.

"I don't need any practise," stated Arabia. "I'm going to beat you all anyway."

Tan laughed. "Somebody will beat you one day."

Arabia laughed louder. "They can try."

"Who knows," said Read, another of the boys from the Loyal Trinity crew. His big smile widening as he fiddled with the shell that hung round his neck on a leather strap. "Perhaps Thom Prow here will beat you – we don't know what he's like yet."

Roscoe looked at Thom, let out a laugh and ran off towards the rigging with the others.

Thom was left with Arabia. They were silent for a few minutes listening to the gulls screaming overhead and the boys' shouts as they climbed up and down the rigging like monkeys in trees. Thom watched with his heart sinking lower, they were all so good already. How would he ever catch up?

"Did you know my father and your father were at school together; they were great friends," said Arabia.

"No, no, I didn't know that." Thom turned to look at him.

Arabia nodded. "I don't suppose you remember much about your parents?"

"No, not much; in fact it seems the older I get the more distant the memories become."

"I'm sorry to hear that. Perhaps I shouldn't have brought it up ..." Arabia went a little red in the cheeks.

"It's fine. It's nice to talk about them. I don't get much of a chance. Gran always becomes so distressed when I mention them, or the ... accident."

"Yes. I'm sure she does. Dad said he and your dad were good mates, shared a cabin and everything. Perhaps you could come back to my family one weekend and meet my dad; he could tell you lots about him."

"That would be great," replied Thom. He had often wondered what his father had been like. His grandparents had told him some things, but it would be good to hear another person's perspective too.

The bell for class rang, interrupting Thom's thoughts.

"Blow it," cried Arabia, standing up. "I was just getting comfortable. Better get back to the ship, we've got sewing, I mean sail-mending, this afternoon."

Thom got to his feet too. "We've got swashbuckling. I can't wait!"

"Watch out for Spike, he doesn't always play nicely – see you soon. By the way, I can't wait to see if you're the one to take my title of best rigging-racer."

Thom laughed, but inwardly cringed.

A shout caught his attention. Angus was waving to him. "Come on. We don't want to be late – we'll get the best swords if we get there first."

"See you later," Thom called to Arabia.

"This is my favourite lesson," cried Roscoe, looking at Thom as he caught up with the others, his face full of mischief.

"Me too," said Angus. "We have to stay on deck for this. Follow me and I'll show you where the swords are kept."

Thom walked beside Angus to the quarterdeck where a large door stood heavily padlocked. It was next door to Captain Ginger's office.

"Captain Ginger is the only one with a key," explained Rufus in a whisper, looking cautiously at the Captain's office door. At that moment the handle to his office started to turn.

Thom held his breath and noticed that all the boys, who had been fidgeting, immediately stood calmly and in single file leading up to the sword room. Many of the crews' faces wore a wary look; even Spike was quiet, head down.

After a few moments Storm appeared around the door, followed shortly by the big boots of Captain Ginger. His beard seemed more orange today in the sunshine, as he growled a 'hello' to the boys.

A young man with long, thick black curls and thick stubble on his chin stepped out from behind Ginger. He wore a loose white shirt; red, velvet trousers and a black leather waistcoat. At his waist he wore a scabbard which held a beautiful handled sword, encrusted with more jewels than Thom had ever seen.

"Who's that?" Thom whispered.

"Master Wainright, Weaponry teacher."

Ginger approached the door which hid the weapons from view and undid the padlock with a key that he had unhooked from his belt.

"Okay, crew, collect your swords and then go and stand on the poop deck – no nonsense or we'll cancel the lesson and do more maths instead," warned Master Wainright.

A groan went round the crew.

"Not McManus!" cried Roscoe. "Anyone but him, I don't want to do any maths today."

Thom watched as Angus, Roscoe and Rufus took a sword each from the Captain, their eyes wide with anticipation.

Thom moved forward to collect the sword that Captain Ginger had in his hand, but the Captain, seeing it was Thom, stopped and frowned.

"Ah, Prow ..." Captain Ginger searched amongst the swords until he finally pulled one out from nearer the back, slightly hidden amongst the others. "This must be your sword, Prow. This one was your father's whilst he was on board the Sudden Ghost just seems right you should have it."

"Hey, that's my sword, I always have that one!" shouted Spike.

Ginger turned and roared at Spike. "I make the decisions round 'ere, how dare you question my authority; your punishment must be to clean and polish all the swords tonight ... under close supervision."

"S-sorry, Captain, of course, Captain," he said politely, but Thom saw him mutter something under his breath. Storm arched her back and hissed at Spike, who glared back at her.

Thom took the sword. He held it in his hand - it was heavy, but felt well-balanced. The handle was golden, a dragon's head protruding in a menacing way towards his wrist. The blade, silver and sharp with a sea-serpent engraved along the curved sword.

"Wow," said Thom. "It's beautiful."

"Just what your father said," said Captain Ginger, a smile starting at the corner of his lips. "I think it suits you." His blue eyes sparkled.

"Thank you," replied Thom, making his way towards the others on the poop-deck.

"Watch she doesn't cut you," Spike sneered as he passed by.

Thom ignored him, it wasn't his fault the Captain had given him this particular sword. It had been his father's after all.

"That's really gonna upset Spike," said Rufus. "He always has that sword, every lesson."

"Well, not this time," replied Thom, holding up the sword and watching the sun glint off the blade. He tried to imagine his father's young hands clutching the sword and wondered if he'd enjoyed swashbuckling – what young boy wouldn't?

Master Wainright had the boys in two lines facing each other. Captain Ginger and Storm stood watching at the other end of the line to Master Wainright, who, with a flourish, drew his sword and held it above his head in a threatening manner.

"This is an attack position," he said.

"Looks more like he's just showing off," whispered Rufus, who stood next to Thom in the line.

Thom laughed, but regretted it straight away.

"You boy!" Master Wainright called, beckoning him to come forward.

"Me, Sir?" asked Thom, looking around.

"Yes. Dare to laugh during my lesson, would you?"

"Sorry, Sir," replied Thom approaching Wainright.

"What do you know about swords, boy?"

"Nothing, Sir."

"Then might I suggest you listen, so that you do learn."

"Of course, Sir."

"Go back in line," he barked fiercely.

Thom quickly returned to his space in the line, but he didn't fail to notice Spike's look of satisfaction.

"Right, Angus and Silver, come on you two, let's show the new kids a bit of amazing swashbuckling."

Angus and Silver stepped forward.

"En-guarde!" called Master Wainright and the boys raised their swords so they touched and crossed. "Right, thrust and parry, boys, thrust and parry."

Master Wainright called commands as the boys fought; their swords clashing and glinting in the sun; their feet doing a dance of sorts around the deck. It ended when Angus knocked Silver's sword out of his hand and pointed the blade towards his chest.

Silver cursed. The crowd cheered.

Thom noticed that, for the whole lesson, Storm sat and watched the fighting; her green eyes seemed to follow every move - she seemed especially to be keeping an eye on Spike

Chapter 8
Facing Fears

Over the passing days, Thom grew a little more used to his life on board the ship. Rising early, doing his chores, going to lessons and getting to know other students and teachers kept him busy enough for time to pass quickly, but thoughts of his grandfather and the map were never far away.

One afternoon before dinner, Thom excused himself from the common deck, where the others were doing homework or playing games, and made his way up to the top deck. He stood staring up at the rigging, dreading the forthcoming races. What made him feel even worse was the fact that he was expected to race Arabia (amongst others) – how could he even compete with such an athletic and fearless young man? Arabia was the unbeaten champion.

Thom took a deep breath and began to climb. *Just don't look down.* He climbed as quickly as he could and found that he could go fast if he didn't think about how far up he was. He looked up at each hold above him and just moved his hands and feet up and up; not once did he look down.

Finally, and breathlessly, he reached the top. *I've done it!* Clinging on to the rigging, his legs were like jelly and he didn't dare look down. Instead, he looked out across the water towards the Hades Rambler. The black, lifeless sails were rolled up, it was as if the crew on board might as well have been living on land in a dark cave, they never seemed to be out and enjoying themselves; always hidden below deck, obsessed with raucous behaviour. They were a miserable, ugly lot.

Thom switched his glance to the Loyal Trinity, which was alive with activity and colour. The sound of a fiddle could be heard playing an upbeat tune to which some of the pirates were dancing a jig and laughter was carried towards him on the breeze.

Thom thought he ought to start climbing down; this was not so easy. To climb down he would need to look down – he froze. He felt frustration grow; he had done so well in climbing up. He *had* to climb down again. Taking a deep breath, he counted to three then gradually uncurled his fingers from the ropes. He glanced down just enough to the next piece of the ratline; he could ... he *would* do this. Steadily he climbed down, not as fast as he went up, but once his feet were back on the deck he felt a strong sense of achievement.

All of a sudden, applause was heard from behind. He turned. Angus was stood there clapping his hands, beaming.

"I wondered if I might have to climb up and rescue you again – but you were amazing that time. How'd you do it?"

"I couldn't bear the thought of racing against Arabia or the others from the Loyal Trinity and getting stuck; that would've been so embarrassing."

"No denying that," he replied, laughing. "I didn't realise you were so competitive. Come on, I'll race you to the top; it will be great practise."

"Ok. One, two, three ... go!"

Thom sprung up onto the rigging as if he was an expert then climbed as fast as he could; Angus was just ahead of him. Thom felt his competitive streak (that he always felt during kite-boarding) kick in and he pushed himself faster up the ropes; if he didn't think about his fear, it would be fine. If he did, it would consume him.

Soon, he was shoulder to shoulder with Angus. They neared the top, although Angus climbed away from him and came in first, Thom was not far behind.

Angus slapped him on the back. Thom and he laughed breathlessly. "Well done, ship-mate."

Thom felt elated and was eager now to take part in the races; he couldn't believe how he had conquered his fear of heights – his competitiveness had helped, that and not wanting to look a fool.

The day of the rigging-racing arrived quicker than Thom had hoped. Although he was feeling more confident, having practiced a few times over the past few days, he was still worried that he might freeze with fear if he looked down at any point during the races.

The boys welcomed the crew of the Loyal Trinity with R.U.M. amongst jeers of who would win. A ripple of excitement ran through the two crews as Captain Ginger appeared from his cabin and addressed the boys.

"Welcome to our neighbouring crew. I can see that our other neighbours are late ... anyone heard from the Hades Rambler?"

"I think we should start without them," called Long Harry.

A voice spoke from the gunwale, "I don't think so." Stanley approached, hands on hips. His mates Gunn and Bart stood fiercely either side of him.

The crews and Captain Ginger turned to see the pirates from the Hades Rambler climbing like spectres over the gunwale, their distorted faces full of the same competitiveness as the others aboard – theirs, much more sinister.

Stanley searched the crowd, spotted Thom and smiled.

"Right. Well now everybody is here I'll give you the rules," stated Captain Ginger. "We'll be starting with the mizzenmast then onto the foremast then, for the finalists only, it will be the main mast," he shouted. "Any cheating, whatsoever and you'll be disqualified and punished. Get your teams ready, we'll be starting in five minutes."

Long Harry gathered his team around him. "Right lads, I want Spike, Angus, Roscoe, Thom and Lucifer; you're all in the first round. I don't know what you're like at climbing Thom or you Lucifer, but I want a couple of new kids on the team this time."

Thom looked around and could see Stanley with a group of other boys. "Who are they?" Thom asked Angus.

"That's Hook, Salty, Springer and Barnie," he replied.

The boys were circling Stanley, and Thom could see the drive in the boys' faces; they clearly wanted to win. There was a lot of growling and snarling from the group.

In contrast, the crew from the Loyal Trinity was quiet and calm but no less determined from the looks on their faces. Arabia had chosen his team: Read, Nesta, Sporty and Sleek.

"Gather round!" commanded Captain Ginger. "Three at a time in each heat – sort your teams, now."

The Captains sorted their teams and gave their orders.

Thom felt his heart sink a little when he realised that he wouldn't be racing Arabia in the first heat, but Barnie and Nesta. He had built it up all afternoon that he would be, had thought that he would lose, but it would be great fun in trying to beat the champion.

As the competitors took their places at the bottom of the rigging, Thom was surprised to see Captain Ginger raise a pistol. He had no idea that there were any guns on board the ship.

"Three, two, one ..." Captain Ginger fired the shot and Spike, Hook and Read sprang onto the ratlines. The boys raced up the rigging. To start with there wasn't much in it then all of a sudden Spike pulled ahead of the others. Read was ahead of Hook who was beginning to slow; he sprung rapidly up the ropes, but Spike won a head and shoulders above the other two. A huge cheer went up from the crew of the Sudden Ghost. Spike was grinning from ear to ear, but Hook looked like he could rip Spike apart with his steel hook. Read looked disappointed, but shrugged his shoulders before climbing back down to the deck.

Stanley could be heard giving his boys a good talking to, reminding Thom of his rugby coach at his previous school, who could not bear to lose a single match. Ginger raised the pistol again: Roscoe, Salty and Sleek sprinted to the ropes and leapt up the ratlines to the top – Sleek won, followed closely by Roscoe and Salty came last.

The races continued, coming first was Angus and Arabia from their teams, then soon enough it was Thom's turn. The butterflies in his stomach fluttered furiously and he hoped that he wouldn't lose his earlier nerve. He lined up next to Barnie and Nesta waiting for the pistol start.

"Three, two, one..." The shot rang out.

They ran at the ropes and Thom threw himself up and onto the ratlines, hand above hand, foot above foot – he climbed not looking down, only up; not sideways at the others. He barely heard the shouts of 'Go Thom' from his crew members below – he just had to get to the top and fast. Breathless, but exhilarated Thom grabbed the top of the mast - he had won.

"Well done, Thom," stated Nesta.

"Hmmph!" mumbled Barnie, breathing heavily beside him, but immediately beginning to climb down.

Thom and Nesta followed more steadily. They were about a third of the way down when they heard a cry from below; Barnie was falling ...

"Cripes," cried Nesta and he and Thom hurried down to see Barnie lying on the deck, his ankle broken. Thom could see he was fighting back tears.

"Get him to the medical quarters and Surgeon Swale!" cried Ginger. "Stanley, go with him, he's yours. You too, Hook."

The remaining crew of the Hades Rambler slunk back over the gunwale grumbling at their luck, preferring, it seemed, to go back to the dark depths of their vessel than to stay and cheer on the crew members of the other ships.

For the second round the five winners of the Mizzenmast heats were racing up the Foremast. Spike, Sleek, Thom, Arabia and Angus took their places. The first three boys to reach the top would go through to the Mainmast final race.

Captain Ginger raised his pistol and they were off.

Arabia sprang into action as soon as the gun had sounded; he was followed closely by Angus whose height was of an advantage. Spike's face was determined, but his efforts could not match those of the first two. Thom and Sleek were neck and neck, bringing up the rear.

The crew of the Loyal Trinity and the Sudden Ghost applauded and shouted excitedly.

All of a sudden, Spike slipped, enabling Thom and Sleek to get ahead of him. Thom knew he had to come in at least third place to get through to the final race. He wanted it more than he had realised, and with that realisation, he powered up the ratlines distancing himself from Sleek and gaining on Angus. The crowd below cheered as Arabia reached the top first, Angus was only a hand behind him and Thom came in third – he was through to the final! The crew of the Sudden Ghost went wild, cheering and chanting for their champions. Thom and Angus descended the rigging together and were swept up in a group hug. Thom's legs were like jelly, so it was good to have the support; his head was spinning with excitement and he had no idea how he was going to start, let alone finish, the final race.

The Mainmast race was the decider for the Rigging-Racer cup. For the past three years it had been won by the Loyal Trinity, namely Arabia. It would be amazing if the Sudden Ghost could take claim of the cup this year for a change. Thom realised that it might be possible as there were two of them in the final race - the odds were good.

Much to Thom's disappointment, Stanley and Hook arrived just in time to watch the final race; this made Thom feel more nervous. He tried hard to forget that his cousin was watching, but a quick glance at Stanley, who smirked at Thom, made his nerves fall to pieces.

Ginger raised the pistol for the final time. Thom took a deep breath and snuck a quick look at the pirates he was up against – Arabia, the reigning champion and Angus who stood a good few inches taller than him. He tried to push the negative thoughts aside, a few days ago he couldn't even climb the rigging without clinging with fear to the ropes around him; now he had raced up and down the ratlines without even thinking about it – anything was possible.

The pistol shot rang out.

The boys were off.

Thom flung himself into the race with all his worth and began to climb. About a quarter of the way up, there wasn't much between them. Angus was just in the lead with Arabia and Thom close behind. Thom heard a cry as Angus slipped, but he caught his footing again and continued to climb, although behind Arabia and Thom now. Thom spurred himself on ... he had to win, he wanted to win.

As Thom gained on Arabia his heavy breathing could be heard beside him, but Thom was tiring too ... he could feel it in his legs. He pushed himself harder, putting as much energy into his legs as possible – they were now about three-quarters of the way up the Mainmast.

"Come on," Thom cried aloud, pumping his legs harder and harder.

Suddenly, he was at the top, Arabia just behind him - a split second between them.

"Yeeesss!" he cried, his legs burning.

"Congratulations, Thom!" said Arabia panting and holding out his hand to shake Thom's. This time, Thom didn't even think about letting go of the rope – he shook Arabia's hand and felt his heart thumping in his chest. The cheers from below made him look down; that was his mistake ... his legs started to tremble, his head went dizzy; he grabbed back onto the rope with both hands.

"You're scared of heights!" said Arabia, but he wasn't smiling. "That's amazing; to climb that well, but to be afraid – you're a brave pirate, Thomas Prow – your parents would've been proud of you."

"Thanks," he replied taking a deep breath. He gradually let go of the rigging and began his slow descent, not wanting Arabia to know he was still shaking.

Back on deck, the majority of the boys were cheering and slapping him on the back and giving 'high-fives' to congratulate the new winner and holder of the trophy. Captain Ginger handed him the cup and shook his hand, then whispered in his ear, "Not bad for a pirate who is scared of heights."

Thom blushed and wondered how he knew. Had Angus or Roscoe told him or had he been watching him practise; discreetly, without Thom knowing he was there?

Arabia shook him by the hand again, a real sportsman in the way he dealt with having to hand over the title of being the best 'Rigging-Racer' of the school, especially to one of the new boys. Angus added his congratulations.

That night Thom felt for the first time that he belonged at the School for Scoundrels. He was beginning to feel more settled and he had made a couple of good friends in Angus and Arabia.

Chapter 9
News

The next morning the Sudden Ghost was anchored in the south-west Pacific. Azure skies and clear waters surrounded the ship which had travelled overnight underwater to its new destination. Thom wondered why the ship constantly moved around the globe. Perhaps it was because they needed to be in different places for learning objectives, but he hoped it was because Captain Ginger was onto something regarding the whereabouts of Grandpa.

During Navigation with Sir Rupert, the teacher whom Thom had come face to face with when he had been searching the Navigation room for the map, Thom's pride at winning the rigging-racing was still in his heart. He felt happy and relaxed sat with Angus, Roscoe and Rufus, learning how to read maps. Thom hadn't anticipated how complicated map reading could be, but he knew he had to remain focused, because if he did find the map that would lead to the treasure map, he would want to know how to read it accurately.

Firstly, he had to learn how to use a compass properly, which excited him knowing the compass his grandmother had given him was safely stowed away in the secret compartment of his large trunk. He would bring it to the next Navigation lesson.

The school's compasses were not as ornate, but some were as ancient and a few had intricate engravings on them. They were given two compasses per group and a map; then it was time to row out to a nearby island and search for treasure. In this instance the 'treasure' was bars of chocolate, not bars of gold.

"What's the point of searching for chocolate?" protested Spike.

"It's a treat. Something to make sure you follow the map and don't get lost or get your selves into danger," said Sir Rupert, pacing the room with his bare feet.

"Danger? How can we get into danger on such a small island?" Spike continued.

"Never underestimate the dangers you might face out on the high seas or any of the lands you visit; haven't we taught you anything, Spike?" said Sir Rupert sternly. "All of your lessons, each day, are designed to help you learn to be safe and wise, ready for the real Pirate World – if you make it that far."

Spike looked sullen, but remained silent.

Sir Rupert continued. "In ten minutes we will be lowering the row-boats to take us to the island where your first practical will take place for this term. First, I want you all to make sure you have got the idea of how to read the compass. Each head of group needs to test the others, when I'm happy that you know what you're doing, I'll send you up to Windbags."

In the classroom, the noise grew, as the excitement of adventure grew. There was lots of laughter and some groans as a few got it wrong.

All of a sudden, the class fell silent and Thom looked towards the door where Windbags was talking to Sir Rupert. He was holding a red bottle in his hand and speaking urgently to Long Harry who'd arrived with him. They looked, with concern, in Thom's direction.

Something was wrong at home.

"Thom," called Long Harry. "There's a message for you."

Thom made his way towards the men, he took the bottle from Windbags and walked out of the class, he didn't want everyone knowing what the message said.

Alone, out in the corridor, he removed the stopper from the bottle and took out the small piece of paper inside.

Dear Thom,
Your grandmother is ill, you must come home immediately.
Skipper

Thom felt his blood run cold. What was wrong with Gran? How could he get home, and fast? He became aware of someone standing next to him.

"What's up?" asked Angus.

"My Gran's ill. I must go home."

"Oh gosh. What's wrong with her?"

"I don't know." Thom felt a tear fall down his cheek and hoped that Angus hadn't noticed. Not Gran as well.

Angus shifted uncomfortably beside him. "She'll be fine, try not to worry."

"It's not just that ... promise you won't say anything to anyone?"

Angus nodded. "Of course I won't."

Thom explained about Grandpa; Angus' expression became serious.

"Come on, we'll tell Captain Ginger, he'll get you home as soon as he can," Angus reassured.

The boys hurried through the ship, with its creaks and groans, towards Captain Ginger's office. They knocked on the door and waited.

"Come in," called Captain Ginger.

"Sorry to disturb you, Captain. I've had a red bottle message. My Gran's ill. I have to go home."

Captain Ginger nodded. "Of course, Prow, we'll get you there as soon as we can. I hope it's not too serious."

"So do I, Captain," said Thom, his head bowed.

150

"Angus, go and tell Long Harry to prepare the crew and ship for subaqueous sailing."

"Aye, Aye, Captain," replied Angus and hurried from the room.

"You'd better grab a few things together; we'll be there in about an hour."

"An hour?" asked Thom, surprised but very pleased he would be home so soon.

"Yes, pretty much anything's possible here. I hope your grandmother is okay. She's probably been fretting about William."

"That's what I thought too," replied Thom. "I feel so bad that I haven't been able to do anything to help Grandpa yet."

Ginger shook his head. "Don't despair, lad, it takes time, that's all."

"I just wish I had something to tell her when I go and see her."

"We know nothing more at the moment, Thom."

Thom sighed.

"Give my love to your grandmother; she was quite a looker in her youth." Captain Ginger winked at Thom, rubbing his bright beard.

Thom managed a smile. "Thank you."

Thom returned to his cabin to throw a few bits into his smaller, weekend trunk. As he was doing this he felt the ship tip and dive down to the depths of the ocean. It was a little easier this time to keep his balance and not quite so alarming.

After closing his trunk he made his way up onto deck. The large air bubble that surrounded the ship was in place again and Thom watched the ocean creatures sweeping past at high speed, unsure whether it was the ship or the fish that were in more haste.

Thom waited on deck, pacing up and down the boards, knots in his stomach. Why was so much going wrong? Why did it all have to happen to him? Was he such a bad person that he deserved such bad luck in his life?

To the side of him, Thom noticed a group of jellyfish, brightly coloured aliens glowing in the dark waters surrounding the ship. It was a whole other world down here in the ocean; fascinating and strange. No wonder his parents had loved to explore this secretive place, full of new and exciting things to discover.

After a while, the ship tilted and the vessel rose up, up, up and out through the surface of the sea; the air bubble popped and the water splashed all over Thom. His heart leapt as he noticed the Isle of Bos in the distance – it seemed deserted; certainly no kite-boarders.

Windbags appeared with a sullen look on his face and dumped Thom's trunk into one of the row-boats. Angus and Roscoe lowered it down into the water. Thom and Windbags climbed down the rope ladder and into the small boat. Windbags grabbed the oars and began to row towards the familiar island. As he approached the small, sandy island, Thom felt the pain in his stomach grow.

"So, the landlubbers can't see the Sudden Ghost?" he asked.

"Nope," replied Windbags. "It's invisible to their eyes in an emergency such as this."

"How?"

"I dunno. I ain't no scholar," he growled.

Stood on the island ahead of them, with his hands on his hips, was the large frame of Skipper, his weathered face and pale watery eyes were full of concern.

"Hello, Thom, welcome home," he said, helping Thom climb out of the boat and pull it up onto the beach with Windbags.

Skipper and Windbags lifted Thom's trunk into Skipper's row-boat before they pushed it out onto the water and headed towards the mainland. Windbags grumbled a goodbye and then set back towards the Sudden Ghost.

"I'll take you straight to the hospital," said Skipper.

"What's the matter with Gran?" asked Thom.

"She's not at all well. You must prepare yourself to see her looking very sick indeed."

"Is she going to die?"

"I sincerely hope not, she's my wife's best friend – who would I have to ensure that Peggy went out the house at least once a week to W.I.

153

and out from under my feet?" Skipper smiled, but his eyes were sad.

Thom felt the tears well up in his eyes as he looked at Skipper's grave face.

The hospital smelled of disinfectant and disease. Thom followed Skipper down through the corridors; he realised he was holding his breath and let out a large sigh.

Entering the room behind Skipper, Thom saw an elderly woman lying in a bed in the centre of the room; tubes and monitors were attached to her. It took him a moment to realise that the elderly woman was Gran. He rushed over to the bed and looked down. Tears welled up and spilled over onto his cheeks. He felt Skipper put a hand on his shoulder, but found no comfort in the gesture. Gran's usual healthy complex was pale and drawn; she looked about twenty years older than when Thom had last seen her. She seemed so small and fragile in the large hospital bed.

"Your Gran's strong, she'll be all right," said Skipper.

"What happened to her? What's wrong?"

"She had a bit of a turn at the bakery; collapsed on the floor and Mrs Lawrence called for the ambulance -"

"Was it a heart attack?" Thom had heard of heart attacks, but didn't understand what one was.

Skipper shook his head. "It was a stroke."

"A stroke? What does that mean?"

"It's when the blood supply to part of the brain is cut off."

"Is she unconscious?"

"She's sleeping. She regained consciousness this morning, which is a good sign, but we don't know what damage has been done yet; the doctors will run more tests."

"What damage could've been done?"

"It's possible she may not be able to talk properly, or have to take time to be able to walk again. But I don't want to speculate too much, only time and the doctors will be able to tell us."

"She might have to be in a wheelchair? How will she cope?"

"I've already told your Gran we'll help," said Skipper firmly.

Thom looked towards his grandmother. "Can I speak to her?"

Skipper nodded.

Walking up to the side of the bed, and trying hard to avoid the tubes and wires that were stuck to his grandmother, Thom gently took hold of her hand. There was no response.

"Hello Gran. Sorry you're so sick. I came as quickly as possible. School is going well. I'm glad that I went, but I miss you and Grandpa." He lowered his voice, aware that Skipper and the doctor were now deep in their own conversation.

Thom looked at Gran and realised for the first time how truly alone he would be if his grandparents were no longer there. He had no parents or siblings, only an uncle of sorts who wanted the Prow treasure, not an actual Prow, a boy, orphaned and alone, unable to look after himself.

Fear gripped him.

"I'm doing my best Gran, to find the map. I will give it to the kidnappers as soon as I do and then we can get Grandpa back. I will find the map, I promise – please don't die." Fighting back more tears, he felt the gentlest of squeezes on his hand. He stared at his Gran, but she seemed to be completely unconscious.

"She squeezed my hand," he said, but a flicker of doubt in Skipper's expression made him think that he didn't believe him, he was certain he'd felt it, positive. He wasn't making it up.

"That's marvellous, a great sign," whispered Skipper.

"She did, honestly!" retorted Thom.

"I believe you," said Skipper. "Come on, I'll take you home. Peggy's got some dinner on for you. I'll bring you back tomorrow. Ellie needs some rest." Skipper guided him out of the room and Thom noticed he turned and gave Gran a sad look, mouthing a silent parting to his old friend's wife.

Later that day, back at the cottage, having been fed by Peggy and Skipper, Thom sat with Skipper together on the sofa in the living room at his grandparent's house. Skipper had told Peggy that he would be staying at the Prow's house with Thom overnight.

"It's weird without them here ... it's too quiet," said Thom. He wanted so much to be brave, but was struggling.

"It'll all be okay, Thom. I've known your grandparents most of my life and they're survivors. You mark my words, within a few weeks you'll be wondering what all this fuss was about."

Thom couldn't quite bring himself to believe what Skipper was saying, but he appreciated his kind words nonetheless.

In bed that night, listening to Skipper's heavy snores from the other room, Thom thought about his grandparents. He couldn't believe how much had happened in the past couple of weeks. There was still no sign of Grandpa being rescued, despite his note. More needed to be done – but what? He could see the outline of the full-moon through his curtains and wondered where the Sudden Ghost might be right now. Waiting just off Bos, or somewhere more exotic?

Back in his familiar room, the School for Scoundrels seemed surreal, but the fact his grandparents weren't here with him, made it a reality.

Thom awoke the next morning to the smell of bacon frying and voices in the kitchen. For a moment, he thought it had all been a dream, a dreadful nightmare and that Grandpa and Gran were both downstairs in the kitchen, safe. But he soon recognised the booming tones of Skipper's voice.

When Thom walked into the kitchen, Peggy rushed up and enveloped him in her fleshy arms. "How are you this morning, sonny? I'm cooking you a big breakfast before you go and visit your gran – Skip here will take you as soon as you're ready."

"Thank you. I would like to see Gran. Perhaps she's a little better this morning."

"I hope so," said Skipper, giving Thom a smile.

Thom raced through his breakfast, eager to get going as soon as Skipper had finished his cup of tea.

When they walked on to the ward, Thom was pleased to see that Gran was sat up in bed. She had a magazine on her lap, but was staring into space.

"Hello, Gran," he said.

"Thom," she said quietly, holding out her arms. She smiled at Thom as he approached, but Thom noticed that the smile was slightly lopsided.

His heart felt like it had stopped in his chest for a moment before it then started to race.

"Are you all right, Gran?"

"Not brilliant, my lovely, but they are looking after me well. Now, tell me how school is going. Any news on Grandpa?"

Thom couldn't bring himself to tell his grandmother that he had no news, it could make her worse. "Captain Ginger thinks he's onto something. He's sure that we will have Grandpa back with us very soon." He hated lying to his grandmother, but she looked so ill that Thom knew she needed to hear something positive.

"Morning, Ellen," said Skipper, kissing Gran on the cheek.

"Thank you for bringing my boy home," she replied, holding on to Thom's hand and caressing it.

"Thought it might cheer you up a little," Skipper smiled at Gran. "Don't you worry, Ellen, William will be home safe before we know it."

Gran smiled another crooked smile.

"I'll stay as long as you like," said Thom.

"Ah, Thom, you're a good boy. I would rather you went back to school as soon as you can. I'm going to be fine and I think Grandpa might need you more."

"I've only just got here, I can't go back already," cried Thom.

"Stay a couple of days if you like, but promise me you'll return to school and help in the search for Grandpa?"

Thom sighed. "Of course, Gran. I want him home as much as you do, but I feel I should stay here with you -"

"Come on, Thom, you know Peggy and I will take care of Gran. You must go back and find your grandfather, he'll be relying on you, you know."

Thom nodded. He felt the heavy burden of responsibility weighing down on his shoulders. He wanted to be there for both his grandparents, just as they had always been there for him, but he knew he needed to return to school; learn to be a great pirate, find Grandpa and bring him home.

Thom spent the afternoon with Peggy, cleaning Gran's house while Skipper went to help his sons bring in the morning catch.

"She won't want the worry of this when she gets home," said Peggy, scrubbing the front step.

"No, of course not," said Thom, who was dusting in the hallway.

"Hello, you two," said Skipper, a bundle of what could only be fish under his arm. "Got tonight's tea."

"Wonderful," said Peggy, standing and stretching her back.

160

"Also found this," said Skipper, handing Thom a red bottle. *What now?* Thom took the bottle, undid the stopper and pulled out the note.

Thom,
Hope your Gran is not too ill. Have found a map that says it will lead us to the treasure map. Perhaps you should return asap. Send message by return red bottle.
Roscoe and Angus. (P.S. Tell no-one).

"More trouble?" asked Skipper.

Thom deliberated. Should he tell them? Angus and Roscoe had said not to tell anyone, but he trusted Skipper and felt he owed them an explanation, besides they may be able to advise what he should do. "They've found a map -"

"Well, we better get you packed then," replied Skipper.

"What about Gran?"

"We will take care of her, Thom," said Peggy. "She will be happy knowing that progress is being made."

Thom felt torn. He didn't want to leave Gran, but he needed to help find Grandpa too. Peggy and Skipper were watching him, waiting for him to make the right decision - whatever that was.

Chapter 10
A Weekend Jaunt

When he arrived back on board the Sudden Ghost, Angus and Roscoe were on deck to greet him. Thom could tell that Roscoe was bursting to tell him about what they had discovered, but Angus spoke first.

"How is your Gran? What happened?"

"She had a stroke, but is on the mend, thank goodness. It scared me though."

"So, she's not going to die then?" asked Roscoe, his face close to Thom's.

"Roscoe, don't you know how to be sensitive?" scolded Angus.

"Sorry," he replied, blushing. "Mum always says I don't know when to shut up."

"It's all right, Roscoe. I hope she won't die, no. She's strong, but the next few hours could be critical, especially if she has another stroke."

"I'm sure she'll be fine," Angus said. "We'll keep our fingers crossed."

"Thanks. Now ... what's this about a map?"

Angus looked around them then whispered, "Not here. Let's wait until we get back to the cabin."

The three of them hurried back to their cabin. As they approached the door, in the dim lamplight, Thom could see the shape of Storm

163

sitting looking at them; she stood and put her tail up in greeting then rubbed all around his legs. Entering the cabin, Storm slinked in after them; she jumped up onto Thom's hammock and settled down into it, purring. Thom watched Roscoe as he went to the corner of their cabin and removed a loose floorboard; from within he pulled out an ancient piece of parchment rolled into a scroll.

Thom held his breath. "Is this the map?" he asked, finally breathing out and peering over Roscoe's shoulder.

He nodded. "I found it in the Navigation room the other day, the day you were called away. I was asked by Sir Rupert to put all the books away and do a general tidy up ... there was a book on his desk and as I lifted it I could see the corner of something inside. I pulled it out and unrolled it. Look."

Thom could see that the map was of an island, mountainous and green. It had lots of illustrations and a couple of trails that led to a large red cross near a forest and a mountain. The illustrations warned of swamps, hideous beasts, a pit of snakes and a river full of man-eating fish. When Roscoe moved his hand away from the edge of the map, Thom read what it said at the top:

Ye mappe of the Prows

He grabbed it from Roscoe's hands. "Crikey," he said breathlessly. "Could this lead us to the real treasure map do you think?"

"It's possible -" started Roscoe.

"I think we should go to the island, we've managed to find it in the atlas, it's 3000 miles south of here, but we can go subaqueous and be there in no time. We just have to persuade Ginger," said Angus.

At the mention of Ginger's name, Storm's ears pricked up and her tail flicked impatiently.

"Do you think he'll let us go?" asked Thom.

Roscoe and Angus shrugged.

"If we can find a good enough reason to go there, then possibly," said Angus. "We'll go and see him at breakfast time tomorrow, he's usually in his office at that time – we daren't wake him now, he'll have us walk the darn plank."

"Come on, we'd better get some sleep, might be a big day tomorrow. Good to have you back, Thom," said Angus, patting him on the shoulder.

Thom smiled and watched Roscoe put the map back beneath the boards. Finally he felt they were getting somewhere.

As he lay listening to the heavy breathing of his friends and the creaking of the ship, Thom wondered about the map and the island. If he could find the treasure map then he could give it to the kidnappers, then they would release Grandpa and that would make Gran better too, or at least, help her towards a speedy recovery. However, how would they convince Captain Ginger to let them go?

The next morning with the Sudden Ghost anchored off the south coast of Italy, the boys found Captain Ginger sat at his desk in his office, eating poached eggs on toast. Storm was now curled up on his lap asleep, having left Thom's hammock in the early hours of the morning. He smiled at them when they entered, his beard coated in crumbs and bits of egg yolk. Thom was glad he hadn't had his breakfast yet.

"Morning, me hearties," he said with his mouth open, bits of egg and toast escaping. "What brings you lads here at this early hour?"

Angus spoke first. "We'd like to go to Plathgem Island for the weekend."

Captain Ginger's fork stopped dead and he stared at them. "Why do you want to go there?"

"We're working on a project about the mythical beast that lives there, the Scorpi, and we need to do some research. We thought if we could go there, it might help," explained Thom.

"It's a long way from here."

"It's our long-term project, Captain, and we want to get good results," interrupted Roscoe. "The deadline is next Friday."

The boys waited while Captain Ginger chewed his mouthful, looking at them through narrowed eyes.

"We thought as it was the weekend, we could do a trip there; build a camp, do some research and perhaps practise our map-reading skills too." Thom hoped he hadn't given too much away, but Ginger smiled.

"Hmmm. All right, why not? We haven't had a jaunt for a while. I'll organise it this morning."

"Brilliant! Thanks, Captain," said Roscoe.

"Thanks, Captain," echoed Angus and Thom.

"But -" he paused, stopping the boys in their tracks. "I want to see your full research results on my desk by Wednesday morning – it had better be good."

"Aye, aye Captain," they chorused, rushing off to breakfast before he could change his mind.

They set sail two hours later. Ginger and Long Harry didn't waste any time in getting the crew organised.

"Once I've given you your instructions for the trip, you're all to adhere to Long Harry's orders. The Sudden Ghost is going on a weekend trip to Plathgem Island to do a research project on the Scorpi."

A loud groan went round the crew.

"It's also a great opportunity to assess your map-reading skills. You're all going to be dropped off at certain points around the island; your task then is to find your way to the 'treasure'."

A cheer resounded.

"What's the treasure?" asked Silver, grumpily. "Not chocolate again?"

"An evening of fun and games then a beach barbeque," said Captain Ginger, his eyes bright.

Another, bigger cheer went round the crew, all except Lucifer, Silver and Spike who looked less than impressed.

The ship sailed subaqueous for an hour – the speed with which they went was incredible, but inside their bubble the speed felt like nothing more than a walk along the soft sands of a beach. Finally, a few miles away from Plathgem Island, the ship resurfaced.

"We can't go any further under the sea, the waters are too shallow," said Roscoe. "We can sail for a few more miles then get the row-boats ready."

Ahead, Thom could see storm clouds gathering. Pointing, he nodded to Angus who turned his head in the direction that Thom was gesticulating and his eyes grew wide.

"That's gonna a be a biggun!" cried Angus. "We must tell Long Harry." He ran off towards Captain Ginger's office where Long Harry had been summoned earlier.

Thom watched the bruise of vapours gather together like a large mushroom overhead. The sea and air around him seemed to still and go quiet ... too quiet.

"Can we turn the ship around?" asked Angus, as he and Long Harry appeared beside Thom.

"It's too late, the storm would follow us and it's too big to go round. We need to batten down the hatches, ship-mates! Angus, Thom, get the crew to haul in the sails," ordered Long Harry.

The boys obeyed their orders and got to work. As they hauled in the sails, a strong gust of wind almost knocked Thom off his feet.

"It's beginning," cried Roscoe, tying rope around some loose barrels, which were beginning to roll around, as the ship was beginning to rise and fall upon the growing waves.

The crew were all summoned and they got to work immediately preparing the ship for the storm.

The clouds became as black as a cormorant's wing and the masts started to creek above them. The rolling of the ship increased. A flash of lightning lit up the sky and sea around them; the white foam and grey spray was a contrast against the threatening heavens. The clunking and clanging of the rigging could be heard overhead. The ship reeled more severely – Thom felt his stomach lurch. He surveyed the ocean from the deck, his eye-line caught the charcoal waves one moment then the menacing skies above them the next.

"Are you all right?" asked Angus.

"Fine. It's sort of exciting isn't it?"

"Exciting? Yes, I suppose it is, but this is just the beginning. I've been through a few storms already, never seen one look quite so menacing as this though."

Thom felt his excitement dwindle a little at the serious look on Angus' face. Should he be more worried? The ship tipped and Angus and Thom lost their balance as a wave crashed over the side, cascading salty water all over the deck. The wind was intense and it wailed round Thom's ears, the spray stinging his eyes.

"We should go below deck," said Roscoe. "Ginger'll be along in a minute, I hope."

"No. We must help Long Harry, we have to get through this storm - we have to find the treasure map," he shouted, his words almost slapping him in the face as the wind threw them back at him.

Having watched in disbelief as Roscoe staggered against the wind away from them, Thom saw that one by one the crew abandoned the upper deck and went below. Thom made his way to where Long Harry was relentlessly trying to keep the ship's wheel steady. He could see Angus above them in the rigging – what was he doing up there?

"Where's Spike?" Thom asked Long Harry.

"Gone below. Angus?"

"He's -"

"You should go too!"

"It's my fault we're in this storm," cried Thom. "I wanted to come to this island to do, em ... research. I wanted to get a good grade to make my grandparents proud. I'm not leaving you up here alone." He hated lying to Long Harry and using his grandparents as an excuse. What was happening to him? He rarely told lies.

"That's very courageous of you, Thom, thank you."

The waves were olive and steel-grey; rising up out of the sea like menacing ocean monsters, intent on attacking and devouring the Sudden Ghost. Thom wondered at his own determination, but felt guilty that he had put the others at risk.

Waves tossed the ship on the water as if it were a toy boat, not an ocean going vessel. The wind screamed around the rigging; the drawn up sails were being battered by the storm; some coming loose - torn and tattered.

"Help me hold her steady. You too Angus," Thom shouted as Angus appeared at their side.

"Not sure the mizzenmast will take it," yelled Angus. "Just been up to check and it's bending like rubber. I hope it will hold!"

"We can't do anything about it now, just hold onto the helm – we must try and keep her from rolling over."

Thom and Angus took hold of the wheel and held it as a large wave crashed over them both, filling Thom's mouth with sea-water. The strong salty taste made him retch.

"We need Captain Ginger, can you make it to his office?" asked Long Harry.

Thom looked at the deck below where some barrels had come loose and were sliding from side to side across the sodden deck.

"Of course," he replied and let go of the wheel, he was immediately thrown down the steps onto the deck below; a hot searing pain shot through his arm and his cheek hit the bottom step stunning him. He pulled himself up and stumbled with enormous effort to Captain Ginger's quarters.

Thom knocked and entered. The door swung shut behind him. Inside the office was still and quiet, as if the storm outside was some separate phenomenon. Thom looked around, but could see no sign of Captain Ginger. Storm was sat on the desk staring at him. Thom frowned. Where was he?

Thom absently stroked Storm on the head, the cat butting his hand with pleasure. Thom hesitated a moment before going back out into the raging weather.

After the quiet of the Captain's office, the storm felt to have increased in intensity. Thunder rolled and crackled around them, the waves were crashing over the side and he could just make out Long Harry trying to hold the helm steady through the driving rain. His eyes stung and he laboured hard to get back to his Tutor and Angus.

"I don't think we can hold it much longer," Long Harry hollered, as the wheel was yanked out of their hands and spun out of control. The ship veered starboard and tipped perilously, almost throwing the boys across the deck and into the black waters beneath. Fortunately, Thom managed to grab hold of the wheel and Long Harry, stopping them from both going overboard. Angus clung to a nearby rope.

"Where's the Captain?" asked Angus, his breathing coming hard and fast.

"He wasn't in his office."

"What? Where is he then?"

"He must be below deck with the others," suggested Thom. "I thought he would be out here with us though, being the captain."

"He may be testing us," said Angus.

"Testing us, *now?*"

"Yes. Sometimes he seems to disappear and that can coincide with when bad things happen. I think he does it to see how well we'd manage, it's his way of assessing us," said Angus.

"Where does he disappear to?"

Angus shook his head. "I don't know."

Thom watched as a black beast of water rose above the main mast, curled like grasping fingers then thrust towards them.

"Look out!" he cried, as he was knocked off his feet and slid towards the gunwale, water sloshing all around him – he knew if he couldn't find anything to grab hold of he would be over the side and engulfed by the sea. If he died, how would he help his grandparents? He scrabbled about trying to grab something that would save him – he didn't want to die.

All of a sudden, he felt a strong hand seize hold of him and was surprised to look up into the large, wet beard of the Captain; his saturated beard now dark red. His hair was stuck to his head, but he grinned at Thom and Long Harry who he had a hold of in his other enormous paw-like hand.

"I've got yer, me-hearties," he laughed, standing steady as the ship around them rocked violently. Angus was still grasping hold of the rope.

Thom couldn't believe that he was laughing. How could he find it funny? They'd almost died.

"Come on boys, below deck for you. I'll take over and see us through this storm ... we're near to the island – we don't want to crash onto the rocks and be shipwrecked. Go and get something dry and warm on; you've done a great job – I'll make proper pirates of you yet."

The Captain released the boys and they staggered back to the stairs that would take them below deck and to a drier place. As they descended the stairs, a sour smell filled the air. Some of the boys were unwell having been thrown around in the storm. As they neared the cabins, Tim rushed past, green in the face his hands over his mouth.

"Poor Tim," said Long Harry, who was shivering. "Get some dry clothes on boys then try and get some sleep. If we make it through this storm, we'll be at the island before long; you don't want to be too exhausted to do your research."

Thom shook his head. He needed to rest if he was to be of any use on the island. As Thom and Angus entered their cabin, they found Roscoe lying in his hammock moaning, his face a worrying pallor.

"Not you as well?" said Angus.

Roscoe groaned as his eyes rolled in his head.

"Better let him sleep," said Thom.

Roscoe barely seemed aware that anyone had entered the cabin.

Thom pulled off his drenched clothes and dried himself on a towel. The storm seemed to be abating, but he was still unsteady. The sound of thunder rolled around the sky like a bowling ball off course, leaving behind it an empty void of silence.

Putting on dry pyjamas, Thom climbed into his hammock. The heavy swaying of the boat gradually became more gentle as the storm outside relinquished its hold over the ship. Thom had never seen a storm like it before and hoped he never would again. However, being on the high seas he doubted it would be the last storm he would encounter, but he had lived through this one at least.

Chapter 11
The Scorpi

"Thom! Thom!" A voice interrupted his dream; a wonderful dream of flying across the waves on his kite-board - the warm sun on his face: free. However, in the distance, dark clouds hung like a heavy blanket above the horizon ... and what was that shape in the clouds? A kraken.

"Are you awake?" asked a different voice.

Thom opened his eyes. They were full of sleep-dust; salt from the storm that had flung itself in his eyes the previous day. He rubbed them, winced at the scratching, and looked around. The cabin was filled with light.

The cabin.

The Sudden Ghost.

THE ISLAND.

Thom was now wide awake staring at Angus and Roscoe who were dressed, their eyes full of anticipation.

"Finally. You took some waking this morning," said Roscoe, thumping Thom on the arm.

"Come on, we're going to the island after breakfast," said Angus shoving Thom's deck shoes into his hands.

"We're here?"

Angus and Roscoe nodded.

"Why do we have to have breakfast first?" he asked, disappointed that they couldn't just get going.

"Captain's orders," said Angus.

"I must have slept deeply," said Thom, pulling on his shoes and climbing out of his hammock. "I didn't hear anyone come to the door."

"Rufus came about five minutes ago to say we had to go to breakfast in ten minutes," said Roscoe, opening the door and walking out into the corridor. "Come on, I'm starving."

Over a breakfast of pancakes (oddly tasting of fish) Thom was bombarded with questions from Rufus.

"What made you guys choose the Scorpi?" he asked. "Can I join your group? That creature is weird."

Angus looked at Thom. He realised it would seem strange if they didn't let him join their group. He had to be honest with him.

"Rufus," Thom lowered his voice. "You can join our group, but there's something you need to know first."

"Oh?"

"We've found a map, which we believe will lead us to my family's treasure map. We told Captain Ginger that we wanted to research the Scorpi for our long-term project, but we aren't here to do that at all. We're going to be searching for the treasure map."

"Wow. I definitely want to join you then," said Rufus, his eyes wide.

"You must swear to secrecy though," said Angus, his face stern.

Rufus nodded his head. "Of course, I won't tell anyone."

Up on deck, the storm had given way to cloudless skies. The Sudden Ghost was anchored just off shore from Plathgem Island. It was covered in an expanse of trees and one, tall mountain, centrally positioned. *A volcano – perhaps still active?* Thom wondered.

The crew's excited chatter was infectious and Thom felt a large smile spread across his face.

"Wow," he breathed.

Long Harry's voice carried across the babble to gain the boys' attention. Their voices grew quiet. "Does each group have their map?" he asked.

After breakfast, Captain Ginger had given each group a copy of the map that should lead them, if their map-reading skills were good enough, to 'treasure', or rather an evening full of games and a delicious barbeque. He told all groups that they should research any signs of the mythical creature, the Scorpi, but map-reading was what they were really being assessed on during this particular venture.

The groups were all given different positions around the island as their starting points. All were given maps, including Thom's group, but they wouldn't be using it, they would be using the Map of the Prows.

Long Harry was to stay on board with Captain Ginger in case any of the groups fell into trouble and needed rescuing. They were each given flares to let off in the event of finding themselves in danger.

"Come on, let's go," called Thom, heading to where the row-boats were being lowered to the water. He touched the pocket in his trousers where his compass sat. Having wolfed down his breakfast, he had returned to his cabin to search for, and pocket, the compass his Gran had given him before he left for the School for Scoundrels. He hoped it might bring him good luck, or at least help him find his way around the island.

Angus and Roscoe took the oars and rowed them towards the island which was covered in thick jungle. The heat beat down on them, although it was only early, and Thom was grateful that they had plenty of water with them. Sitting next to Rufus he drew the map out of its tube and spread it across his lap.

"According to *this* map, the treasure map is in a cave at the foot of the mountain, behind the waterfall. I think we'd be better off following the lower trail south of the island to start with.

There's a freshwater pool there, where we can refill our bottles."

"Looks like there's a pit of snakes to the north of the island too, which I'd like to avoid," added Rufus, with a shudder.

Roscoe laughed. "Yes, me too, I'm not very keen on snakes either."

"There are some bogs, or quicksand we need to steer clear of when we go the south side," said Thom, pointing at an illustration they knew from their map-reading classes meant bogs or quicksand. "Certainly don't want to get trapped in one of those and suffocate."

"Any other inhabitants on the island, apart from the Scorpi?" asked Angus.

"Not that we can see," stated Rufus.

"That doesn't mean that there isn't," interrupted Roscoe.

Thom looked at the rocks that surrounded the island. Beneath the surface of the blue-grey sea, dark shadows moved around close to the shore – Thom didn't want to think about what they might be. They were headed for a small stretch of beach that sat nestled amongst the rocks – hopefully it would be a safe place to disembark.

Thom's anticipation rose in him like the giant waves of the storm the previous evening. He was excited, but anxious too – what if they couldn't find the map? What if somebody had beaten them to it?

"Can you row any faster?" he asked the boys.

"Come on Roscoe, put your back into it!" called Angus.

Roscoe scowled at him in return, but pulled harder on the oars nonetheless.

A couple of metres from the beach, Thom and Rufus jumped out into the shallow water that lapped onto the soft white sand. The earlier shadows seemed to have moved on. Small waves rushed to shore then retreated back to the sea as if burnt by the hot sands of the beach and wanting to find comfort in what they knew.

Thom felt the coolness of the water seep through his canvas shoes and grabbed the rope at the front of the boat. The two boys pulled the row-boat onto the sand where the others jumped out and helped to shift the boat further up the beach where the arms of the waves could not reach out and drag it back into the ocean.

They set the map down on a flat rock that protruded from the sand and rolled it out to take a closer look.

"If we follow the southern-most trail it will take us north-east past the bogs and round the fresh water pool. From there can go west through the forest where the Scorpi is supposed to reside. Or, we can go further north past the snake pit then south-west to the foot of the mountain and into the cave from there," said Rufus.

"What if the others follow us?" asked Roscoe.

"Hopefully, they won't. Their maps are very different – the treasure they are supposed to be finding is up near the swamp area, with the pool where the flesh-eating fish are," said Angus. "I certainly don't want to be going anywhere near there."

"Coward," called Roscoe, grinning widely.

"Coward? I'm not the one afraid of the beast in the forest, probably doesn't even exist," Angus retaliated.

Roscoe shoved Angus playfully and the boys wrestled in the sand covering themselves and the other two in tiny grains.

"Come on, cut it out, we've no time to lose," said Thom. He snatched up the map, got his compass out of his pocket and stomped up the beach.

The boys scrambled to their feet and caught up with Thom. They kept a rapid pace up the rocky hill to the top of the cliffs. Out in the bay, they could see the Sudden Ghost anchored. The sea was calm, the sky clear. On deck, Thom noticed the glint of the sun on a spyglass lens – their progress was being watched. From their vantage point they could see one of the other groups who had only just reached the island. Thom had heard them squabbling about who was going to row as they had set off. He was pleased to see they were ahead of everyone else. The other groups were still rowing out to the island.

"Come on, let's keep moving," said Thom. "If we go west from here, we'll fill our water bottles at the fresh water pool then decide if we're going to go through the forest or up to the snake pit."

The sun was warming up now and Thom realised that the heat would only increase in intensity as the day progressed. He was anxious to cover as much ground before lunchtime as they could. For a while they headed along another beach, the sand was hard going, their feet continually sinking – their progress slow. After a while, they came to a stony path which was much easier to walk upon. They passed trees and shrubs on either side; birds and other creatures could be heard amongst them - some familiar, most strange and alien. Finally, they reached the freshwater pool and splashed water over their hot heads; drank in gulps and filled their water bottles to the brim.

"Which way should we go from here?" asked Rufus, sweat beading on his forehead despite having just washed his face.

"I think we should go north to the snake pit, doesn't sound as terrifying as the Scorpi," said Roscoe.

"We would save a lot of time if we go through the forest. We don't even know if the Scorpi is still living on the island, or ever was – it is a mythical beast."

"That's just it," argued Roscoe. "No-one knows for sure if it *is* mythical – it seems to be that there is some truth in most 'myths'.

"The quicker we find this map, the quicker we can find the treasure," Thom snapped.

"Look Thom," said Rufus. "I know it means a lot to you, and I'm willing to help, but you have to realise that we get nothing out of this," said Rufus. "So stop being so bossy."

Thom turned on Rufus. "If you don't want to help, get lost! I can do this alone, if necessary."

Rufus' face flushed red and he stomped off ahead of the group.

Angus placed a hand on Thom's shoulder. "Thom, we're here to help you, but please don't take your frustrations out on us."

"Looks like it's the forest then," said Roscoe as he watched Rufus, turn west into the thick, evergreen forest: alone.

"I need to apologise to him," said Thom in a low voice, his cheeks glowing.

"I'd leave him to calm down a bit first," reasoned Angus. "He gets irate at times. Perhaps you should tell him about your grandpa too."

Thom nodded and sighed. He felt bad about snapping at Rufus, but he felt so close to getting what he needed to get Grandpa back, it wasn't the treasure he wanted, but Rufus wasn't to know that. He looked at the compass and then at the map. "We need to keep heading west."

As they walked deeper into the forest the silence became very loud. At the edge of the forest, the birds had sung in subdued tones and everything was still around them. Now, as they walked further into the trees the creepers and fauna became thicker. The vines felt like arms trying to entangle the boys in their snares as they walked amongst them.

Thom realised that they had lost sight of Rufus.

"Come on we must try and keep up with Rufus, it's not safe for one of us be alone," said Angus, staring around him in all directions.

It was humid. Thom was in the lead when, all of a sudden, he put up his hand to indicate to the others to stop. Silently, he placed a finger to his lips and the others grew quiet. Unexpectedly, an awful stench permeated the air.

"What is it?" Angus whispered.

"I thought I heard a noise -" Thom returned in a hushed voice.

"It's probably Rufus," said Roscoe moving forward. As he did so, a huge roar broke the silence, followed by a boy's scream.

"Rufus is in trouble," cried Angus, breaking into a run.

Thom and Roscoe followed, but their progress was impeded by the thicket. They fought their way towards the scream which brought them to a clearing, where the trees and creepers had been broken and arranged to make some kind of nest.

The boys halted.

In the clearing standing as still as a statue, his face full of terror, was Rufus. Facing Rufus, its enormous body just a few feet away, was the biggest beast any of them had ever seen. The creature had the scaled body of a dragon; the head of an eagle with a forked tongue which flicked in and out of its beak like a snake's; it's scorpion-like tail was raised over its back ready to strike.

The Scorpi.

"It does exist," squeaked Roscoe.

"So much for being mythical," said Thom, finding it hard to breathe.

The beast turned its peculiar face towards the three boys and opened its beak. The strangest sound surged forth through the jungle like an untuned violin. It turned its full attention back to Rufus, it crouched, its eyes unblinking.

Rufus didn't move, but his eyes were full of fear and he was whimpering like a puppy.

"We have to do something!" cried Roscoe.

"What?" asked Angus.

Swiftly, from amongst the green, came a flash of black; large and feline. It pounced on the back of the Scorpi and dug its claws into its scales. The Scorpi flapped its wings trying to escape, but the puma had a good strong grip on it. The Scorpi flicked its tail trying to sting the puma, but the large feline dug its teeth into the Scorpi's feathered neck.

"Quick, let's get out of here," shouted Angus.

The three boys ran towards Rufus, who was stuck to the spot, mouth agape. They pulled him along with them through the jungle and away from immediate danger. They ran until they felt they were at a safe distance then stopped, panting and perspiring.

Angus was the first to speak, his breath coming in short, sharp puffs. "Wow. That puma was amazing; came from nowhere. I'm so glad it was hunting the Scorpi and not us."

"What if it's still hungry after stuffing the Scorpi?" asked Roscoe, trying to catch his breath too. "It might come after us."

"I'm not sure it was hunting the Scorpi ... look -" cried Thom, indicating above the trees that were now thinning nearer the edge of the jungle. "I think it might have been trying to protect us."

Above the boys, the Scorpi flew; it's wings strong and strangely graceful. It flew overhead of them, but the boys could see it was injured, blood oozed from a large gash in its neck.

"Where's the puma now?" asked Rufus, his whole body shaking.

"Let's not hang around and find out," said Angus, setting off again at a fast pace. "Roscoe, bring up the rear with your sword at the ready."

Roscoe pulled his sword from its scabbard and walked unsteadily backwards, eyes alert.

Thom glanced above him as they came out of the forest. There was no sign of the Scorpi now, but ahead of them in the near distance a large black mountain surged upwards out of the island. He wondered, again, if the volcano was still active ... he hoped not, although now there was a small wisp of smoke winding its way skywards.

"Not far to go now," said Roscoe. "The mountain looks quite close."

"I think it's further than it looks, but according to the map we need to go north-west towards it then take a south-west turn at the foot of the mountain until we come across the waterfall. The cave is behind the waterfall and the map, apparently, is in there."

"I'm hungry," said Roscoe. "Can we stop for lunch?"

To Thom's disappointment, the others nodded in agreement. He wanted to keep going, he wasn't hungry, but the others were slowing and it would do them all good to fill up, rest then continue.

Roscoe pulled sandwiches out of his rucksack and the boys sat on the dry grass to the side of the track and started to devour their lunches.

Thom looked at Rufus, but he avoided his eyes. "Rufus, I'm sorry, I had a go at you. I should've realised that it could have put you in danger. We stick together from now on, okay?"

Rufus remained silent, but the others nodded.

Thom sighed, he had to tell the others the truth, he hated leading them on. "Rufus, Roscoe, there's something I need to tell you."

Roscoe looked at Thom with interest, but Rufus remained aloof.

"The reason I need to find the map ... is that my grandfather has been kidnapped. Unless I find the map and give it to the kidnappers they're going to kill my Grandpa."

"Blimey," said Roscoe. "Why didn't you say so before?"

"It's difficult to know who to trust when you start at a new school, you should know that Roscoe," said Angus.

"At least that explains your great enthusiasm," said Roscoe. "We will help you all we can, won't we Rufus?"

Rufus nodded, but did not look at Thom.

"Well, at least we can honestly say we did see a Scorpi," said Angus, his mouth full of sandwich.

"Yes," said Roscoe. "But where did that big cat come from? I'm not sure if it was hunting the Scorpi, or was protecting us, it was strange."

"I don't know," said Angus. "But I'm sure glad it came along when it did. Although, I'm still worried that it could still be lurking in the jungle somewhere - hunting us!"

"We'll finish lunch and keep moving. I think that would be the safest thing to do right now," said Thom.

After a hasty lunch, they continued through the tall grass towards the mountain ahead of them. Thom wondered if any of the other groups of boys were around. They should all be in different directions around the island, but if they had seen Thom's group going this way then they may have followed, not bothering to look at their own maps and realise that they were going in the wrong direction; just piggybacking off the other group, eager to find the 'treasure'. Thom felt guilty about lying to Long Harry and Captain Ginger, but he knew he had to find this map and set his grandfather free.

Sometime later, they reached the bottom of the mountain. Up close, it was evident that the black rock was from previous eruptions, the volcano above them was now breathing out large puffs of smoke.

191

"I hope it doesn't erupt whilst we're here," said Roscoe, gazing up at the smouldering mountain.

Thom got out his compass to check the direction on the map, then indicated to the others which way to go. They continued round the base of the mountain; nearby he could hear rushing water – they must be close. Thom's heart beat faster in his chest as the noise increased.

"We must be nearly there," said Angus, smiling.

They turned the corner and there above them stood a towering, gushing, waterfall. As they approached, the spray struck Thom in the face, cool and refreshing after the humidity of the jungle.

Finally.

Beneath the cascade of water, Thom could see the coal-black mouth of the cave. Depositing his rucksack and taking out his torch, he walked behind the torrent and entered the gloomy cavernous hole. He was drenched, but he didn't care.

"Wait for us!" cried Rufus, hurrying to catch up.

"Where do we look now?" asked Roscoe.

"I don't know," said Thom. "The map doesn't make that clear. I guess we just search."

The torch beams stretched out towards the backs and sides of the caves; it was vast.

Stalagmites and stalactites took on eerie forms in the shadows, the smell of damp earth and the dripping of the water created strange sounds.

"I don't know what I'm looking for -" said Roscoe.

"A map," snapped Thom.

"I know that, but it wouldn't be just sitting on the floor, not in this damp place, it wouldn't last a single night," insisted Roscoe.

"Look for a box ... I don't know either," said Thom, his earlier anticipation dwindling.

A noise startled them.

"What was that?" asked Rufus.

"It sounded like footsteps," said Angus.

"Do you think somebody got here before us?"

A shadow glided across the back of the cave.

"Who's there?" he asked.

A laugh echoed round the walls of the cave.

"Who is it?" asked Angus, his own voice echoing the same question.

Thom felt his irritation rise. He had wanted to find the map and get back to the Sudden Ghost so he could continue his mission to find his grandfather.

Another laugh resounded round the walls. There was more than one person, or was it just echoes?

"Show yourselves!" commanded Angus.

They could hear footsteps and laughter grow fainter as they retreated.

"Who the hell was that?" asked Rufus.

"I've no idea, but look," said Roscoe, pointing his torch to a large mound at the back of the cave, where a wooden box was perched.

Thom swallowed. Could it be the map? Had the others missed it, or was it now empty? Was he too late? Hastily, he crossed the damp, uneven floor towards the box and grabbed it. Unexpectedly, it opened easily. Surely if it had been there for over a century, or more, then it would be rusted ... something didn't feel right. Shining his torch into the box he could see a small scroll tied up with a leather thong. He took it out, dropped the box to the floor which echoed all around them, and opened it up.

As Thom read, he thought he was going to vomit.

Ha Ha! Tricked you!
Did you really think that the map was real?
I'd never tell you if I had the real treasure map, you fool.
Stanley

Thom's mouth went dry. His body grew rigid and tears pricked his eyes. How could he have been so stupid? He had thought he was so close to finding the treasure map, now he was back to square one with no idea where Grandpa was, or how to rescue him. Without the map, Grandpa's kidnappers had said they would kill him.

Humiliating tears ran down his cheeks. Angus put a hand on his shoulder, but didn't say a word. Thom shrugged it off, threw the scroll to the ground and ran out of the cave. This time he went straight through the waterfall; the cold of the water a shock to his warm body. He ran full pelt back the way they had come. He didn't care where he was going, but he had to run off his rage, separate himself from the others. He had never felt so foolish in all his life. Everyone would be laughing at him.

The evening drew in around him. However, Thom could not face returning to the ship. He sat hidden among the long grass and felt his sorrow overwhelm him. How could Stanley be so cruel? Didn't his family have enough money already? What would happen to Grandpa and Gran now? He had failed.

In the distance, he could hear some of the boys calling his name. He knew he should go back, but he felt such an idiot. It wasn't his fault, he realised; Stanley had planned this, obviously to humiliate him. Angus would understand, but what about Roscoe and Rufus, would they be angry with him, or with Stanley? How would they explain his absence to Captain Ginger and Long Harry too? It was such a mess.

After a while, a rustle in the grass nearby startled him. Something was making its way towards him; the long grass swayed and whispered as whatever it was approached. Thom held his breath. A flash of black amongst the green made his heart leap.

Storm.

Thom let out a sigh of relief. "What are you doing here? How did you find me?" Storm rubbed round his legs and purred; her tail straight up in greeting.

"She was trying to find where you'd got to," said Captain Ginger, stepping out in front of Thom.

Thom sprang to his feet. "Captain!"

"Relax, Thom. Angus told me what's happened, it was a cruel trick – Stanley will be punished, severely, when I can find him. There's no sign of the Hades Rambler at present, but I have sent some dolphins to see if they can locate the ship."

"I'm sorry, Captain," said Thom, unable to meet the Captain's eyes.

"Well, I have to say I'm disappointed that you all lied to me. Researching the Scorpi indeed, I should've smelt a rat!"

"We didn't think you'd let us come if you knew the truth," said Thom.

"You were right, I wouldn't have, but not for the reasons you think."

"Oh?"

"I know a lot about plenty of things, but you're following the treasure map because you want to save your grandpa which is admirable, but you're letting your heart rule your head – it should be the other way round, hence the pirate training. If you're meant to find the treasure map you will."

"But what if it isn't 'meant to be'?"

"Then I'm afraid, lad, it's not."

Thom felt even more despondent. He wanted so much to find the treasure map, surely he would find it, but then his parents hadn't, had they? Besides, they had died trying to - was that to be his fate too?

"Come on, let's get you back to the ship, I think you've had enough adventure for one day," said Captain Ginger, picking up Storm and making a fuss of her, she purred and butted into his bright beard.

"I don't want to go back ... I'm too embarrassed."

"If embarrassment is the only thing holding you back, then you need to find an inner strength, lad. At the end of the day, it doesn't matter what people say about you, or what they think, you have to be true to yourself; that's what makes you strong."

Captain Ginger marched back through the tall grass the way he had come, holding Storm who stared at Thom over his large shoulder, green eyes unblinking.

Thom took a deep breath and followed his Captain. He knew he was right, he was just being silly. He would prove to the crew that he was brave and that he was still determined to find the treasure map and set his grandfather free.

As Windbags launched the row-boat, a large explosion shook the island and the water around the boat rippled furiously. Great clouds of smoke permeated the sky above the volcano, amongst it red rocks were hurled skywards and a fountain of lava rained down, just missing the boat. Windbags cursed and threw his puny weight into rowing them away from Plathgem Island.

While Thom watched the dramatic display of red, orange and black, he wasn't sure how much more *adventure* he could take.

Chapter 12
The Search for Long Harry

Windbags rowed Captain Ginger and Thom back to the Sudden Ghost muttering miserably under his breath. As they neared the ship they could see that something was wrong on board. The crew were milling around the deck like ants in a panic. Had some of the red-hot lava rained down on the ship? Was the ship on fire?

Thom and Captain Ginger exchanged a glance.

"Pass me that spare oar, man!" roared Captain Ginger to Windbags, and taking the oar he plunged it into the sea making the little boat move more quickly towards the ship.

Angus was at the top of the rope ladder when they climbed aboard.

"What's happened? Where's the fire?" asked Captain Ginger, a frown crossing his brow.

"There is no fire, Captain. It's Long Harry ... he's been taken," said Angus, his face deathly pale.

"Taken? Taken where?" asked Thom.

"We don't know. When we returned to the ship we found this ..." Angus held out a note. "It was stuck to the main mast with a dagger."

Thom's blood ran cold.

199

Captain Ginger snatched the note and held it up so Thom could read it too.

Captain Ginger,
We don't think you, or your motley crew, are taking this seriously enough. So, as well as William Prow, we've taken Long Harry hostage, just to ensure you know we're serious.
Give us the treasure map and we'll return them both unharmed.
Keep it and they're shark bait!

"Who's it from?" asked Thom.

"I don't know," sighed the Captain. I thought it might be the Hades Rambler turning mutinous. After their actions today and now their disappearance, they must be involved in some way, but they know we don't have the map. It doesn't make any sense."

"Do you think it was the Hades Rambler that took Grandpa and have hidden him away? It's been them right from the start?"

The Captain shrugged his broad shoulders and shook his head.

"What will you do?" asked Angus.

The Captain's face turned red. "I will search the oceans until I find my grandson and William Prow, then those scoundrels will be fed to the sharks. I will not tolerate mutiny. The School for

Scoundrels is at risk if I do and I will not rest until I know my ancestors' school is safe once more." Captain Ginger growled in his throat and thumped the palm of his hand with his other fist. He turned and with Storm swaying unsteadily on his shoulder, stomped across the deck to his office, disappearing inside with a slam of the door.

Thom felt Angus' eyes on him. "How're you doing?" he asked quietly.

Thom looked sheepishly up at him. "Ok. I suppose. I-I'm sorry."

"No need to apologise. It was a cruel and nasty trick you had played on you today; you have every right to be angry, but don't be angry with yourself. I understand."

"You do?"

Angus nodded. The two looked at each other and Angus punched Thom lightly on the arm and they laughed.

"Come on we should turn in. We'll let Captain Ginger sort this out. He'll be sure to let us know more of what's going on in the morning. He'll most likely call a breakfast meeting – don't worry, he'll get your Grandpa and Long Harry back safely."

The two boys walked across the deck and descended the stairs to the cabins below. Thom realised how exhausted he was. Entering the cabin, they found Roscoe stood next to his hammock holding a yellow bottle.

"Thom, a message for you …" he handed him the small bottle, a look of concern on his face.

Thom was glad it wasn't red, as that would alert him to the fact that things might have taken a turn for the worse at home. He unravelled the small piece of paper and read the message:

> *Thom,*
> *Gran wants you to know that she is feeling much better. They may let her come home in a couple of days. Great news. Hope you're getting on okay at school?*
> *Skipper.*

Tears welled up in Thom's eyes. He couldn't let Angus and Roscoe see him cry. He left the room and hurried up the corridor back towards fresh air – hopefully the rest of the crew would be asleep by now.

Tears fell as he ascended the stairs. It was such a relief after the awful events of the day to know Gran was getting better. He had been so pleased and excited that the treasure map was so close at hand that when he had discovered it was all a hoax he experienced anger, so intense, like he had never felt before in his life.

No progress had been made in his grandfather's rescue and he now knew that he had to be more careful, more vigilant of those around him. He trusted Angus, Long Harry and pretty much Roscoe too; the others he wasn't so sure about. Even Captain Ginger seemed a little dubious at times ... in fact, what was he doing right now? Thom wiped the tears from his face and observed the Captain.

The light was fading from the sky, the moon was rising and it cast an eerie light aboard the Sudden Ghost which was now sailing calmly eastwards. The Captain had walked out of his office, carrying a long tusk, a narwhal's tusk, and hurried to the stern of the ship. Thom watched as he placed the narwhal's tusk to his lips, like a trumpet, and blew.

No sound came from the tusk – what was the point of blowing it? Or, was it like a dog-whistle where only dogs could hear the high-pitched sound? Thom wondered what creature could hear this silent call.

Creeping up to the portside of the ship, he slipped behind some barrels. Thom didn't want the Captain to see him lurking about on deck; he should be asleep by now. He was aware that he had lied to the Captain and didn't want to be found breaking any more rules. Cautiously, Thom looked over the gunwale.

Captain Ginger blew the tusk for a second time, again there was no sound, but he stood and waited peering out to sea. A few minutes later a large school of dolphins appeared at the stern –

they flipped their tails so that they were treading water.

"Yes Captain?" asked the biggest dolphin in a high-pitched voice.

"I need your help," called Ginger, his voice anxious.

"Anything for the Sudden Ghost's Captain," replied the dolphin.

"I need you to search for the Hades Rambler; they've turned mutinous. I need you to find Stanley Teach then report back to me."

"In trouble, is he?"

"The worst kind. I also need you to discover if anyone knows of the whereabouts of William Prow and my grandson, Long Harry."

"Of course. We'll start immediately, Captain."

The dolphins dived back under the surface; their dark shadows slipping away from the ship.

Captain Ginger walked back to his office. When he had closed the door, Thom emerged from his hiding place. However, he stopped dead when he saw Spike slip out from behind some rope curled up on the deck and descend to the lower decks. So, he had been watching too?

Thom squeezed himself out from behind the barrels then walked towards the opposite stairs that led below. As he walked across the deck, something rubbed up against his leg and he heard the distinctive mew of Storm.

"Hello, Storm after some more milk?" he asked, bending down and picking up the cat, it butted his nose and purred.

"Come on then," said Thom, glad of the distraction and the affection from the cat.

Having given Storm some milk, he walked back to the cabin. Roscoe and Angus' snores were loud as he entered and he was relieved that he wouldn't have to talk to them again that night. Storm slipped through the open doorway and jumped effortlessly onto Thom's hammock. Climbing in beside her Thom fell fast asleep to the soothing sound of her purring.

Just as Angus had predicted, Captain Ginger called a breakfast meeting in the dining deck the following morning. The whole crew from the Loyal Trinity and the Sudden Ghost were present. There was a lot of speculation about what was going to happen.

Thom lowered his voice and spoke to Angus and Roscoe whilst Rufus collected his breakfast. "I saw Captain Ginger summon the dolphins last night. He told them to see if they could find the Hades Rambler, but also if there are other clues to Grandpa's and Long Harry's whereabouts."

"It must be serious if he's got the dolphins involved," suggested Roscoe. "He suspects Stanley Teach, but there is definitely something else afoot."

"Someone has Ginger's grandson and the Captain won't rest until he's been rescued," said Angus. "Your Grandpa too."

Thom nodded towards the door and put his finger to his lips. The whole room went silent as Captain Ginger entered; his face pale and his eyes fierce.

"Captain, has Stanley taken Long Harry hostage?" asked Rufus, sitting down with a plate of toast at Thom's table.

"It seems likely after yesterday's events that it has to be Stanley's crew that has taken my grandson," snarled Captain Ginger. "But I'm not sure that there isn't anyone else involved because the Hades Rambler know that we don't have the map they're after."

"What are we going to do?" asked Roscoe.

"Anything we can do to help?" offered Captain Blake, who had joined the teachers' table for breakfast.

"I'm awaiting news on the whereabouts of the Hades Rambler. When I know where they're hiding, I will decide what to do next. I cannot endanger my grandson's life."

Captain Ginger paused for a moment before continuing. "In the meantime, we carry on as normal, but we will move around more trying to locate them. However, lessons will continue as normal. I have an important meeting, on shore this afternoon, with your Aunt Petra, Rufus, she wants to discuss, again, the idea of having female pirates in the school. I don't think the Department for Pirate Education or O.U.S.T.Ed will ever agree though."

"I think it's very short-sighted of them," said Captain Blake. "I think that girls can be a great asset to any school."

Roscoe whispered, "That's because they like books so much and Captain Blake teaches literature."

"I don't think it would be such a bad idea," called Nesta.

Overnight, the Loyal Trinity had joined their sister ship having heard by red bottle, what had happened.

Some of the Sudden Ghost crew nodded in agreement, but there was also a lot of disapproving noises from others.

"I know that a lot of your generation don't have so much of an issue with female pirates, but many of the older generation still do," continued the Captain.

"It does seem a bit old-fashioned," said Thom.

"Well, the rule still stands, at the moment. Right, let's get breakfast finished and then I will see the Sudden Ghost crew in the classroom. Today you've got literature. I hope you've all read Treasure Island?" said Captain Ginger.

A lot of worried faces looked at each other.

Angus shrugged and took a large bite of toast and marmalade, a smug smile on his face.

The crew of the Loyal Trinity took their time over breakfast, stalling, afraid they might miss something.

"I can't believe they've taken Long Harry," said Nesta. "It's not the same without him." He looked down at the half-eaten porridge in his bowl.

"Captain Ginger will make sure he's found ... although I wouldn't want to be your cousin when Ginger does find him," Arabia said, looking hard at Thom.

"He's not my cousin," scowled Thom. "I shall never call him that again!"

"Come on, Thom, Roscoe, let's get to class before we're really late," said Angus, standing up.

Thom strolled with Angus and Roscoe out of the dining deck, appreciating Angus' subtle ways.

Spike and Lucifer were already in the classroom, speaking in hushed voices, heads together, when they arrived. The two boys stopped and stared as Thom entered the room, watching him and Angus with narrowed eyes.

"Good morning," said Angus.

"Ain't nothing good about it," sneered Lucifer.

"Where's Long Harry, Spike?" asked Thom fiercely. "You must know something."

"Haven't a clue what you're talking about," said Spike.

"Weren't you with Stanley yesterday, at the cave?"

"No, I heard what happened though," he smirked.

Thom felt rage rise within him, he would love to wipe the smirk off his face, but Angus put a restraining hand on his arm, guessing at his thoughts.

"If you know anything of Stanley's plans to kidnap Long Harry, you'd better tell the Captain," said Angus, stepping closer to Spike. He was quite a bit taller than Spike close up and Spike looked a little unnerved.

"Like I said, I don't know nothing ... all I know is when we all got back to the ship, he were gone. I didn't see Stan at all yesterday."

"Hmmm. Not sure I believe you," stated Angus, stepping even closer.

"Leave him alone," said Lucifer. "You heard 'im, he don't know nothing."

"Well, if it's discovered that you're hiding something then it'll be the plank for you," said Thom. "You know that don't you?"

The boys turned as more of the crew filtered in full of talk about the Hades Rambler and the disappearance of Long Harry.

"I bet he does know something," Roscoe interrupted, glaring at Spike.

"Yeah, Spike, you'd better tell Ginger if you know anything," said Rufus. "We want Long Harry back safe, or you're gonna get it!" Rufus clenched his fist and went for Spike, but Lucifer stepped in his way and pushed him to the floor.

"WHAT is going on in here?" a voice boomed.

The boys fell silent as Captain Ginger's large hulk entered.

"We think Spike knows something," said Roscoe, his face reddening.

"Well?" Ginger stared hard at Spike. "*Do* you know something?"

"No, Captain, I swear, I don't know nothing about where Long Harry is ... I had no idea that Stanley was planning anything," Spike looked like he was about to cry. Either that or he was a good actor, Thom thought.

"Right. Well then, you'd better get on with the lesson." Ginger glared round at the class as if daring any of them to say something. "We must not blame anyone until we know more, does everyone understand that?"

"Yes, Captain," the boys chorused.

"Where's Captain Blake?" he asked, looking round the classroom.

"I'm here. Sorry Captain," said Captain Blake shuffling in, carrying a lot of books, his glasses slipping down on the end of his nose.

"Get on with the lesson, Captain Blake, these boys need distracting."

"Of course, Captain. Sorry Captain."

The boys took their seats at their desks ready to listen. Thom wondered if the Captain had had any news this morning about Long Harry; if he had he was keeping it close to his chest. Thom tried to retune his attention to Captain Blake when he realised the teacher had already started the lesson.

During lunchtime, Captain Ginger was taken ashore to meet Aunt Petra. The Sudden Ghost was now anchored off southern Spain. The Loyal Trinity had been invited aboard the ship for lunch.

"Loyal Trinity here again?" said Rufus, as he joined the group of boys, which included some of the crew of their sister ship.

"Safety in numbers. I think the Captain is keeping us all close at hand ... probably worried that the Hades Rambler might attack us," said Angus.

"I'm surprised that Ginger is going to his meeting this afternoon, but I suppose if he expects us to get on with our lessons then he must continue doing his job too," said Roscoe.

"Well, *I* think there should be girls on board," stated Rufus. "My sisters, especially the youngest, are fierce ... she might be quite petite, but she takes no nonsense ... I should know."

"I agree," said Arabia. "Girls have a lot to offer too and can be as strong and feisty as some of the boys, more so than some of them." He looked in Tim's direction.

Angus laughed. "I don't have a problem with girl pirates either. Although I imagine Spike and Lucifer would, look at their faces; black as a Devourer's mouth!"

Nesta shuddered. "Uh, don't talk about Devourer's; they're awful creatures."

"What's a Devourer?" asked Thom.

It's a creature made almost entirely of water - waves in the ocean - they have a mouth and teeth that are like cut-throat razors."

"Have you seen one?" asked Thom.

"I have" replied Nesta. "Once, and that was enough. My parents were in their yacht and we were going through a huge storm when one opened its mouth and nearly swallowed us whole. If it hadn't been for the help of a Griffin, who pulled us to safety by a rope, it would have eaten us alive.

"The noise was terrible, like someone with disgusting eating habits, gulping and slurping – vile. Also, it being so close, you could smell its bad breath; like someone who hasn't cleaned their teeth in years – the stench of decay was awful."

"Cool," said Roscoe, laughing.

Nesta glared at him.

During Weaponry later that day, Master Wainright was demonstrating how to clean the cannons to both the students of the Sudden Ghost and the Loyal Trinity, when a commotion at the stern of the ship caught their attention. Thom could see that Captain Ginger had a red bottle in his hand. He wondered if it could it be another message about his grandmother, or a message from the captives of Long Harry and Grandpa. Ginger unrolled the note and his face grew a livid red.

"Gather round, crew," he bellowed across the deck. Everyone fell silent and surrounded their Captain.

"What is it?" asked Thom.

The Captain read aloud:

"If you want to see Long Harry or William Prow alive again, bring us the Prow treasure map that you got from Plathgem Island yesterday and we'll let them go.
You have 12 hours."

Thom felt his fury increase, but also confusion. If the Hades Rambler knew about the map being a fake, how could they expect him to give it to them?

He heard a few whispers go round the room, "Who's William Prow – relation of Thom?" Many eyes turned on him.

"Twelve hours?" said Angus. "That's never enough time to find a map that's been missing for a hundred years."

Captain Ginger took a deep breath, his face scarlet. "There's more ...

"We *are holding them captive on the Isle of the Dead in the north*"

"It's signed ... by the crew of the ... Elusive Wolf!"

Shocked exclamations rippled through the pupils.

"The Elusive Wolf took Long Harry, not the Hades Rambler?" said Angus. "I don't understand."

"They must've got wind of the treasure map being discovered somehow, I suppose they haven't yet heard it's a hoax," said Captain Ginger.

"I thought the Elusive Wolf wasn't around anymore," said Roscoe.

"It does appear on rare occasions, especially when there might be treasure involved. They are rather a motley crew and would give the Hades Rambler a run for its treasure." said Ginger. "Only, on this occasion, it's the Prow's treasure they're after."

Thom felt all eyes turn on him; his cheeks reddened and he felt like he just wanted to run away. It seemed as if everyone wanted the treasure of his ancestors, everyone that was, except him. Thom just wanted the map so he could hand it over to the kidnappers and get his grandfather back.

"We must support Thom in his quest," said Captain Ginger eyeing Thom kindly. He must have seen Thom's awkwardness. "The treasure was stolen from their family over a hundred years ago."

"Thom's great-great-grandfather died trying to defend the Sudden Ghost and the treasure. You will all honour Thom with the respect he deserves – he comes from a family of decent pirates; very generous pirates, I'll have you know."

Lucifer sniffed loudly. "Is he gonna share the treasure with us then? If he finds it, I mean."

Spike stared at Thom, a fierce, greedy look in his eyes.

Thom felt sick. Everyone was looking at him with expectation in their eyes; some with more greed than he would have liked to see amongst the crew members of the Sudden Ghost and the Loyal Trinity.

Captain Ginger glared at Lucifer. "If I know a Prow, there will always be generosity, possibly not always where you might expect, Lucifer, especially for those who are just plain greedy."

Thom took a deep breath before he spoke. "I know that this is all about *my* family; but I wasn't involved in the mutiny or have had any control over what's happened in the past. However, now I am involved, whether I like it or not.

215

"Long Harry is not the only person the Elusive Wolf has taken: they have my grandfather too. That is the real reason I came to this school, to save him."

Both students and teachers gasped.

Thom continued. "The most important concern at the moment is to find both my grandfather and Long Harry. The treasure map can wait. At least we know where they're being held prisoner now and the Elusive Wolf doesn't know that we don't have the map. We're in a good bargaining position."

A lot of heads nodded, some shook.

"If you help me do this, once we know they're safe then we can look for the treasure map. Then, and if, we find the treasure map and then the treasure, I will give some to the school, but we have to consider that the treasure may have already been found and taken."

A loud cheer went up around the ship. Captain Ginger's face was full of pride. Angus hugged Thom. The only one that looked on darkly was Spike; he slunk away below deck, but not unnoticed by Thom.

Captain Ginger bellowed his command, "Come on crew. Get this ship ready to sail subaqueous – we need to reach the Isle of the Dead, before Long Harry and William Prow get buried alongside the ones already there."

The crew got to work, pulling up the sails and attending their stations. Captain Blake and the crew from the Loyal Trinity went back to their own ship to prepare to sail alongside their comrades. The two ships would stick together.

As Thom stood at the wheel, he felt a hand on his shoulder, he turned to see Captain Ginger facing him with a smile under his bright, ginger beard – it was so thick, Thom wondered if he had ever had a shave.

"That's the spirit, Prow. I know you have a good heart, now let's go and find our families."

Thom felt the ship tip and dive; he hoped that they wouldn't be too late.

Chapter 13
The Isle of the Dead

In no time at all, it seemed, the ships reached the waters a few miles from the Isle of the Dead. Unfortunately, the seas surrounding the cluster of islands, that stood sentinel around the main island, were treacherous. About five miles from the islands, the Sudden Ghost resurfaced. They could go no further under the sea unless they wanted to be shipwrecked on the ragged rocks. They would have to sail closer to the island upon the surface. The row-boats were prepared, for when the time came, for the selected crew, to go and search the island for Long Harry and William Prow.

In the distance, blood-red, capped mountains came into view. The Isle of the Dead looked very much alive and menacing as they approached its shores.

Thom's anticipation was growing. He wanted to find Grandpa so he could return him to Gran and make her feel better. Finding Long Harry was important to him too, he'd become fond of his Tutor, of his forthright ways. Long Harry was someone Thom felt he could depend upon.

They were not far from anchoring the ship when, out of nowhere, a loud explosion was followed by a warning shout. He turned to see a cannon ball heading his way, he ducked down. Fortunately, the ball lost speed and dropped heavily into the water, missing the Sudden Ghost. As he looked to the distance he noticed a ship with red sails, firing more cannon balls at them.

"It's the Elusive Wolf!" cried Angus.

The enemy ship was getting closer; its crimson sails were billowing in the wind. It was gaining on them.

The crew of the Sudden Ghost got to work, letting down the sails fully to catch the wind and pick up speed. They would have to skirt round the other side of the island to see if they could lose their pursuers. Captain Ginger stood at the helm; his solid form firm, bellowing out commands.

Thom realised that they had to get to the Isle of the Dead and fast. They didn't have the treasure map – had no idea where it was, therefore they had to rescue the prisoners before they were slain by the crew of the Elusive Wolf, or they themselves became prisoners too.

As the Sudden Ghost rode the waves around the headland of the Isle of the Dead, from the deck Thom watched the gangs on board the other ship fire more cannon balls in their direction. Fortunately, they missed, but the nearness of them unnerved Thom.

Suddenly, a cannon ball ripped one of the sails on the main mast; the white sail flapped in the wind like a ghost floating above them; a foretelling of doom?

"What in blazes ..." shouted Captain Ginger.

"Torn sail," cried Roscoe, running at once to tend to it.

The ship immediately slowed a little and Thom turned to see that the other ship was gaining on them.

"Anchor the ship here and get the row-boats ... we're close enough to the island to row the rest of the way," called Captain Ginger. "I'll stay on board and fight to protect the ship. I want Thom, Fergus, Angus, Roscoe and Lucifer to go ashore; see if you can find William and Long Harry, they have to be on the island somewhere. The rest of you all hands on deck!"

The captain held something out to Thom. "Take this map of the island to help you." He thrust the map into Thom's hand. "They could be anywhere, but I have a feeling it might be worth looking in the Fearsome Forest. However, beware, even the best map readers can get lost in there!"

"Aye aye, Captain," said Thom, making his way to the row-boats where Windbags was waiting. His thoughts turned to Lucifer; it seemed a bad choice of the Captain's to have him along with them. He didn't trust him.

The five boys climbed down the rope ladder as Windbags lowered the row-boat for them. "Me bloomin' back! All this toin' and froin'; I should get paid more!" he moaned, but nobody was listening.

As Angus and Roscoe rowed the boat, Thom unrolled the map of the Isle of the Dead. "They must be the blood-capped mountains," he said pointing at some dark grey, rocky, mountains that were capped with what looked like sticky red blood.

"They're disgusting," called Fergus. "Is it really blood?"

"So it's believed," said Angus. "The pirates who die are buried here in the Pirate Graveyard on the south side of the island. It's believed that the blood of those dead pirates caps the mountains."

Fergus shuddered.

"It's probably some other natural type of phenomenon and that's just a myth to frighten people away," said Thom.

"It's working," said Fergus.

"Don't be so soft," said Lucifer, nudging Fergus with his shoulder which made the boat rock.

"Careful!" said Thom in an authoritative voice. He glanced back at the Sudden Ghost, could see cannon balls being fired at the Elusive Wolf from his own ship; the crew managing to hold the ship back. What he also noticed was a handful of pirates, from the Elusive Wolf, rowing towards the Isle of the Dead too.

"We must hurry," said Thom. "We're almost there."

Soon enough, the boys were shin deep in the freezing waters that lapped at the edges of the island, pulling the boat up the beach.

"We're being followed, we must get ahead of them," said Thom pointing at the other row-boat which was gaining on them. "Come on, I've planned a route. I just hope we find them quickly."

As they made their way up the beach, the boom of canon fire could still be heard behind them. The island was eerily quiet and it was bitterly cold, unlike the Island of Plathgem.

"Which way?" asked Angus, rubbing his upper arms.

Ahead of them, lay the blood-capped mountains, but there was a clear valley path that they could follow at the foot of them. As they got nearer to the mountains, they could see the grey-blue waters of a frozen river to their left; the mountains lay to the right of them. They walked swiftly, following Thom's lead.

After a while, Thom stopped and showed them the map. "We're heading for the Fearsome Forest, but we have to be very careful near the swamp, see here?"

The others nodded.

"I don't want to get stuck," said Fergus.

"If we're careful, then we should be fine, if we stick to the banks of the river, which are

223

frozen, the ground should be hard enough to walk on," said Thom confidently, although inside he hadn't got a clue whether or not the ground would be frozen at that point, he'd just assumed so.

They trudged on. Thom pulled some chocolate bars out of his pockets which Cook had stuffed in his hands just before they'd climbed down the rope ladder to the row-boat.

The boys ate hungrily as they continued. The ground got more challenging to climb as the valley began to slope uphill.

When they reached the top, they could see more of the island below them. The Frozen River spread out into a partially frozen lake beneath them. More blood-capped mountains could be seen on the other side of the island and an impenetrable forest as dark and deep as any Thom had ever seen was over to the west. Would they ever be able to penetrate those walls of trees, so thick and close together? If anybody did get in, there was no certainty that they would ever be able to get out.

"Whoa!" said Lucifer. "Look at that forest."

"A good place to hide someone -" said Angus.

"I'm sure those trees are watching us," cried Fergus.

"Pull yourself together," said Angus.

Thom peered behind him. He could just make out the other pirate youths from the Elusive Wolf a short way to the rear of them. They stared at the boys, their faces, which were painted red, full of determination. "Come on, we'll see if we can get into the forest and give them the slip," he urged.

They slipped as they descended the slope keeping close to the edge of the lake at the bottom, away from the swamp. Thom had been correct about the ground being harder and frozen - they didn't sink.

About half an hour later they had reached the edge of the dense Fearsome Forest.

"Follow me," said Thom, squeezing his way between the tightly packed trees, the evergreen needles scratching at his arms and face like an aggressive cat as he passed through them. With his compass in his hand, he tried to keep as north-east as possible.

After a while he saw something move in the trees ahead of him and after their meeting with the Scorpi on Plathgem Island he stopped dead in his tracks and held up his hand.

"What is it?" hissed Roscoe.

Thom stayed silent while he tried to adjust his eyes enough to see what creature it was that was dashing through the trees towards them. Thom could see a hairy back, brown and black.

A wild boar.

"It's okay, it's just a boar," he said. "But we had better get off the pig-track before it mows us down." The boys stepped off the track as the wild pig ran off through the trees away from them.

The boys continued through the almost impassable trees; it was dark amongst them and they could barely see the sky, certainly no sunlight. It was a forbidding place.

"Over here," said Angus.

"What's up?" asked Thom.

"Look, the tree branches are broken here." He walked in a different direction. "And again here ... and here ... they are freshly broken too, so it has to be recent."

"So?" asked Lucifer.

"So, this shows something, or someone has been through here recently. I used to go deer hunting with my grandfather sometimes and we'd follow trails like these to tell us which way the animal had gone."

"So we're following a deer right now?" asked Fergus, rolling his eyes.

"No, I don't think it can be a deer; deer don't wear deck shoes."

"What?" asked Fergus.

"Look on the ground, here ... see? Someone has come this way in deck shoes a short time ago."

"Perhaps we're close," said Thom. "Let's try shouting."

"Long Harry!" shouted Roscoe. "Long Harry, are you there? Can you hear us?"

"Grandpa!"

Nothing.

"Long Harry. Grandpa!" shouted Thom, raising his voice.

There was no response.

"Come on, let's follow the trail further," suggested Angus, setting off.

Maintaining an easterly direction, according to Thom's compass, they searched for more tracks or signs that might lead them to the prisoners.

After a while the trail stopped dead.

"Damn," said Angus.

"*Now* what?" asked Fergus.

"I think we should give up and go back to the ship," said Lucifer. "They're not here.

"Give up?" snarled Roscoe, pushing Lucifer in the chest. "Give up on Long Harry, never!"

"No, no I didn't -" started Lucifer.

"We are NOT giving up. I will not give up until I've found Grandpa," said Thom searching wildly for another clue. "How could the trail just *end?*"

"I don't know ... unless ..." Angus tipped his head and looked above them. "Up there!"

Gazing up into the trees, they could just make out a tree-house perched on the branches above them. It was small and well concealed with evergreen branches camouflaging it.

"Hello!" called Thom.

Again nothing.

"Is there anyone there?" called Roscoe.

"How are we going to get up there?" asked Lucifer.

"There must be a way up," said Fergus.

"There is ..." said a voice behind them. "But we're not telling you how."

Thom turned and saw a tall, lanky, young pirate with a red painted face and a patch over one eye; he wondered if there was actually anything wrong with his eye or if he was just wearing the patch for effect.

"Where's Long Harry?" demanded Angus.

Another two red-faced pirates came forward out of the trees swords raised ... three more behind them. The crew of the Sudden Ghost placed their hands on their scabbards. Releasing their weapons they stood ready to fight.

"Where are they?" Thom demanded.

The crew of the Elusive Wolf sneered.

The lanky one spoke again: "Where is the treasure map?"

"We don't know," squeaked Fergus.

"I don't believe you," said another Pirate. He was tall, but broader and had a huge scar down his left cheek. His eyes glinted with a look Thom couldn't quite fathom, but decided it wasn't good.

"It's true. I'm Thomas Prow," said Thom stepping forward a couple of paces. The others raised their swords higher. "I haven't any idea where it is. We were tricked yesterday; it was all a hoax. Stanley Teach planted a fake map to get at me."

"Liar!" spat Lanky.

"Surely you know where the map is. Why else would they have you aboard the Sudden Ghost this year?" asked Scarface.

"So I can learn to be a pirate, just like the rest of you," said Thom.

"Well, let's see how well you're doing." Scarface raised his sword in a combat position forcing Thom to stand firm and ready.

The sound of metal clashing on metal echoed through the silent forest; the crews of the two ships collided in combat that was fierce and aggravated.

In his peripheral vision Thom could see Angus brawling with Lanky as he had lost his sword; Lanky was now on the floor underneath Angus who held him down.

Thom fought with skill; his sword seemed to know what he wanted it to do; it sailed through the air as light as a feather, but Scarface was strong and also an accomplished swordsman. Thom felt his strength dwindling as the fight continued, would he be able to hold out?

Roscoe soon had his opponent in a fierce grip against a tree; he tied his ankles together then went over to Angus and they did the same to Lanky.

The look of terror on Fergus' face indicated he was being defeated. The fearsome looking pirate he was fighting growled and snarled at him like some kind of demented dog.

Thom felt a strong stinging sensation on his upper arm and was alarmed to see blood immediately soaking through his shirt. "Angus, I'm cut," he called.

Angus, who had been helping Roscoe tie up the pirates that they had conquered, seized his sword and rushed to help Thom in his bid to beat, or make surrender, Scarface.

"Well, Prow, still need a bit more practise I see," he scoffed maliciously, swiping his sword towards Thom's neck. Thom jumped out of the way just in time and Angus tripped Scarface up. He landed on the ground with a thump.

"Ouch!" he cried. "That's cheating!"

"There's no need for us to be fighting in the first place," cried Angus. "We don't know where the map is, so even if you capture each and every one of us, which you won't, we couldn't give it to you because we don't have it."

Scarface tried to stand up again, but Thom knocked him back to the floor.

"You need to tell us where they are, right now!" seethed Thom, wincing at the pain in his arm.

"Why should I?"

"Because we don't know where the map is, so you have no reason to keep hold of them," stated Roscoe.

The other pirates had stopped fighting and seeing the members of their crew held captive, ran off into the trees.

Gradually, Thom became aware of knocking, as though somebody was banging wood against wood. He realised that the sound was coming from the tree house above them. "Up there," Thom said, pointing. "Come on, we should be able to find a way up."

Roscoe grabbed Scarface by the throat. "How do we get up there?" he growled.

Scarface grinned.

"There's a rope," said Lanky looking at the ground. "It's camouflaged. You have to look carefully amongst the branches of pine that are concealing the tree-house."

Scarface threw him a glare full of blades.

Thom and Angus were first at the base of the tree which had more thickset branches than the rest of those that the tree-house was attached to.

The boys from the Sudden Ghost searched thoroughly for a rope that would enable them to climb up to the tree-house and free the prisoners.

"I've found it," called Fergus, untangling a rope ladder from amongst the branches.

"Brilliant," shouted Angus.

Thom made his way over to the rope and looked at Angus. Angus nodded at him. "You go. You're the fastest up a rope, if your arm can take it."

Thom nodded fiercely and began to climb the knotted rope. He hoped that Grandpa and Long Harry would be at the top. The rope was frayed and he wasn't a hundred per cent sure that it would support him all the way to the top. His arm throbbed and he was still aware of the warm sticky sensation of the blood soaking through his shirt and down his arm. He tried to ignore the pain, concentrating on the hope that he was about to be reunited with his grandfather.

When he was almost at the top, a long way from the ground, he suddenly found himself falling; the rope had frayed even more. Despite the pain in his arm, he held on tightly ... to fall from this height ... the words of Pirate Notts ringing in his ears. "*A good knot could save your life; a bad knot could kill you.*"

Abruptly, he was jerked to a halt – the knot had held by a thread. With his heart in his mouth he started to climb again – he must fix that knot before he descended the rope.

At the top he clambered onto the deck on which the tree-house was built. The cabin was shoddily made from logs and planks of wood, a door – padlocked from the outside – stood shut against him.

"If you're in there, you need to step aside, I'm going to kick the door in." He waited a couple of moments. He heard a small movement inside then he raised his foot and kicked the door as hard as he could. It gave way much more easily than he had anticipated and he landed flat on his back, the pain in his arm unbearable.

Long Harry, his face more bearded that usual, was tied into silence by a scarf twisted and secured across his mouth. Behind him, huddled in the corner, was Grandpa, grey-faced and thin. Thom sprang to his feet and untied their gags.

"Am I glad to see you, boy," said Grandpa, smiling at Thom as he undid his hands which were tied tightly.

"Are you all right?" Thom enquired.

"Hungry and I probably stink, but I'm okay. What's been going on? Was the map real or a hoax?" Grandpa looked from Long Harry to Thom.

Long Harry explained. "When Angus returned to the ship without you yesterday, Thom, he told Captain Ginger and I that you'd found it, but it was a hoax, that's why Captain came to find you."

"That's right, it was a hoax. The map which was supposed to lead us to the treasure map was a forgery made up by Stanley."

"What? That's outrageous, even for a pirate," said Grandpa. "But then nothing surprises me about that family."

"I know, but at least I know not to trust him ever again. He may be my cousin by blood, but I will never call him family."

Grandpa looked sad.

"Are there others here?" asked Long Harry.

"A few. Come on, we need to get back to the Sudden Ghost, that's if the Elusive Wolf hasn't destroyed it. It was firing cannon balls at us earlier."

"Yes, we heard the canon fire, wondered what the hell was going on," said Long Harry. "It sounds like there is a proper mutiny within the school. Captain Ginger will not tolerate this."

After they had secured the frayed knot on the rope, Long Harry and Grandpa followed Thom back to the others. The crew members from the Elusive Wolf had disappeared, except those tied up.

"Let's get back to the Sudden Ghost and take these traitors with us," said Long Harry.

"Aye, Aye," said the crew.

They retraced their tracks back through the Fearsome Forest, dragging their bound prisoners with them, past the swamp and the blood-capped mountains and onto the beach. Their row-boat was where they had left it and the Sudden Ghost was afloat on the grey seas just off the island.

Thom could just make out the bright orange beard of Captain Ginger who was leaning on the gunwale, his spy-glass to his eye – he waved at them.

There was no sign of the Elusive Wolf – Thom hoped it had been obliterated.

Chapter 14
A Hidden Message

As the rescuers returned to the Sudden Ghost they received a hero's welcome. The crews were ecstatic to see Long Harry returned unharmed and were pleased for Thom to have found his grandfather too.

Captain Ginger grinned widely as he embraced his grandson. "I can't thank you boys enough. You have done a great thing in rescuing Long Harry." He turned to the crowd of crew members on the deck. "I would also like to welcome aboard a special guest, one of the best students the School for Scoundrels has ever seen, William Prow."

Applause swept through the teachers and students as Captain Ginger gripped William's hand, shaking it enthusiastically. The two men regarded each other jovially, despite Grandpa's pallid colour.

"What should we do with the prisoners?" asked Roscoe, who held onto Lanky from the Elusive Wolf.

"Shackle them and put 'em in the hold until I can decide what to do with them," stated the Captain, glaring at the crew members from the other ship who shrank back in fear.

"Where's the Elusive Wolf now, Captain?" asked Thom, looking out to sea, but unable to see the ship with red sails.

"They've retreated, but I will ensure the rogues are dealt with by the Ministry. If I get my hands on them, they won't live to see another day."

A roar of approval ran through the crew of the Sudden Ghost and the Loyal Trinity.

"QUIET," roared the Captain. "As a way of thanking you all, we're to have a marvellous feast tonight and plenty of R.U.M. But, for now, perhaps we can return to some sort of normality before we start the search for the other two ships. I want an end to this mutiny within my school. We've had a lot of excitement over the past few weeks, but tonight, we celebrate the return of our two family crew members. Tomorrow we search the seas for those treacherous traitors."

Another roar, of excitement this time, rang through the crowd of boys on the deck of the Sudden Ghost.

Thom called for silence and all eyes fell on him. "I also want to thank you all for helping me find my grandfather. I couldn't have done it without you. I'm so pleased he's safe and will shortly return home to my Gran."

The crews applauded.

Long Harry then addressed the crowd: "I want to thank those of you who came to rescue me; you all put your lives at risk, be assured that I would do the same for you, without hesitation. Now, let's head for warmer climates where we can swim and have some fun."

Captain Ginger gave further orders to the crew, who sprang into action to ensure the Sudden Ghost and Loyal Trinity went subaqueous and got them away from the dark and dismal Isle of the Dead and to an island of paradise.

Thom and Grandpa had been invited to Captain Ginger's quarters where he had hot food brought up from the galley. Steaming plates of roast wild boar and all the trimmings were placed in front of them. Thom tucked straight in, starving after all the adventure. Grandpa too.

"You look like you could do with this, William," stated the Captain, He cut off a little piece of meat and fed it to Storm who sat by his plate expectantly. "I got Arabia and Nesta to help Cook with dinner, once the Elusive Wolf ran out of cannon balls and had departed."

"Thank you, Captain Ginger," Grandpa replied. "I want to thank you too for helping Thom rescue me. When I was taken that day, I couldn't think how anyone would ever find me. Those scallywags just put a bag over my head and forced me off my boat. I struggled, but I'm not getting any younger."

Ginger laughed. "Me neither. Anyway, you know the School for Scoundrels looks after its own." He piled up his fork and took a great mouthful.

Grandpa nodded as he ate hungrily.

Thom wasn't sure how to tell Grandpa about Gran and was grateful when Captain Ginger took the lead.

"I've a bit of bad news, William."

Grandpa looked from the Captain to Thom.

"Ellie's been ill. She's much better now and is home from the hospital -"

"Hospital?" Grandpa looked alarmed.

"Yes, Grandpa, she had a stroke, but she's okay. Skipper and Peggy have been looking after her. I visited her a few days ago, but I had to get back to school and try and find the map and rescue you ..." Thom felt hot tears prick the backs of his eyelids.

"Don't you upset yourself, boy. None of this is your fault," said Grandpa firmly.

Thom hung his head.

"He's right, Thom," said the Captain. "This feud is deep-rooted in history and, unfortunately, you are now caught up in the middle of it. However, let's hope that the next few weeks we can restore some kind of order to our school and punish those responsible."

"I should think so too," said Grandpa. "And, if you want my grandson as part of this school, then I need your word Captain that you will see to it that he succeeds in his studies."

"I swear by the Pirate Code, William." He spat on his hand and held it out to Grandpa, who tentatively took it, then shook it firmly. "For now, I want you to rest, enjoy the festivities tonight then tomorrow I will drop you and Thom off home so you can see Ellie. I've sent a red-bottle message to Skipper to let them know them you're safe."

"Thank you," said Grandpa. "Now, if you'll excuse us, I'd like to talk to my grandson, alone."

"Of course. I'll see you tonight."

Grandpa and Thom left the Captain's quarters and walked down to Thom's cabin. Storm followed close behind, obviously pleased to see Thom safely back on board.

Once inside the cabin, Thom hugged Grandpa tightly. "I was so worried about you and Gran."

"I'm all right, boy, just a good night's sleep will see me right. Now, tell me about Gran, is she really all right?"

"I had a message from Skipper and he seems to think she's much better, but I was scared, Grandpa. If anything happens to you two -"

"Grandpa hugged him closer. "Hey now, we're all right, aren't we?"

"Yes, but -"

"No buts, boy, just remember we're all safe now. Forget the what-ifs, buts and maybes."

Thom nodded, safe in Grandpa's embrace.

241

The next day, the Sudden Ghost resurfaced near the Isle of Bos where Skipper could be seen waiting on the beach. The early morning sun shone orange in the sky.

Windbags dropped Grandpa and Thom onto Bos then, reminding Thom he only had forty-eight hours before he would be collected to return to school, Windbags rowed miserably back to the Sudden Ghost.

Skipper embraced Grandpa and they held onto each other for a few moments before Skipper coughed loudly, thumped Grandpa on the back and smiled kindly at Thom, his eyes moist.

"Ellie's so looking forward to seeing you. It was all I could do to persuade her not to come out to meet you both. She wants you home, to see with her own eyes that you're safe," said Skipper.

"I can't wait to see her either," said Grandpa. "Come on, let's go."

Gran opened the front door and her arms widely as Thom and Grandpa hurried up the path. She started to cry when she had them in her arms, but Thom peeked out to make sure none of the neighbours were watching. They all walked into the house, laughing as they all tried to fit through the doorway at the same time.

"It's so good to have you back safely," said Gran, blowing her nose and smiling widely.

Thom noticed the slight slant of her smile.

"It's good to be home," said Grandpa, folding Gran into his arms again.

"I'll go and put the kettle on," said Thom. He walked into the kitchen. The first thing that he noticed was that there were no cakes on the side. It was the only time he could ever remember there being no baking, but a packet of pills, with Gran's name on it, sat on the side next to the kettle. He tried to read the label but the words were too complicated for him to decipher.

So used to having tins full of home-made cakes, Thom struggled to find some biscuits in the larder, but he found some chocolate digestives tucked away.

Thom could hear his grandparents talking in lowered voices in the lounge. He waited for the kettle to boil, knowing they must have a lot to say to each other. Gran looked pale and both she and Grandpa looked far frailer than they had a few weeks ago.

Thom made the decision that he must stay at home and help to look after them. He would not return to the School for Scoundrels. He had Grandpa home safely, so why did he need to go back? Not for the treasure map that was for sure, hadn't it caused enough problems over the years? But the thought of Stanley or the crew of the Elusive Wolf searching and actually finding his family's treasure filled him with anger - they had no right to the treasure of the Prows.

Thom returned to the lounge with a tray full of tea and biscuits. His grandparents stopped their conversation and looked at him.

"We're so proud of you, Thom," said Gran, smiling at him.

"We certainly are, boy."

"I could hardly leave you out there, could I?" asked Thom, blushing.

Grandpa poured them all tea. Thom noticed that his hand shook a little as he did so.

"I've decided I'm not going back to the School for Scoundrels," Thom announced.

His grandparents looked at each other then back at Thom.

"We feared you might say that," said Gran.

"What's stopping you?" asked Grandpa.

"I thought I'd lost both of you. I don't want to be away from you. I can stay here and help. I want us to be together, as a family."

Grandpa placed his cup back on the saucer and set it on the coffee table. "I understand how you must feel, but didn't you enjoy the school, despite being there in the first instance to rescue me?"

Thom nodded. He had enjoyed the different lessons; his new friends and yes, despite his grandfather's life being in danger, he had enjoyed the adventure too.

"Gran and I'll be fine here. I'll take care of Gran until she's better, so will Skipper and Peggy. You have to think of your future, Thom, as I've said to you before."

"But I'll miss you."

"Go, Thom. Go and make your old grandparents even more proud," said Gran. She looked tired.

"I'll think about it," agreed Thom. "But I'm not promising anything. I want to stick around for a few days at least, just to check you're both okay."

"It's your choice in the end, boy, but we think it would be better if you did return ... it's what your parents wanted too, remember?"

Whilst finishing their tea and biscuits, Gran said, "Look, while you're here, why don't you go and see your friends, go kite-boarding while you've got the chance. I'm sure they'd love to see you."

The idea of kite-boarding excited Thom and he immediately went to phone his friends to see if they were free. It would be good to give his grandparents some time on their own, either to chat or rest - whatever they needed. It would also be amazing to get out on his kite-board, to have some fun without the dangers of the School for Scoundrels interfering.

Sam gave Thom an enormous hug when he arrived at his house.

George was also there, but punched Thom on the arm. "Hugging's for girls," he stated.

Thom felt elated by the sight of his friends; he had missed them. He liked his new friends, especially Angus, but he'd known Sam and George all his life and their friendship was familiar, secure; safe.

They rowed out to Bos, the weather perfect for kite-boarding. They arrived on the island, carrying most of their kit on their backs with their brightly-coloured boards tucked under their arms. Thom couldn't help but think about the Sudden Ghost and how it unexpectedly appeared up out of the water from beneath the waves – it seemed unreal now that he was here, back with his friends.

"So, what's your new school like?" asked Sam, as he withdrew his kite from his pack and started to sort the strings which had become entangled.

"It's great," said Thom, squinting as he looked up into the bright sky.

"How can school be great?" asked Sam. "Don't tell me you're becoming a swot!"

"No, no," laughed Thom. How could he tell them about the school? The school where he learnt to climb rigging, read maps, have adventures and fight with real swords against real pirates?

"The after-school clubs are the best. The lessons are the usual boring poetry and stuff, but we have great clubs at weekends too."

"Such as?" asked George, fighting against the wind to keep his kite on the beach.

Thom climbed into his harness. "There's fencing and climbing; we even go on excursions sometimes and do orienteering." He was *almost* telling them the truth. He hated lying to them, but the School for Scoundrels was for pirates only and had to be kept top secret, besides he wasn't sure they would believe the truth even if he did tell them.

"Sounds better than ours already," said Sam, a little wistfully.

"Come on, aren't you ready yet?" asked George, he was always the first to be geared up.

"You get going, we'll join you in a minute," stated Sam.

Thom watched George as he ran down the beach and into the water. He was soon riding the white waves that rolled and curled towards the beach; the wind direction was ideal. George was now speeding through the water, twisting, spinning one-hundred-and-eighty degrees; three-hundred-and-sixty degrees; always resulting in a stomp. His strength and energy which resulted in good air-time allowed him to do the tricks he desired.

Sam joined him in the waves, steering clear of a kook who looked out of control; a young lad with all the gear and no idea.

Once Thom had got all his kit into the sea he was soon riding his board through the water, enjoying the feel of the wind and sun upon his face - free. Sheeting his kite, he used the side-shore wind to get air-time before looping himself through the strings of the kite, dreading that it would end in a hindenburg and he'd crash into the sea with the sound of Sam and George's laughter ringing in his ears.

He landed safely, edging through the water, toe-side. He could hear the whoops of joy from his friends and the gulls around them too. His heart felt full, his worries temporarily forgotten.

A while later, exhausted, but exhilarated they dragged themselves out of the water and sat on the beach to have their picnic. They ate the delicious treats of crisps, apples and sandwiches.

Thom felt that the Sudden Ghost had just been a dream; this was his reality on Bos with Sam and George kite-boarding. However, as the afternoon drew to a close, the sun getting lower in the sky, he began to feel the pull of his grandparent's health again. He was worried about them; he knew that they weren't getting any younger. The weight of his concerns fell once more upon him.

That evening, after dinner, Thom sat together with Grandpa reading Samuel Taylor Coleridge's 'The Rime of the Ancient Mariner'; just as they had when Thom was a young boy. Gran had gone to bed early, saying that she was exhausted. Grandpa and Thom took it in turns to delicately turn and read the pages of the ancient, abridged, beautifully-illustrated children's version that belonged to Grandpa and his grandfather before him. For generations fathers and grandfathers of the family would have read the book to their children at family gatherings. It was an heirloom, full of adventure and mystery, just right for a child training to be a pirate upon the high seas.

Grandpa read Part IV:

> *"I fear thee, ancient Mariner!*
> *I fear thy skinny hand!*
> *And thou art long, and lank, and brown,*
> *As is the ribbed sea-sand."*

Thom relished the comfort of his grandfather's soothing voice as he read the familiar, well-loved tale written by Samuel Taylor Coleridge in 1798. This time, however, it seemed a little more sinister as a whole new world had been opened up to Thom. A world he had known nothing about; was only just beginning to get to grips with the fact that it did exist, and was not just in the pages of adventure books as he had imagined.

At ten o'clock Grandpa said he was tired and needed to go to bed.

"Aren't you going to watch the headlines?" asked Thom. Grandpa always watched the news at ten.

"Not tonight. I saw the 6 o'clock news; I don't think much has happened since then. Goodnight, boy."

"Goodnight, Grandpa."

Thom watched the elderly man shuffle out of the lounge and heard him struggle up the stairs. He felt bereft. His grandparents weren't anywhere near as fit and healthy as they used to be. So much was changing.

Thom was tired, but didn't feel like going to bed. He glanced down at the illustration of the portrait of the Ancient Mariner just inside the front cover of the book that sat on his lap. It was a face he'd looked at many times over the years; an artist's impression of the poet's ancient sea-man. The grim mouth, slightly open as though it would speak a strange language; a long, hooked nose like a mountain surging up out of a hairy, bearded face – sideburns as bushy as his eyebrows. The longing, haunted eyes were deep-set like pools in his ancient, lined face. Primeval, wrinkles like crevices ... like contours on a map.

Immediately, Thom sat straight up in his chair, wide awake. He looked more closely at the face of the ancient sailor. Yes. The nose looked like a mountain because it *was* a mountain; the bushy beard and eyebrows, forests; his deep-set eyes, pools and the wrinkles ... contours. Thom traced his fingers along a track, which if you followed it carefully took you around the island and towards the mouth - a cave!

Those bushy sideburns, which almost joined the moustache, they were no forest - they were lazy, hairy beasts ... there to protect ... but to protect what? A treasure map?

Thom had to pinch himself. Had he fallen asleep? Was he dreaming? No, no he was very much awake. Could it be that he had just stumbled on the map that would lead them to the treasure map? It had been in front of his family's eyes for decades and nobody had known, not until now.

His mind was spinning. What should he do? He wanted to race upstairs and tell Grandpa, but he couldn't, didn't want to disturb his much needed sleep. He wished Angus was here too, so that he could share his find with someone. Should he go straight back to school now? No, he couldn't do that to his Gran, she was thrilled to have him back. He almost laughed aloud when he remembered his earlier reluctance to return to the school. Yes, he would miss Gran and Grandpa, but the sense of adventure and the possibility of finding the treasure map, was now enticing him back to school.

Thom felt torn, he didn't want to leave straight away, wanted to spend a few hours with his grandparents as he had promised. He would just have to be patient. A few more hours and he could go back to the Sudden Ghost. A few hours wouldn't matter, surely, not after all this time?

Chapter 15
Who to Trust?

Soon enough, the time arrived for Thom to return to the Sudden Ghost. He had packed up his things, including a cake that Peggy had baked because Grandpa had forbidden Gran to do so, much to her frustration.

"Ready?" called Grandpa standing in the hallway as Gran embraced Thom in the lounge.

"Almost." Thom gave Gran one last squeeze and walked through to the hall. "Grandpa, I wondered if I could borrow your book, 'The Ancient Mariner'? We're supposed to be bringing our favourite book in to discuss with the others for Literature."

Grandpa looked doubtful.

"I promise I'll take great care of it. I know how special it is to you. It means the world to me too, the hours we've sat together reading it. I swear I'll guard it with my life."

Grandpa still looked dubious. "Well ... I suppose it's going to be yours one day anyway, but you must look after it."

"Of course, thank you," said Thom, flinging his arms around his Grandfather and holding him tightly, before going off to the bookcase to retrieve the ancient book.

Skipper arrived. Grandpa was still too weak to row a boat, so Thom finalised his farewells with his grandparents, before putting his travel trunk on the small barrow and following the old fisherman down to the harbour, where the row-boat awaited them.

Skipper rowed in silence out to the Isle of Bos. It was dark, but the sea was calm and lapped gently around the boat. Thom felt sad that he was leaving home again so soon, but his anticipation about the map overrode those feelings quickly. He wasn't sure what he was going to do yet, but he thought he might speak to Angus and Long Harry first – they would know what to do and he trusted them. Angus was always there for him and had earned his trust, almost from the start, and although he was beginning to trust Roscoe too, he felt that he was a little too impulsive at times. Long Harry knew the history of his family more than most and he sensed that he would be on his side not that of Stanley's.

What he must ensure was that Spike didn't know anything about the map, he would just tell Stanley: wherever in the world he was right now.

Angus and Roscoe were thrilled to see Thom, especially when he unpacked the cake Peggy had given him. They sat in their hammocks, the ship moving at speed under the water, eating the delicious chocolate cake in the dull lamp-light.

Most of the rest of the crew were sleeping, but Angus and Roscoe wanted to hear about Thom's weekend back home.

"How are your grandparents? asked Angus. "I bet it's good to know that they're back safely at home together."

"They seem much older, but they are both getting better. Grandpa was very weak when we picked him up from the Isle of the Dead. Gran looks better than she did in the hospital too," replied Thom.

"Did you manage to meet up with your other friends at all?" said Angus through a mouthful of cake.

"I did manage to go kite-boarding with Sam and George which was awesome," replied Thom.

"I'd love to have a go at kite-boarding, perhaps we can get Captain Ginger to add it to the curriculum," said Roscoe, cutting himself another slice of cake.

"It's not up to Ginger. O.U.S.T.Ed would never allow it, far too much like having fun. Imagine all that fresh air and exercise - bad for one's health," laughed Angus, chewing on a flapjack. "Of course, it's much better to be sat in a darkened cabin looking at dusty, old manuscripts about pirates of the past."

Thom sighed. "I do find that quite interesting."

Roscoe laughed at him. "Give it a year or so. Anyway, Ginger's away at the moment; gone on a convention to do with O.U.S.T.Ed and the 'Girls Aboard' campaign. I don't think they'll ever allow it though."

"It wouldn't be so bad," said Angus. "Girls can be pretty fierce, some might make good pirates. I can imagine Rufus's Aunt Petra as a young and lively girl, disguised as a boy climbing the rigging and keeping some of the boys on their toes during swashbuckling."

Thom nodded and laughed.

"You two are soft," stated Roscoe. "I'm going to get some R.U.M., I'll be back soon." He climbed down from his hammock and went out of the door closing it quietly behind him.

Thom waited a few moments before speaking. Angus was rocking himself to and fro in his hammock. "You asleep?"

"Not even tired," said Angus. "Glad you're back, been a bit dull around here without you."

"Yeah, I missed this place too, kinda grows on you. Although it was good to see my grandparents, and spend some time with them after everything that's happened, it does feel good to be back on board," replied Thom.

"Yes, I'm glad your Grandpa's been found, shame he didn't stay a pirate, I think he'd have been amazing. Would have been great if he was one of the teachers here." Angus paused. "I did wonder if you might not come back at all."

"I nearly didn't."

"But?"

"I've, em, got something to show you."

"What is it?" Angus pulled himself up into a sitting position.

Thom went to his trunk and undid a clasp. From a compartment in the base, that was not easily visible, he extracted a false board and pulled out his grandfather's copy of the 'Ancient Mariner'.

Angus took it from him, handling it carefully Thom was pleased to see.

"This looks like it's been around a few years. I know the story of course, but what a lovely book ... look at the illustrations – I never thought black and white pictures could be so amazing, creepy too."

"It's a beautiful edition. Here ... look at this picture of the character of the Ancient Mariner. Notice anything unusual?"

Angus studied the picture. "Hmmm, not really, what am I looking for?"

"What does his face remind you of?"

"An old fisherman?"

"No, take another look."

Angus looked at the face of the character, but shook his head, looking questioningly at Thom.

"I think it's a map. Look." Thom pointed out the features of the Mariner's face and explained what he had discovered.

"You think this might be the map that will lead you to the treasure map?" Angus' face was concerned.

Thom nodded, excitedly, but Angus seemed wary. "You don't think it's another fake?"

"No, not this time, this book has been in my family for generations, passed down from father to son; in my case, grandfather to grandson."

"I see."

"I'm thinking of asking Long Harry to help. If Captain Ginger's away then we can perhaps take a trip to this island and see if we can find the map."

Angus' dark eyes looked troubled. "I'm worried that if you have another disappointment you may leave the school for good. I've got used to having you around."

"I made a promise to myself, in honour of my parents and grandparents, that I would get my F.Q.P. certificate. I've no intention of leaving the School for Scoundrels, even if I don't find the treasure map, but I have to try."

"You can certainly trust Long Harry, but I'd keep it from the rest of the crew, for now anyway."

The latch on the door lifted and Roscoe came in clutching a tray with three tankards on it.

Thom hurriedly put the book away, back into the secret compartment.

"I've got the R.U.M."

"Brilliant," said Angus quickly, distracting Roscoe away from what Thom was doing. "Pass it here, then."

"All right, give us a chance."

Roscoe now handed one to Thom too, who had climbed up into his hammock, hand outstretched.

"What have we got first thing in the morning?" asked Thom. "I'm still not quite used to the timetable yet."

"Weaponry," said Angus.

"Brilliant," said Thom, taking a large gulp of R.U.M.

The next morning, straight after breakfast, Thom went in search of Long Harry. Angus said he would cover his chores so that he could have the time to speak to their Tutor. Thom discovered Long Harry in the classroom preparing for a lesson later in the day.

"Morning, Thom," said Long Harry, smiling at him as he entered.

"Morning, Sir."

"Everything, all right? Got a problem with your chores this morning?"

"Angus is covering my chores because I needed to speak to you urgently," said Thom, feeling his cheeks grow warm.

"Of course, what's up?" Long Harry placed the board pen on his desk and gave Thom his undivided attention.

Thom lowered his voice. "I need to tell you something, but it must be kept a secret."

"I see."

Long Harry gesticulated to a chair and Thom sat down; Long Harry sat opposite him.

"When I went back to my grandparent's this weekend, I discovered a map. I think it might lead us to the Prow's treasure map."

"What makes you think it's not another fake? Captain Ginger told me how hard you took it last time – what if the same thing happens again?"

Thom looked at Long Harry. He was right, he had taken the hoax badly, but what if it was real this time? Surely nobody had been able to fake this map, it had been in his grandfather's possession his whole life, Thom's too and their ancestors before that.

Thom explained where he had found the map and why he thought it was genuine. He watched Long Harry closely, his face grew more and more intrigued and then he smiled.

"I think you might be onto something here."

"I hope so," said Thom. "I'd like to find the treasure map before anyone else does."

"Thom, I know it's important for you to find the treasure map, but you must remember, we don't know that the treasure's not been found already and well ... stolen."

"I had thought of that, but had forgotten in the excitement of finding this map," said Thom, his heart sinking to his stomach like a heavy stone.

"I don't want to alarm you, but you need to be prepared for any eventuality in this situation. Many a pirate has gone mad for treasure; it's not always a good thing, quite often it is the curse of many pirates."

Thom nodded slowly. "So, you won't help me?"

"I didn't say that. I'll help you in any way I can, but I just want you to be prepared for disappointment this time."

Thom knew he was right; it made a lot of sense. However, he knew he still had to go on with it. He must find the map and then, hopefully that would lead him to the family treasure which was, according to history, rightfully his. He had to get to it before Stanley or the crew of the Elusive Wolf stole it. What he would do with it after that he didn't know. He had no idea how much there would be, perhaps just a few hundred pounds worth of gold? Or perhaps a chest full of nothing but sand.

"If you want to go through with it, Thom, then we must keep it very quiet. If the Hades Rambler or the Elusive Wolf were to discover this knowledge then you could be in a lot of danger. Does anyone else know about it?"

Thom nodded. "Just Angus."

"Your grandparents?"

"No."

"Who on this ship do you trust, apart from Angus?"

"No-one."

"You need more than just you and Angus to go on this trip, IF I decide to let you go."

"What about you?"

Long Harry smiled. "I can't come with you, because I'm needed here while Captain Ginger's away campaigning for 'Girls Aboard' with Aunt Petra. If I sail the ship to the island then more people will know and we can't take that risk. This has to be top secret."

"I suppose Roscoe and Rufus are the other two I trust the most."

"Right, well, leave it with me for now. Bring the map to show me tonight, nine o'clock. We'd better get to Weaponry before the boys start trying to get swords out, without supervision, could get nasty."

"Sure," said Thom laughing and following Long Harry back up to the top deck.

Angus eyed Thom as he walked towards him. Thom nodded slightly trying to prevent Roscoe from seeing the look that passed between them.

"Later," whispered Thom, as he stood next to Angus.

The student pirates were all waiting in line to be issued with their swords for the lesson. There was lots of excitement amongst them as it was the favourite lesson of many, including the Loyal Trinity crew who had joined them.

"Fancy being my partner?" asked Arabia, who stood a few people ahead of Thom and Angus in the queue.

Thom was unsure. What if Arabia was as good at sword fighting as he was at rigging racing? He had only had one lesson so far and Arabia was probably highly skilled already. However, he had beat him at rigging-racing, hadn't he?

"Sure," he said. "If Master Wainright will let us."

Angus laughed.

"What?" asked Thom.

"He's brilliant, just watch out."

"Yes, but you said that about him rigging-racing and look what happened there."

Angus smiled. "Ok, just don't say I didn't warn you."

Long Harry handed Thom the same sword as last time, which again felt great to hold;

effortless and balanced like it was a natural extension of his arm.

Thom was pleased to find himself face to face with Arabia; he stood tall and confident the blade in his hand wide and curved – there was a look of mischievous challenge in his opponent's eyes.

The lesson began with Master Wainwright instructing them on how to thrust and parry; working on their footwork and defence. Tim had been given a fine, long sword, but he got a bit carried away and ended up slicing Sonny Boy's hand.

"I'm gonna kill you!" cried Sonny Boy, as he gave chase around the deck after Tim who fled in terror.

Finally, Master Wainright managed to calm the situation. Tan, a first-aider, was called upon to stitch Sonny Boy's hand, with him swearing and cursing at Tim, who kept a low profile for the rest of the day.

Five minutes before the end of the lesson, the students were allowed to fight each other, using the skills they had learnt during that lesson. There were strict rules to abide by and any student who disobeyed them had to spend a night in the hold, alone with the rats and the prisoners from the Elusive Wolf.

Arabia was quick on his feet and was superb at dodging any lunges that Thom sent his way; his sword sliced through the air towards Thom with terrifying accuracy.

"Bitter that I beat you at the rigging-racing?" asked Thom, laughing – but secretly rather anxious about Arabia's amazing sword skills.

Arabia laughed. "I got an A* for Weaponry last term."

"Now you tell me!" Thom ducked another speeding blade and blocked the sword with his own.

"Great block!" said Arabia.

Thom jumped back and found his balance again before raising his sword; he saw a weakness in Arabia's gait and brought his sword up towards his neck.

Swiftly, Thom's sword was knocked clean out of his hands and he found himself on his back with Arabia's sword at his chest, unaware of how he had got there.

Applause broke out amongst the other pirates. Thom hadn't realised that they had spectators and he blushed as Arabia removed the blade from near his chest and then held out his hand to help him up. Thom didn't take the offered hand, but jumped quickly to his feet, his face burning.

The crowd cheered and then started to disperse.

Angus thumped Thom on the back. "Arabia certainly put you in your place," he said with a chortle.

Thom smiled. "He certainly did. I think I might take him on this voyage with us. I imagine he might be very useful," he said, lowering his voice. They were behind the rest of the group that were making their way down to the lower deck for lunch.

"Long Harry is letting us go?" asked Angus eagerly.

Thom guided Angus to the gunwale out of earshot. The wind, although warm, was beginning to pick up and a threat of rain could be felt on the air.

"Long Harry is worried that I might be in for another disappointment, but I need to do this Angus."

"Has he banned you from going?"

"No. I'm going to speak to him this evening, take the ..." Thom looked around. "... the map. He asked who I might like to take along with me if he does give his permission."

"What did you say?"

"Well, that I only trusted you, but he insisted that I should take others as well, perhaps Roscoe and Rufus. Then I saw how Arabia was just fighting with his sword and I think he should come too – he'd be great to have along."

"He certainly can fight and he's great at other stuff too," agreed Angus. "Sensible head, but brave with it."

Thom nodded, "Come on, let's get some lunch. I'm starving!"

At nine o'clock that night, Long Harry was sat in a comfortable armchair eating an apple when Thom, dry mouthed, entered his cabin clutching 'The Rime of the Ancient Mariner' close to his chest. Storm was curled up on the arm of the chair, she opened one eye when she heard Thom come in, eyeing him suspiciously. The cabin was full of bits of driftwood furniture; pictures of mythical sea-creatures hung from nails in the walls; shells of all shapes and sizes lined the shelves around the room; the hammock was swaying gently by the port hole.

"Come and sit down," said Long Harry, pointing to another armchair next to his.

"Thanks," replied Thom, taking a seat.

Long Harry looked at him. Hesitating, Thom handed over the old, well-loved book.

"It's just inside the front cover ... a picture of the Ancient Mariner."

Long Harry flipped the book open to the page Thom had said. "Whoaaaa."

"What is it?" asked Thom, afraid now that Long Harry would tell him that it was, indeed, another fake.

"It's amazing, beautiful," said Long Harry. "You know, I think you could be right. When you first glance at it, it just looks like any other portrait I've seen before that was sketched during this time, by this artist, but on closer inspection I can see the mountains, the lakes, the contours. Magnificent."

Thom let out a sigh of relief. He felt his skin grow tight with goose-bumps. Maybe, just maybe they were finally onto something authentic.

"You need to think carefully about who you want to take with you, Thom. Don't just take them because you like them, only take them if you can trust them and they will be useful to you."

Thom nodded.

"I've decided to let you go and search the island, see if you can find the treasure map. However, like I said, even if you find the map, the treasure could've already been stolen; you must prepare yourself for that. At the moment you are looking for a treasure map, nothing more."

Thom looked at Long Harry. "I will try. I know it's possible that it could've gone, but I still want to try. I feel I owe it to my family."

"Of course. Now, tell me the names of the crew members you want to take with you. I think I'll have to limit it to five. I haven't told Captain Ginger and your team must keep this top secret. I'll tell the rest of the ship that you've been invited to a school in Thailand for a few days to practise

268

rock-climbing. The rest of us can then spend some time map-reading and swimming off Singapore, so we're close, but not so close anyone will become suspicious. If I keep them busy, they won't smell a rat."

"Rock-climbing?"

"Well, Pirates do have to go on land sometimes too, you know that."

Thom laughed then both were quiet for a moment or two.

"I know who I want to take with me," said Thom.

"That's a good start, who?"

"Angus, Roscoe, Rufus ..." he hesitated.

"And?"

"Arabia and Tan."

"Why some from the Loyal Trinity?" Long Harry gazed at him.

"Arabia is an amazing swordsman and Tan is great at first aid."

"I see. What about Roscoe and Rufus? Angus I completely agree."

"Roscoe is silly at times and Rufus a little hot-headed, but they worked well with me last time and I'm pretty sure I can trust them not to run off with the map. I don't know them all that well but they are the ones I trust more than any others in the crew. If I took Spike or Lucifer for instance, although good pirates, I wouldn't trust them not to stab me in the back."

"It sounds like you've given this some considerable thought," said Long Harry.

"It's very important that I have the right crew. Look what happened to my great-great-grandfather!"

"Well, I'm a little apprehensive about letting you all go, not sure Captain Ginger would approve."

Storm sat up, stretched and yawned widely, then moved towards the door. Long Harry got up to let her out.

"She often comes and visits me too," said Thom.

"Yes, she's rather sweet and keeps the mouse population down, the rats too."

"What about a boat?" asked Thom. "How are we going to get to Mariner's Island from Thailand?"

"It needs to be done discreetly so no row-boats, but there is another way."

Thom waited. He could see a small smile playing on the corners of Long Harry's lips.

"Come on, tell me."

"Seahorses."

"*Seahorses?*"

"Yes. You can ride seahorses to the island. They are quick, reliable and fierce, so if you get into trouble they can get you out of there quickly."

"But I've never ridden a horse in my life, let alone a seahorse, besides aren't they tiny?"

"Some are, but others are enormous. It doesn't matter that you've never ridden before, you just hold on tight."

"Won't I drown?"

"No, it's the same as the ship going subaqueous. You can breathe underwater all the time you're on the seahorse. If you come off though, you could drown, so you have to make sure you climb straight back on."

"Crikey," said Thom.

"Now, I've things to organise. Make sure you keep the book safe, don't tell anyone, not even Angus, what you're about to do. I want to confirm the details before you let the others in on the secret and you never know who is listening." He glanced towards the door. "I'll see you all tomorrow straight after breakfast. I'll ensure that the others know about the meeting, so don't mention a word."

"Thank you, Sir," said Thom.

"Goodnight, Thom," said Long Harry. "It's good to have you back on board."

The following morning, just after breakfast, the crew that Thom had suggested to Long Harry, were all waiting outside Captain Ginger's office, wondering why they had been summoned. All that was, except Thom. He knew that Long Harry was inside the Captain's office waiting to call them in and give them the news. He hoped that they would all be up for the adventure, but had suddenly grown nervous that perhaps they wouldn't want to, especially after the last fiasco. Thom realised, for the first time, that this was a very personal quest. Just what would the others gain and why *should* they help him?

Thom knocked on the cabin door.

"Enter," called Long Harry.

They crossed the threshold of the Captain's office one by one. The room was no less gloomy than when Captain Ginger's great hulk seemed to reinforce the darkness. Oil lamps were burning on the walls and a lantern sat upon the vast desk. Storm was curled up on a map – she peered out of one green eye at them.

"That cat always unnerves me," whispered Tan to Thom. "She always seems to be watching me."

"I think she's like that with everyone," Thom returned in a whisper.

"Good morning, crew," said Long Harry, cheerfully.

"Good morning, Sir," they chorused, a hint of anxiety in the tone.

"I expect you're wondering why I have called you here."

They nodded.

"Well, I have a top-secret mission that I need you to help with," he took a sip of his coffee before he continued. "You see, you all know that

Thom has been given the task of finding his family's treasure map."

Rufus groaned. "Not this again!"

Thom's heart sank. Perhaps Rufus had been the wrong choice after all? He thought back to their conflict on Plathgem Island when Rufus had stormed off, had he been too hasty in getting Rufus involved in this new adventure?

Long Harry looked at Thom. "After all these years, the actual map to find the treasure map of the Prows has been found."

Tan gasped.

"How do we know it isn't another fake?" asked Roscoe, solemnly.

"We don't think it is this time." Long Harry went on to explain about the book and how it had been under Thom's family's nose the whole time.

Thom showed them the portrait of the Ancient Mariner.

"It's just a picture of an old seaman," stated Tan.

"No, look more closely," said Arabia, pointing at his nose.

Long Harry pointed out other landmarks in the Mariner's face and finally where the treasure map should be hidden.

As the waves of excitement came off the others, Thom felt his excitement grow.

"This is amazing," said Arabia. "But what if the map has already been taken?" He looked at Thom sympathetically. "Or the treasure, come to that."

"I'm prepared for that," he said.

"So how can we help?" asked Angus.

"Thom needs a reliable, trustworthy crew to help him on his journey to Mariner Island. It may be treacherous at times and you will come up against all sorts of challenges. If you would like to go, great, if not, you need to leave this room now and never mention anything to anyone about it ever again. If you do, you will be discovered and the punishment would be severe."

The others all looked at one another and then at Thom.

"I'm in," said Angus and Arabia, simultaneously.

"Me too," said Roscoe.

"And me," stated Tan.

They all looked at Rufus, who just looked at his feet.

"It's all right, Rufus. If you don't want to come that's fine," said Thom. "We'd love you to. You're a valued member of the team."

Rufus looked up at Thom and nodded. "Okay, I'll come, but I won't be bossed around."

"Thom will be your captain, if you can't handle that Rufus then don't go," said Long Harry, sternly.

Rufus remained silent for a few moments before he sighed and said, "I'll go. I promise to do my best by you, Thom."

"Thank you," said Thom.

"So, when do we get going?" asked Angus.

"Yes. When does the adventure begin?" asked Arabia.

"There are some preparations that need to be done today, but you will be leaving by the full moon tonight," said Long Harry. "For now we continue the farce of sailing to Thailand. On this occasion we're not going subaqueous, I don't want the crew to think we're in a hurry, they will get suspicious; so might the other ships if they are spying on us. I will tell the crew that we need practise of ordinary sailing."

Excited chatter filled the cabin. Storm glared at them for having disturbed her sleep as Long Harry dismissed them back to lessons.

Thom, although elated about the forthcoming adventure, felt that the moon couldn't rise quickly enough.

Chapter 16
A Loyal crew

The Sudden Ghost sailed the seas towards Thailand. Thom was aware that no-one on board knew of what was going on – they just saw it as another exercise in Pirating. Those who did know kept it to themselves, although when they came across each other on board, or in lessons that day they gave each other a secretive, excited look.

Unfortunately the journey felt slow and Thom found it near impossible to hide his feelings of excitement, but also of frustration. He spent the morning in Sail-mending followed by Carpentry after break; the minutes ticking painfully by.

During lunchtime the boys sat together on deck eating their lunch and enjoying the hot sun. They continued sailing through the Indian Ocean, the warm air and bright sun made Thom sleepy, but the noise of the others talking and shouting kept him awake. He felt he needed to sleep, to conserve some energy for the adventure ahead of them. Gently, he slipped his ear plugs in which lessened the noise and he was able to drift off to sleep amongst the chatter of the other boys.

When Thom opened his eyes he noticed that the sky had changed from clear blue to dark grey. How long had he been asleep? At first the Sudden

Ghost was so quiet it appeared to be deserted, but the crew *were* there … all fast asleep. The ship rocked forcibly. There was no sign of anyone awake. Baffled, Thom stood unsteadily and looked around. Bodies of the sleeping crew were curled up on the deck. Angus was beside him, mouth wide, snoring. He shook him, but got no response. Close by Roscoe and Rufus were sleeping too. What was going on? Why couldn't he wake them?

Remembering the ear plugs, he removed them. Instantly he became aware of a beautiful serene singing. Voices so pure that his mind began to blur …

Sirens!

Swiftly, he replaced the ear-plugs and walked to the side of the ship.

Looking over the gunwale, he was conscious of sharp, jutting rocks that were dangerously close. The surf was crashing in titanic waves against them. He stared upwards at the high cliffs towering above him like an army of stone giants. He heard a muffled shout from his left and noticed the Loyal Trinity edging itself between the Sudden Ghost and the jagged, black rocks.

Without a crew the Sudden Ghost would be wrecked upon the rocks within minutes. The Loyal Trinity were obviously trying to put themselves between the Sudden Ghost and the cliffs to prevent the Sudden Ghost from smashing against them. But he realised that the Loyal Trinity would be thrown against them instead.

Thom was bewildered. How was the Loyal Trinity not in the same predicament? Why was its crew unaffected by the singing? Had they realized what was happening and had inserted their ear plugs in time?

The Loyal Trinity were trying to protect their sister ship, but in doing so they were putting themselves in perilous danger. They would be destroyed too if they didn't get their ship out of the treacherous waters and away from the rocks.

Thom sprang into action. He ran across to the helm and dragged it as hard as he could to get the ship away from the cliffs. As he did so, a member of the crew from the Loyal Trinity, swung across on a rope to the Sudden Ghost.

Nesta ran from student to student placing ear-plugs into their ears.

From the wheel, Thom could see that the Loyal Trinity would be smashed upon the rocks any moment if they didn't get away from them.

"What on earth is going on?" Angus shouted to Thom as he joined him at the helm.

"Sirens."

"Sirens?"

"We're going to be wrecked if we can't get the crew to pull the ship back out to sea. Look."

Angus looked to where Thom was pointing. The Loyal Trinity was being hauled further and further towards the rocks and was now in far more imminent danger than the Sudden Ghost.

"We have to help them," shouted Angus.

"We have to get the ship to safe waters then we can go back and rescue them," said Long Harry, appearing at their sides rubbing his eyes. The Sudden Ghost was alive once more with activity; students and teachers alike were all hands to deck.

Now the sails were loose, Long Harry took the helm and tried to steer the ship away from the rocks. Although the crew could not hear any orders being shouted, because of the ear-plugs, they seemed instinctively to know what to do - working together as a team. Fortunately, the wind picked up and they were able to shift back out to sea, to a calmer place away from the predatory rocks.

Looking back Thom could see that the Loyal Trinity crew were trying to drag the ship away from the cliffs, but were struggling against the pull of the powerful surf. Suddenly, it got caught in the grip of a powerful wave, and they watched in horror as the ship collided with the cliffs with immense force – shattering and splintering. Terrified squeals were carried towards them on the wind. The main mast snapped like a twig and the colossal waves grasped at the ship like a frenetic fiend, threatening to devour it and the crew in one final slug.

Thom felt sick. The Loyal Trinity had saved the Sudden Ghost crew; put themselves and their own ship between them and the rocks that would have wrecked the Sudden Ghost if they hadn't been there.

The crew stood silent, gaping at the catastrophe before them. Already parts of the ship and some bodies were being washed away from the Loyal Trinity and taken up onto a nearby beach.

Thom removed his earplugs and indicated that the others do the same.

"Anchor the ship!" shouted Long Harry.

"I'll do it," shouted Rufus, who was now stood with Thom and Long Harry, and dragged Tim along with him.

"Right, we need to send in the life-boats. I need some crew to come and help," continued Long Harry. "Whatever you do, take your earplugs, just in case they start to sing again." He selected Angus, Thom, Roscoe, Lucifer and Fergus to man the life-boats and help with the rescue. "Master Wainright, Sir Rupert you go too".

They lowered the life-boats into choppy waters. Ahead of them they could see what was left of the Loyal Trinity, being tossed about on the inhospitable waves.

With his heart in his mouth, Thom started to row with Angus pulling hard on the oar next to him. The boys were silent.

As they approached, Thom could see barrels, crates, wooden buckets, broken parts of the ship and clothing from the crew all scattered on top of the water.

As they neared the shore, to his horror, he spied a few bodies floating on the surface; some were thrashing around in the water, tiring; others held desperately onto pieces of wood from the ship.

Thom dived into the water and swam towards a limp body upon the waves, praying they would not be dead. It was Tan. He took hold of him and swam with him back to the boat, thankful for his life-saving skills.

Angus helped heave the injured Tan aboard he was coughing and spluttering, thankfully alive.

Thom became aware of more people on the nearby beach, where the waves were calmer. They were either lying down or were sat, coughing and retching. He swam for shore hoping he would be in time to rescue some more of the crew that could be seen floating in the water.

In the shallows more of the crew from the Sudden Ghost jumped out of their row-boats and waded through the water, pulling the bodies up onto the shore.

Thom found Arabia face down in shallow water. He feared it was Arabia from the curly, dark hair, the blue scarf swollen with air next to him on the water – Thom hadn't realised Arabia's hair was so long. He turned him over ... it was Arabia ... his eyes were shut.

With his heart in his mouth he pulled him up on to the beach and laid him on his back. Thom tried to remember more of what he had learnt on the life-saving course he'd done with Sam at the beginning of the holidays at the insistence of Sam's mum. With all of the kite-boarding they did it seemed silly not to. Taking a deep breath to calm his nerves, he started CPR, methodically breathing and pumping Arabia's chest, he continued as he'd been taught then sat back on his haunches and waited a moment.

As the moments passed, Thom began to lose hope, but then Arabia coughed and spluttered out a whole load of water. Opening his eyes he stared at Thom. "What-what happened?"

"You're going to be okay, Arabia. You're okay. The Sirens, they ... the Loyal Trinity ... it's ..."

Arabia sat up and looked around, then burst into tears; great gulping sobs. Thom placed an arm around his shoulders; he was surprised how slight he was, but he knew of his strength, had witnessed it during the rigging-racing and sword-fighting.

Thom looked around him; other members of the crew from the Loyal Trinity were coughing and crying. Suddenly, from out of the water Captain Blake appeared and stumbled, saturated, up the beach with seaweed entangled, long wavy hair, weeping.

Thom felt his breath catch in his throat, there was no mistaking from the shape of her that Captain Blake was a *woman.*

"Oh my girls; my poor, poor girls!" she cried running from one crew member to another.

Suddenly, there was uproar of shouts and exclamations.

"GIRLS?" cried Angus, wide-eyed.

Read sat next to him looking pale and shocked.

"Girls!" cried Roscoe, jumping to his feet in an attempt to get away from Sporty, whose headscarf had come off in the water. There was no mistaking the fact that she was a girl, with flaming coiled locks.

The crew of the Sudden Ghost were on their feet gaping at the crew of the Loyal Trinity who, all of a sudden, were silent. It was now, quite apparent, that they were, most definitely, all girls.

An uncanny stillness enshrouded the two crews. The Sudden Ghost crew were gawping at the girls and the girls stared at Captain Blake with a panicked, questioning expression.

"Oh my, oh dear, oh no ..." cried Captain Blake, her hand over her mouth, her eyes wide with shock, water still cascading down her ashen face.

"I think we all need to stay a little calm," said Captain Ginger's voice from behind Thom.

He turned and saw the Captain stood in the shallow waves, his face serious, but composed; Storm perched on his shoulder like some sort of feline parrot.

How had he got here so quickly? Thom wondered.

"But Captain, how did you ... and they're all girls," said Roscoe shrilly. "Girls aren't allowed in the School for Scoundrels, it's an ancient rule. They bring us bad luck. Look at all this ..."

Captain Ginger nodded, rubbing his large, red beard with a rough, calloused hand. "I know."

"Did you *know* they were girls?" asked Thom.

Captain Ginger sighed. "I had my suspicions a while ago, but only recently did the matter become more apparent. Aunt Petra has been trying for years to get girls on board, she says it is discrimination for us to exclude them – I've been trying to persuade O.U.S.T.Ed., and the Ministry, but they'll not hear of it. I'm afraid that the deceit of Captain Blake and Aunt Petra will deter them even further."

"Do they already suspect that the Loyal Trinity are all female?" asked Rufus.

Captain Blake had stopped snivelling and said: "No, they have no idea. The girls are good pirates and I don't want to hear any bad words said against them, is that clear?"

"But they *lied* to us," said Thom, feeling angry that he and his crew had been duped by girls. Girls of all things.

"Only out of necessity. If we were allowed to attend the School for Scoundrels there would be no need for this secrecy," said Tan, indignantly.

"They'll bring us bad luck," called Spike. I don't want 'em on the Sudden Ghost, see what they've done to their own ship! How can you call them good pirates when they can't even look after their ship?"

"That's enough, Spike," said Captain Ginger, sternly.

"But they *helped* us," said Rufus. "They put themselves in danger to help us."

"Excuse me, Captain." Arabia looked up at him, fear evident in her eyes.

Captain Ginger looked at Arabia who was now getting to her feet, her tear stained face, determined. "We may be girls and we may have made a mistake today, but we are good pirates, better than some of these boys. Therefore, I'm happy to write to my father and ask him to pay to replace the Loyal Trinity. I know he would want us to have another ship, he is all for girls becoming pirates. However, he will make one stipulation ... O.U.S.T.Ed must allow female pirates in the School for Scoundrels from now on."

A round of applause from the girls on the beach started as a steady clap from a few; it became more enthusiastic and then more of a crescendo as some of the boys and teachers joined in too. Tim started to clap, but soon stopped when Spike growled at him.

Captain Ginger held up his hand and the crews grew silent. "I'll do what I can. Now the secret's out and they can see for themselves what great pirates girls make, who knows, their actions today should go in their favour."

At dinner that evening, the girls were subdued. Now that their disguise was no longer necessary it was as if they weren't quite sure how to behave. Spike, Lucifer and Fergus ignored the girls, taking their dinners back to their cabin to eat away from them.

Arabia and Tan approached Thom's table, their faces were pale.

"Can we join you?" asked Arabia, her voice quiet.

Thom was unsure what to say, but Angus immediately moved round in his chair to allow the girls space to sit down.

Arabia smiled at Thom, but he remained stone-faced. Why had they felt it necessary to lie?

"So, we've known you for a year and didn't realise you were girls," stated Roscoe laughing. "Got to give you credit for the disguise."

"All our ancestors have been pirates so why should we be excluded?" stated Tan, sternly. "It's discrimination."

"It's a good argument," said Angus. "I don't have a problem with girls being part of our pirate school. Do you Thom?"

"I ... em," replied Thom.

"You don't, do you?" asked Arabia, looking directly at him.

He felt his cheeks flame. He shook his head. "It's just the deceit, the lying. I don't like lies ..."

"Oh," said Arabia, her cheeks turning pink.

Thom had to get away, he felt angry, but also guilty that he did so. He excused himself and went up on to the poop deck. The night sky was full of stars, so many stars. He looked up at the constellations wondering if he could spot any he knew that Grandpa had taught him. He felt the tears well up – he so wanted to find the treasure map, so wanted Gran and Grandpa to be okay and for them to go back to how things were – but then things had changed so much – could they ever be the same again? He knew if he could find the treasure map, and then the treasure, he would hopefully have enough to pay for his grandfather to buy a new fishing boat, a good one to see him through until he retired.

Thinking of his grandfather, he wondered again why he had lied to him about his parents – why did people tell lies?

Thom felt a presence approach and stand beside him.

"They're beautiful, aren't they," said Arabia. "Oh, look. A shooting star, Thom, make a wish."

"Funny, I was just thinking about what I wish." Thom hung his head.

"Sometimes wishes come true."

"Not always."

"No."

They remained silent for a few minutes.

"Does this mean you don't want me to come to Mariner's Island with you? I'd understand."

Thom remained quiet. The sound of a few voices carried from a lower deck. The creaking of the ship and the jangling of the rigging wasn't so alien to him now. "I would still like you to come. You and Tan, but no more lies – promise?"

"No more lies, Thom. I'm sorry we had to lie in the first place, but it was the only way. I hope you can see that."

Thom began to realise that he could.

"Us girls have all wanted to be students at the School for Scoundrels for years, most of us have brothers or fathers, cousins, uncles, grandfathers that have studied here. We wanted the rules to change, but they didn't, despite Aunt

Petra's efforts. We're just as loyal to our ships and crews as you boys, sometimes more so."

"Yes, I'm sure if it was the other way round, I would feel the injustice of it. Not sure I'd disguise myself as a girl though."

They both laughed.

"If you want something badly enough you'd do anything, Thom."

"You're right, Arabia."

"Come on, let's go and find the others. We should try and get some sleep before we set off for Mariner's Island and see if we can make your wish come true."

Chapter 17
The Guardians

"They're gigantic!" Tan squealed.

The sea-horses were not as Thom had expected – nothing like the delicate little ones he had seen at the Sea Creature's Visitor centre back home. They were huge, at least fourteen hands, encased in dark, iridescent armour like the horse of a medieval knight. They were proud creatures, their heads held high, their manes all the colours of the rainbow; graceful, but powerful too. Their tails, just on the surface of the sea, curled forward like a fleshy ammonite and they drifted on top of the sea swiftly towards the boys.

Windbags had dropped the young pirates off in the water and rowed away immediately he had seen the seahorses coming. Thom and his small crew were all eager to start their adventure, but as soon as they saw the seahorses it was if Captain Ginger had roared a command of silence; they gaped at the sight approaching them and paled.

"Our transport," said Thom.

Rufus looked rather alarmed, but Angus and Arabia's faces lit up.

The seahorses stopped just beside the young pirates and bowed low. The largest of them spoke first. "Which of you is Thomas Prow?" Its voice was light, musical; it didn't suit the size of the beast.

"I am," replied Thom.

"Then we take our orders from you, Thomas Prow."

"Oh, right. Well, let me introduce you to the crew first then we can decide who will ride each of you." Thom introduced the members of his crew one at a time.

"Pleased to meet you," said the largest seahorse. "I am Ventricaria and these are my friends." He pointed at each in turn as he spoke their names: "Kelp, Halimeda, Coralline, Padina and Algae. We are here to assist you in any way you require."

"Well, first we need you to take us to Mariner's Island," stated Thom, feeling rather important as he gave the first command.

"Of course. You need to climb on our backs, take a deep breath and then we dive beneath the waves."

"Goodness, how are we going to breathe?" asked Tan.

"Don't worry," said Halimeda in a soft, whispery voice. "You will be able to breathe in the same way as when your ship travels the oceans underwater."

"Are you sure?" asked Rufus, frowning.

"Of course," said Halimeda, nodding.

Thom looked at the others. "I will ride Ventricaria. Each of you must choose a seahorse to ride."

The crew chose quickly. Angus got onto Kelp; Arabia chose Halimeda; Tan chose Algae – the smallest of them. Roscoe and Rufus started squabbling, both wanted to ride Coralline, who was the second largest seahorse. However, when Corralline tried to nip Roscoe on the shoulder he climbed onto Padina's back instead.

"Everyone ready?" asked Ventricaria.

They all agreed they were.

Thom took a deep breath and felt the cold water close over his head. He was a little apprehensive, not knowing how long to hold it for.

Quite soon Ventricaria turned his equine head and nodded to Thom. He took this as a sign that he could now breathe; that and the fact that an air bubble had encompassed both him and the seahorse.

"Are you all right?" asked Ventricaria, as he rode through the water.

Thom was surprised that they could still communicate under water. "Yes, yes, I'm fine." He turned and looked behind him. The others were all looking comfortable, except Tan who still appeared rather startled.

"How long will it take?" asked Angus, riding up alongside Thom and Ventricaria.

"Quite a while, you might as well all try and get some sleep. Just put your heads down and we'll make sure you don't fall off," said Ventricaria.

293

"Sleep?" said Arabia. "I can't sleep, there's so much to see and think about."

"I think you should try," said Angus. "I think we're going to need all our strength once we get to the island."

"Angus is right, try and sleep now while we can," replied Thom.

One by one the crew fell asleep. Although there were no saddles or stirrups the pirates remained seated, heads leant against the long necks of the sea-horses. Thom waited until they were sleeping then tried to get to sleep himself; it took him quite some time.

When Thom awoke, sunlight was streaming through the waters above him. He sat up, his neck was stiff and he was hungry. He looked around at the others. All were still sleeping, except Arabia.

"Good morning," she said, smiling.

"Morning, Arabia," Thom replied.

"We'll be there soon," said Halimeda.

"Thank you," said Thom, feeling his stomach grumble. He couldn't help thinking about the sausages and eggs that were in his watertight backpack. Breakfast could be cooked as soon as they arrived on the island – they would need all the strength they could muster.

"Can I ask you something?" asked Arabia, in a low voice.

"Sure."

294

"Why did you choose me to come along? I thought maybe after you found out I was a girl you would think less of me, of my pirating skills too."

"I think you're an amazing swordswoman and I thought you'd be a good member of the crew. You're sensible, but adventurous and I believe that you can work well in a team."

Arabia blushed. "Oh, thank you."

"Morning," said Angus, yawning and sitting up on Kelp's back.

"This is quite good fun, isn't it? Riding seahorses I mean," said Arabia, cheerfully.

"Sure is," said Angus. "When's breakfast? I'm starving."

"Hallimeda just said we won't be much longer now," Thom told him.

One by one the other members of the crew awoke, all complaining of stiff necks and being hungry.

"So what's your plan when you get there?" asked Ventricaria.

"Cook breakfast," stated Roscoe, sleepily.

"Yes, breakfast then we'll decide which route we'll take across the island to find the treasure map," said Thom.

"If it's still there," Rufus reminded him.

"Of course, Rufus, I hadn't forgotten that bit, thanks."

"There's only one way to find out," said Angus. "That's why we're here, together, to help Thom."

The others nodded in agreement, but Rufus still looked miserable. Not for the first time did Thom wonder if he'd made the right decision in including Rufus in his crew. Rufus had agreed to come, so why was he still so glum? Perhaps he was still sulking about the way Thom had spoken to him on the last trip? Or maybe he didn't like the fact that Thom was in charge this time?

Soon enough they surfaced and saw an island a short way ahead of them. Protruding up, in the middle, was a large, nose-shaped mountain, surrounded by thick forest on the south side, just like the beard in the Ancient Mariner's portrait.

"This is where we leave you, Thomas, you'll have to swim from here," said Ventricaria. "All you have to do to call us is blow a conch shell, you'll find plenty on the beach. We'll be here in no time."

"Thanks for the ride," replied Thom. "Come on guys, let's get some breakfast."

They watched the seahorses disappear under the water then swam towards the island. It appeared to be deserted and Thom hoped it was. They stripped off their wet-suits and laid them on some low branches of a tree that grew up out of the sand at the edge of the forest. In shorts and t-shirts they collected wood for a fire over which to cook the sausages and eggs for breakfast.

Once a good fire was going, Tan and Roscoe took charge of the cooking whilst the others poured over the map. Thom un-wrapped the book carefully from its waterproof cover, still concerned that it might have got a little water damaged; he was relieved to find that it was completely dry.

Thom traced his finger over the old man's wrinkles, explaining that he thought that this was the track that led to the cave.

"It could be very overgrown," he told the others. "We needn't take all our kit, just what we need to make the journey. We need to head for the mountain and cave in the middle of the island, here." He pointed at the nose.

"We should take swords, food, water and courage," said Angus. "We'd better take Long Harry's pistol too."

"Long Harry's pistol?" asked Thom.

"He gave it to me before we left. I'm the only one whose parents paid extra for me to have secret shooting lessons."

"You lucky ..." said Rufus.

"Great, that will certainly come in handy, if there are large and ferocious beasts like the Scorpi!" cried Tan. "I wish my parents could've paid for *me* to have had private lessons. It's not fair."

"IF we find the treasure map, and the treasure, and if there's enough, I'll pay for us all to have private shooting lessons, how's that?" suggested Thom.

A hoot of excitement went through the young crew, but was interrupted by Angus' strangled cry as he stared out to sea. The crew followed his gaze where, in the distance, they could see another ship headed towards the island.

"What the ..." cried Thom, leaping to his feet and dragging a spyglass out of his bag. He moved the scope to focus the distance. It was only a speck on the horizon, but there was no mistaking the colour of the ships sails.

Black: the Hades Rambler.

Thom threw his telescope into his bag. "Quickly, gather our things. Are those sausages ready yet?"

"Yes, ready," said Tan.

"Forget the eggs, we eat as we run. Roscoe, put the fire out, cover it up with sand and try to stop it smoking."

"How on earth did they find us?" cried Angus.

"I don't know," said Thom, feeling panic rise in his chest. "There must've been spies, or somebody followed us."

"I bet it was those seahorses, I didn't trust them from the start," said Tan, handing each of them hot sausages in rolls.

"I don't think so," said Angus. "They seemed all right to me."

"Come on, guys, let's move," commanded Thom. "Rufus, Arabia, hide the other belongings in the trees and let's get going."

Thom's heart was beating hard in his chest, he didn't feel like the others were moving fast enough, more interested in their food than in the approaching rivals. He stuffed his own sausage in his mouth and chewed, quickly swallowing, but barely tasting it. Finishing the last bite, Thom pulled his silver compass out of his pocket, opened the book at the map and headed off in a north-west direction.

"Wait for us," cried Arabia. "We should all stick together we'll be stronger that way."

Angus and Arabia stomped either side of Thom. Roscoe and Rufus bringing up the rear, through the trees, until the path became too narrow to walk three abreast. Then, each of them pulled out their swords to cut back the thick undergrowth that encumbered their passage. Slicing through foliage, that grew like curled snakes around larger trees, slowly choking the life out of them. Surrounding the crew, strange, unseen-creature's cries unnerved them. However, the knowledge that the Hades Rambler was now on their heels, made them more determined to get to the mountain faster than ever.

They trekked for what seemed like hours. It was hot and humid. Thom's arms and legs were scratched and itchy from the plants that assaulted him.

"I've run out of water," cried Tan, shaking her flask upside down.

"Me too," said Rufus. "We need to get more water, Thom."

Thom stopped and looked at the crew they were beginning to look very weary and extremely hot. "There are some pools not far from here," he said, studying the map. "It's a bit of a detour, but we must stay hydrated."

They took a path to the east, it seemed clearer than the path they had diverged from, as if something had been using it regularly, something large. Thom wondered what it could be, perhaps one of the hairy beasts that were depicted as sideburns and beard on the map of the Ancient Mariner.

Angus was leading the way ahead of the others, he stopped abruptly, raising his hand then placing a finger over his lips. The others stopped and were quiet. Angus turned and beckoned Thom forward. Slowly, carefully, Thom tiptoed to Angus' side. He pointed.

Thom's gaze came to rest on a deep, blue pool. He made to go forward, but Angus placed a hand on his forearm to stall him. Thom looked again, this time he saw a very odd creature. It was about the size of a large hippopotamus, but it was woolly like a sheep. The wool was green, like a shrub – good camouflage in a jungle, thought Thom to himself. The beast was drinking steadily from the pool through a short trunk. Thom looked at Angus who shrugged. Was it dangerous? Should they approach the pool and refill their flasks?

Tan moved and as she did so a twig snapped beneath her feet. The creature's head shot up out of the water, immediately alert. It looked in their direction then growled and hissed like a wild cat, showing large fangs in a cavernous mouth, but instead of running towards them in attack, it turned and fled into the undergrowth - extremely fast and agile for a creature of its size.

"That is the strangest creature I've ever seen," said Roscoe.

"What *was* that?" asked Tan.

"I've no idea," said Thom. He could hear his heartbeat in his chest, but it was the only sound he could hear, all other birds and creatures were silent.

"Let's not hang around in case it comes back and brings its friends." Rufus ran towards the pool with his flask.

"Let's get water and get out of here," said Tan, unscrewing her flask lid and filling it with cool water.

Having filled their flasks, Thom led the way back towards the north-west route he knew they needed to take. The jungle around them was still and silent. Angus tried to keep some conversation going, but all, except Thom, were now subdued.

After a while, they came to a clearing in the trees. Here, the atmosphere felt more stifling and there was a strange, regular, rhythmic sound in the distance that they hadn't heard before. Thom took out the map and his compass, but he was astonished to see that the compass needle was spinning out of control. "Look at this," he cried.

The others stared.

"What's it doing?" asked Roscoe in alarm.

"I don't know," admitted Thom.

"Do you know which way we need to go?" asked Rufus looking round.

"No," stated Thom.

"Can we see which way to go, just by the map?" asked Roscoe, peering over Thom's shoulder.

Thom looked at the map then up and round the clearing, confused. Which way had they come from?

"*Can* you?" repeated Roscoe, impatiently.

"I'm not sure," said Thom.

"We can put our heads together, we've all done map reading at school, we just need to work it out, that's all," said Arabia.

"Yes, yes," agreed Angus. "Now, which way did we come into the clearing?"

They all looked around and then at each other, shaking their heads.

They were lost.

"Look," said Arabia. "Over there, that's where we came in. I remember seeing that large rock and thinking it looked like a sleeping baby giant."

"I hope it isn't," said Rufus, his face white.

Thom laughed. "It's just a rock, Rufus."

"We were travelling in a north-west direction," continued Arabia. "So that's north-west." She picked up a twig and made an arrow pointing in the direction of north-west. "Now we have to see which way we need to go on the map."

Thom closed his mouth and opened the book, studying the map. "We need to head towards the mountain; then south towards this cave here ... this is where I think the treasure map may be hidden." He could hear the rhythmic sound again it seemed to have changed direction and was getting louder.

"Right then, if that is north-west, we need to go west towards the mountain, so that must be ..." Arabia paused, turned and then pointed. "This way."

Thom looked at the map and had to admit that she did seem to make sense. "Ok, crew, let's go."

They trudged through thick undergrowth, swinging their swords and cutting a path ahead of them; the sun was high in the sky and their water bottles were only half full again. Their steps were slower and Thom was worried that the crew of the other ship might now be on the island too, following them, catching up. He held the book in his hands having no idea about the scale of the map – how far had they come? How far until they reached the mountain?

Then suddenly, ahead of him, he could see the tip of a rocky mountain peeping out from above the tall trees of the jungle.

"Look, there!" he cried.

"Yesssss!" cried Roscoe, punching the air.

"Brilliant," said Angus. "Not far now then."

"No, we have to take the south path from the nose, directly down to the mouth - the cave," said Thom, quickening his pace.

The sight of the mountain seemed to have spurred the crew on. Thom was pleased to notice that they were definitely picking up speed.

After about half an hour, they were at the foot of a grey, rocky mountain which jutted out skywards and looked exactly like the knobbly nose of an old man. Thom wondered whether the island actually looked like the 'Ancient Mariner' from above.

From here the ground seemed to slope upwards, the earth beneath their feet became much softer and a strange, brown grass covered the path. The rhythmic sound was now close and seemed to be coming from inside the mountain.

"Can you hear that?" asked Thom.

"The drums?" asked Arabia.

"Yes, that's what it is, drums."

"Who and why would anyone be banging drums here?" asked Angus.

Thom shrugged. "I guess that means that there are others here. Perhaps they know we're here too. Maybe it's a warning to others that we're approaching, stay alert everyone." It suddenly made him feel uneasy.

Then - as if they had been heard talking about the drums - they stopped. The crew all looked at one another, the silence felt unnatural.

Unexpectedly, the ground beneath their feet started to shake. Tan cried out as she lost her balance and tumbled over. Thom bent down to help her up, but the ground moved again making him miss her hand ... this time Rufus fell down too. The ground continued to move and shift beneath their feet.

"What's happening?" said Roscoe.

Tan shrieked.

"What is it?" asked Arabia.

"The ground, it's ... it's ... look!" she cried.

Thom stared at the ground to where Tan's hands were clutching the dry, brown grass. Although, on closer inspection, he realised that it was not grass at all, but hair: stiff, wiry hair.

Thom looked at the ground as it continued to shift, it was rising up; he had to sit down to stop from toppling off.

"It's a creature! We're on the back of some animal," cried Roscoe. "Look, I can see its ears."

Sure enough Thom could see large, furry white ears like those of a cat, but more rounded with tufts at the tips. As the creature moved again, a great lollop of a gait, the crew all ended up on their bottoms. Tan yelped and this time the creature turned its head towards them. Great spherical, purple eyes stared widely at them; a black nose from which grew lengthy red, sinewy, whiskers and a large mouth which housed many sharp teeth and two fangs at the front, gazed down at them. A high pitched screech came forth from its throat and it shook fiercely to rid itself of the children on its back, as if they were parasites.

The crew ended up in a heap on the sandy soil beneath the beast's belly. It turned slowly so its face was only a metre or so away from the terrified crew. It opened its mouth wide - the high pitched sound came again, piercing and alien.

A voice, abrupt and peculiar, came from the trees above them. It addressed the beast, who stepped back a couple of metres, obeying an obvious command.

"Who are you? What do you want?" The voice asked the crew.

Thom could not see who was speaking because of the dense foliage. A moment later his eye caught something in a branch above and he realised that they were being spoken to by a squat, ancient-looking man. He stood above them with a spear and shield in his hands, he wore a furry loin cloth and his face was painted in greens, greys and browns; garlands of leaves were at his ankles. He was the size of an average Year Two student, no taller.

"We mean no harm," stated Thom, still cowering from the jaws of the beast. "We didn't realise that the island was inhabited."

"Why shouldn't it be?" questioned the miniature tribesman.

"W-We come in peace," Rufus stammered.

Angus gave him a quizzical look. "We're doing a school project and em, we're investigating strange creatures."

"We have plenty of strange creatures here on the island, but they are *not* for scientific experiments." The man raised his spear.

"No, no, of course not," said Thom. "My great-great-grandfather, Seamus Prow, told tales of how -"

"*Seamus Prow*, the murdered pirate ... he was your great-great-grandfather? Well, why didn't you say so?" The man gave him a broad, blackened smile then started shouting in his strange language again at the creature.

The enormous beast, with purple eyes, lay flat on its stomach and started to purr like a cat. Unexpectedly, many other miniature tribesmen started appearing in the tree tops where they had obviously been camouflaged amongst the leaves. An excited chatter ran amongst them.

"What is your name?" demanded the first man, clearly the leader, their Chief.

"Thomas. Thom Prow."

"Then you are very welcome, Thom Prow. Now, you can drop the pretence, we know exactly why you're here and we will help you as our ancestors promised Seamus that they would. I'm chief Gwallop."

A sudden shout from a high treetop caught everyone's attention. A tribesman shouted urgently in their own language.

Chief Gwallop looked back at Thom. "Who else is with you?"

"Nobody, it's just us," said Thom.

"There are others approaching," he continued.

Realisation dawned on Thom. "It's probably the crew of the Hades Rambler, Stanley Teach and his mates."

"The Hades Rambler. Teach, did you say?" said the chief.

"Yes. I think they must've followed us."

Chief Gwallop started yelling commands at the other members of his tribe.

Angus shot a look at Thom. "They sound angry. Do you think we should leave?"

Thom shrugged as the dissonance of shouts continued, aggression becoming more evident amongst the tribe. He tried to gain the attention of the rest of the crew, to indicate that perhaps they should make a run for it, although how they would outrun all the little tribesmen, let alone the beast, was beyond him.

Arabia grabbed his wrist. "Look."

Thom glanced up and noticed that most of the tribe were swinging on creepers through the trees away from them. The chief stayed where he was, with a few men stood around him – spears raised. The beast thundered through the undergrowth following the tribe above him in the trees, issuing its high pitched squeal.

"Where are they going?" asked Roscoe.

"To stall the crew of the Hades Rambler. We must get you to that map Thomas Prow – we will be honoured to help you."

"Why would you want to help me?" asked Thom.

"Your great-great-grandfather, Seamus Prow, he gave us a home, here on Mariner's Island. His kindness meant we had a home after Teach took over our old island. It wasn't just Seamus Prow that Teach betrayed ... he had many enemies, Thom."

"Seamus Prow gave you this island?"

"On one condition."

"That you safeguard the treasure map?" replied Thom.

"Exactly." Chief Gwallop nodded, grinning. "It will be my honour to guide you the rest of the way." He swung down from the tall tree to the ground and bowed low before Thom.

"Thank you," Thom breathed, taken aback at his sudden good fortune.

Chapter 18
Ghost Captain

The crew followed the miniature tribe along a rocky trail that led from the nose-mountain, south. The muted tones of the late afternoon sun spread a golden glow on the rocks and shrubs around them.

The chief was chatting animatedly to his tribesmen, glancing back now and then at Thom which made him feel a little apprehensive. What were they saying? Were they really trying to help him find the map, or were they luring him and his friends into a trap? Thom struggled not to be so suspicious, but after Stanley's appalling ruse he found he was unable to fully trust the little men whose laughter grated his already stretched nerves.

"Do you think we should trust them?" whispered Tan, mirroring Thom's thoughts.

"I was just thinking the same," added Roscoe.

"I think they're all right," said Angus, "They know all about Thom's history and they seem genuinely glad to be able to lead us to the treasure map."

"Or to our deaths," said Rufus.

"If they're leading us to our deaths, at least we have the advantage of height and swords over them," said Arabia. "I'm sure we can fight our way out of here if necessary."

"They may be small, but I don't think we should underestimate their ferocity," said Roscoe.

"And what about their creature?" asked Tan.

"I'm sure it'll be fine," said Angus. "Look, they're slowing down."

The tribesmen came to a halt.

"We're here," said the chief, smiling proudly at Thom.

"Where's the cave?" asked Thom, instantly becoming wary. There was no evidence of an opening that he could see.

"It's concealed beneath the undergrowth. Over the years the shrubs have all grown up around it, we decided it was safer that way, more hidden from prying eyes," replied the Chief. He lifted a knife, hidden in leafy gaiters around his ankle, and began hacking at the knotted foliage around their feet. The other tribesmen started chopping too, so Thom and his crew stepped forward to help.

After a few minutes carving away at the undergrowth, a dark hole became apparent in the ground.

"It's an *underground* cave," said Angus, staring in bewilderment at Thom.

"Keep cutting," called Thom, continuing to cut the foliage, but with more vigour.

Out of the blue, a piercing squeal shattered the steady severing of the plants. The tribesmen all glanced at one another with concern.

"What was that?" asked Tan, her eyes wide.

"That was the Delchale beast. She's warning whoever is upsetting her off her island."

"Would she really hurt Stanley?" asked Roscoe.

"She would kill him, if necessary," replied the Chief, curtly. "But usually her fearsomeness gets rid of any unwanted guests."

"She's loyal to us and to your great-great-grandfather," continued Chief Gwallop. "Seamus saved her great-grandmother's life too. Her species were hunted almost to extinction, but your great-great-grandfather saved them and for that she's very loyal. There are now nearly twenty Delchale beasts alive today, spread across the isolated islands of the Southern Hemisphere."

Agitated babble, in the tribesmen's language, was heard from a nearby tree where one of the tribesmen was looking through his telescope out towards the sea.

"What's he saying?" asked Rufus.

"He says the Hades Rambler is preparing to leave. Your cousin's row-boat is propelling across the waves as if the devil himself is after him."

The tribe and student pirates gave a cheer.

"Great," shouted Thom. "Let's continue." He imagined the Hades Rambler sailing away from the island, its black sails billowing, Stanley's face, full of fury, as he watched the island, and his chance of obtaining the map, growing more unlikely with each stroke of the oar. However, Thom was not naïve enough to think that this was the last he would see of his dishonest and greedy cousin. For now though, he had to focus on the task in hand and find the treasure map – if it hadn't been filched already.

As the entrance of the cave became evident, Thom's heartbeat increased. Presently, the crew found themselves stood in a gloomy cave, their torches the only light to see by. The Chief lit some lanterns that were fixed to the walls of the caves which gave additional light; revealing paintings of men with spears running after the Delchale beast. Whereas, other pictures depicted men having killed the beast and were stood over it spears raised, gloating.

Thom stared around the cave, but couldn't see anything that resembled a map.

"Do you know where it is?" Thom asked the Chief.

The little man nodded and beckoned for Thom to follow. "Just Thom," he stated. "The rest of you wait here."

"I want Angus with me," said Thom.

The chief looked at Angus with suspicion, but nodded slowly.

Angus and Thom followed the chief to the back of the cave and down a long, narrow passage. It was chilly and had an odour of damp earth. Thom's stomach was tight.

At the end of the passage, the Chief turned right and they found themselves in an insignificant chamber. It was bare except for a cavity in the wall, halfway up. The chief was unable to reach it, so he motioned to Thom to shine his torch inside.

Thom stepped forward and shone his light into the hollow. On a natural shelf there stood a brass tube about the length of Thom's spyglass.

"Is that it?" he asked, his stomach churning. Had he been duped again?

With a trembling hand, he drew the brass tube towards him and pulled off the lid – it took quite some effort, but finally it popped off with a satisfying sigh which whispered around the cave like a spectre. Something was rolled up inside the tube; he pulled on a corner and extracted a roll of fabric: leather.

"Hold the torch," he said to Angus, who did as he was requested. Thom unrolled the dry, square of leather ... his heart raced as he realised that it was a map.

Angus gave a sharp intake of breath.

Thom stared at the illustrations and words upon it. It was certainly a treasure map, not dissimilar to the one that had led them to this place, but written at the top, in red ink was the name, Wilfred Seamus Prow.

"Wilfred?" said Thom.

"Yes, Wilfred was Seamus Prow's grandfather. The treasure had been in your family for many generations until Greybeard decided he would try and steal it. Fortunately for you, he never found it. He murdered your great-great-grandfather; stole and wrecked his ship, but he could never find the treasure. Now, perhaps you will."

Thom felt determination grow within him. Yes, yes, perhaps he could.

As they emerged from the cave, Thom was greeted by the eager faces of his crew. He held the map up above his head and they all cheered and rushed forward. Thom laughed as they hugged him.

"Steady on."

"Is it the real one?" asked Rufus.

"I don't know for sure and I guess we won't know unless we search and find the treasure, or not – it may be that somebody will have beaten us to it."

"That's not going to stop you from searching though is it?" asked Arabia, her eyes sparkling.

"No way," said Thom.

"Are we going in search of the treasure now?" asked Roscoe.

"If the Captain will let me take a crew," Thom replied. He hadn't thought much further ahead than finding the treasure map so far, but now he had found it, he wanted to get going.

"And if Captain Ginger refuses?" asked Angus.

"I go anyway."

That afternoon, the crew enjoyed a feast that the tribe presented them with, in honour of Seamus Prow and his family. Great fires were lit and wild hog roasted. Fruits and berries with honey were served to the hungry, happy crew who were waited on by the miniature islanders. A sense of celebration filled the warm afternoon.

The moon was high in the sky and the fires a red glow on the beach, when Thom raised the conch shell to his lips and blew for the sea-horses to return. While they waited, the small crew from the Sudden Ghost thanked the tribe for their hospitality and getting rid of Stanley for them.

"It's been our honour," said the Chief and bowed low to Thom's knees. "I wish you luck, Thomas Prow."

The boys and girls walked down to the water's edge and waited for the equine beasts to arrive, leaving the tribesmen to party.

"What a day," cried Arabia, standing in gentle waves that sloshed over her feet and ankles, relishing in its coolness.

"Amazing," said Tan. "Best adventure I've ever had at the School for Scoundrels so far. Thanks for having me along, Thom."

"Yea, thanks shipmate," said Rufus grinning, but looking like he was about to fall asleep.

"I'm so glad you got what you were looking for," said Angus.

"I still can't quite believe it myself," replied Thom, looking up at the full moon.

The eerie neighing of a horse interrupted him. Ventricaria and the silhouettes of the other sea-horses could be seen about two hundred metres out in the bay.

"Come on, we have to swim out to them," said Rufus. "Boy, am I looking forward to a nap on the back of Padina?"

The crew swam out to the sea-horses. The water was black beneath the silver light cast upon the surface by the moon. The ocean was warm, but the crew were tired and were slow in reaching the sea-horses.

"Everything all right?" asked Ventricaria, tossing his colourful mane.

"Great, thanks," said Thom climbing onto his colossal back. "We got what we came for and now we need to return to the ship for the next part of the adventure."

"Aye, aye, Captain!" Ventricaria replied and Thom felt the waters closing over his head. Then he slept.

Everyone was asleep as they clambered aboard the Sudden Ghost. It was now past midnight, so they crept around the deck so as not to wake the others.

"I'm going to let the Captain know we're back, if he's returned, if not, I'll speak to Long Harry," whispered Thom. "You lot get to bed, and ... guys ... thanks, thanks for all your help today, I wouldn't have been able to do it without you."

"No problem," said Arabia, through a huge yawn.

"My pleasure," murmured Roscoe.

Rufus and Tan smiled at Thom as they walked towards the steps leading down to their cabins.

"Do you want me to come with you?" asked Angus.

"No, no, I'll be fine, thanks," replied Thom, placing his hand on Angus' shoulder and giving it a squeeze.

"Anytime," replied Angus, with a sleepy smile.

Thom tiptoed towards the Captain's cabin. He knocked gently and hearing a noise from within, entered. There was no sign of Captain

Ginger, but Storm was curled up on his desk next to an oil lamp, possibly enjoying the slight warmth that emanated from the glow. She didn't stir, but opened one green eye. She knew he was there.

Thom started to turn away from the Captain's desk when he saw a shadow start to appear in the Captain's chair. It was very slight to start with then seemed to darken and become more substantial. He stared incomprehensibly as before his eyes, Captain Ginger's form materialised into the man himself. Thom stepped backwards.

Captain Ginger smiled. "Did you find the map?" He spoke as if nothing out of the ordinary had just happened.

Thom nodded. Had he just imagined it? Was he that tired that Captain Ginger had been sitting in his chair the whole time and Thom hadn't realised?

"So, you now have the map of the Prow treasure. What are you going to do next?"

"I - I'm not sure ..."

"Are you all right, Thom, you look like you've seen a ghost." Ginger smiled at him again as he stroked Storm who began to purr loudly.

Thom shivered at the irony. "I think perhaps I should sleep, Captain. I can think straighter when I'm less tired. I will need a plan."

"Yes, yes of course. Just let me know if you need me to do anything."

"Thank you, Captain." Thom started to back out of the Captain's cabin watching Ginger and Storm the whole time. He was very, very tired. "I'll come and see you again in the morning."

"Very well, Prow. I'm never far away. Goodnight."

"Goodnight, Captain."

Thom left the Captain's cabin with a thought forming, but his tired mind just couldn't quite grasp what it was trying to tell him.

A voice startled him. "Are you all right?"

"Oh ... it's you, Long Harry." Thom's heart thumped in his chest.

"Goodness, I didn't mean to make you jump so much, sorry."

"It's just, it's ..." stammered Thom.

Long Harry looked at Thom and then back at the Captain's cabin door.

"Everything okay?"

Thom was quiet, he didn't know what to say, Ginger was, after all, Long Harry's grandfather.

"I, er ..."

Long Harry frowned. "Did you find the map?"

"Yes, I did."

"That's great. You must keep it safely hidden."

"Of course, Sir." Having hidden it in the waistband of his trousers, Thom could feel the leather pressing against his waist. Now he had found it, he wouldn't be letting it out of his sight.

"You look like you could do with some sleep."

Thom nodded and started to walk away.

"Oh, this arrived for you." Long Harry handed him a green bottle.

Thom took the bottle then walked back to his cabin, stopping en-route to read the message it contained under the dim light of a lantern.

> *Dearest Thom,*
> *Sorry about the green bottle, we didn't want to worry you. We hope that you are still enjoying school and working hard? Your grandfather and I have decided to go on a short holiday, somewhere warm. The doctor says that we are both fit enough to travel, so that's a good sign. We will see you soon.*
> *Much love,*
> *Gran and Grandpa. xxx*

Thom's spirits rose, things were beginning to come together. However, feeling lethargic Thom wondered if he'd ever wake up in the morning, so he hurried back to the cabin where Roscoe and Angus were already asleep. Within moments he had joined them.

The next day during breakfast, Thom noticed that there was a celebratory air about the Sudden Ghost, although nobody was supposed to know that he had discovered the map. What could this excitement, amongst the other members of the crew, be about if it wasn't the map?

The presence of Aunt Petra - a woman aboard - and an official from O.U.S.T.Ed made Thom think it had to be something about the 'Girl's Aboard' campaign.

As breakfast was finishing, Aunt Petra stood, head raised at the teacher's table. Her face was flushed, which made the jagged scar on her left cheek more prominent, but she was smiling so widely that Thom began to wonder if her cheeks had become stuck.

She tapped loudly on a tankard with a spoon. The room fell silent before she began. "After years and years of campaigning for girls to be allowed to study at the School for Scoundrels, it is my greatest pleasure to announce this historic event: that is, that girls, yes girls, WILL be allowed to study at the school from this day forwards."

Applause, shouting and laughter followed, with a few boos and hisses, from some of the boys who looked astounded at the very idea of girls staying on in the school.

The O.U.S.T.Ed inspector looked as if he had just swallowed something sour.

Captain Ginger stood with his tankard raised. The other teachers followed suit, faces either smiling or scowling depending on what their opinion of allowing girls on board was.

"I must add ..." started the Captain. "That I, would personally like to congratulate Aunt Petra on her hard work and success that this day has brought. Also, to welcome, officially, the girls to the most amazing school to sail the high seas ... the School for Scoundrels."

Further applause with shouting and stomping from the student crew filled the dining cabin. Captain Ginger tried to speak again, but even his notable voice was drowned out by the excited hoots of the student pirates.

When he finally managed to speak, he said, "We are abandoning lessons for today. I can see there is far too much excitement for any serious learning to be done. Therefore, today is a day of sporting activities and celebrations. He raised his tankard once more and his eyes locked with Thom's. "Here's to adventure, me hearties."

At mid-morning a red bottle was brought to Thom whilst he was playing volley-ball on the top deck. He felt his legs weaken beneath him. Was it Gran, had she been taken ill again?

He popped the cork and hurriedly uncurled the message inside:

*Don't think I'll give up that easily, Prow. My
spies tell me you now have the map, but I
shall take it from you yet – the treasure will
be mine!*
Stanley

Thom felt fury mount in him. How dare Stanley
think he can have the treasure that belonged to
his family?

He didn't notice Angus at his side, until he
spoke.

"Is it your Gran?" he asked.

Thom shook his head and handed him the
message.

Angus read it then was thoughtful for a
moment. "What are you going to do?"

Thom felt himself grow in stature. He had
discovered 'The Map of the Prows' that had been
missing for over a century; had succeeded where
others had failed. He wasn't scared of Stanley and
he would do anything to stop him from getting his
hands on the Prow treasure. Seamus Prow had
wanted the treasure to say in the family, for the
Teach's not to get their filthy hands on it. In that
moment, Thom realised that he was about to
embark on another exciting, but dangerous,
adventure.

Thomas Prow couldn't wait to get started.

Acknowledgements

I would like to say an enormous thank you to the following people who read my early manuscript. Thank you for your time, constructive criticism and ideas, without which I would still be stuck on the first draft.

Harry Cooper
Tara and India Nimoneser
Matthew Bayless

Dan Bayless and Danny Hopes for their insight and ideas from an adult perspective; although still both very young at heart!

Thank you to Alice Cowell and Claire Collins for your editing and proof-reading skills; even English teachers get it wrong sometimes.

Thank you to Mr Soutar and the children at St. Lawrence (C of E) Primary School, Lechlade in allowing me an audience for School for Scoundrels, and a fun session of pirates and poetry.

Thank you to Luke Stevens for the amazing map illustration for the cover of the book and to Sam, his son, for lending it to me from his bedroom wall.

Thank you to my husband, Paul, my daughter, Isolda; my family and friends for their constant and unwavering support.

Sandra has lived and worked in the Cotswolds for 12 years; having moved there from her childhood home county of Kent. She writes for adults and children; along with historical articles for local magazines and for radio.

Sandra gained an upper second-class degree (with Hons.), in English and American Literature, from the University of Kent in Canterbury. Her love of literature and language led her first, into a teaching career, and now into private tutoring and writing. Her passion for learning and for literature drive her to write so people can enjoy a good story, but perhaps learn something along the way too. She is an advocate for keeping people of all ages and abilities reading.

This, her debut novel for children, was inspired by her passion for getting and keeping the younger generation reading for pleasure and remembering how much she loved an adventure story as a child herself.

More of her work can be found on her website: www.sandradenniswrites.wix.com/sandra-dennis

You can also follow her on Twitter @sdenniswrites

Lightning Source UK Ltd.
Milton Keynes UK
UKOW06f1123161017

311063UK00005B/719/P